Devoured

USA TODAY BESTSELLING AUTHOR

IVY SMOAK

This book is a work of fiction. Names, characters, places, and incidents are fictitious. Any resemblance to actual persons, living or dead, events, or locales is purely coincidental.

ISBN: 978-1-942381-39-6

Cover design copyright © 2023 by Ivy Smoak

2023 First Edition

To my husband and editor, Ryan.

For making sure I never made James say something too feminine.

Chapter 1

Saturday

A loud banging noise made me groan. Or maybe it was my pounding headache. It was like I could feel my heart beating behind my eye sockets.

I put my arm over my eyes as the banging intensified. *What the hell?*

My phone started buzzing incessantly.

The noises collided in my head like the worst symphony in history.

"Darling."

The word was a nightmare. Mainly because of the woman speaking it. *Isabella.* My stomach churned at just the thought of her beside me.

But it was just a dream. Isabella wasn't here. I'd started over. I was in Delaware. Safely in my bed. I had Penny... My thoughts came to a halt. I didn't have Penny. I'd fucked everything up. I scrunched my eyes tight.

The pounding noise and buzzing made my skull ache worse than my chest.

"Darling, are you awake?" Isabella's cold hand touched my bicep.

My eyes flew open. She was staring down at me with a fake smile plastered to her face. It wasn't a nightmare. She was here. And I wasn't anywhere even close to being safe in my bed back in Delaware. Because I was ass naked in Isabella's bed.

No. No, no, no. What the hell did I do?

Isabella reached out to touch my face and I pushed myself backward. I fell off the bed, tangled up in her sheets.

Fuck.

"James, the bed is getting cold."

The sound of her voice combined with the word bed made me dry heave.

"What are you doing on the floor? Let's go for round two."

Round two? What the fuck? I didn't even remember round one.

She pushed the strap of her satin nightgown off her shoulder, exposing her breast.

I stood up and my elbow collided with the lamp on her nightstand. It fell off and shattered.

"What the hell, James?!"

I put my hand out to block my view of her while I held my other hand in front of my junk.

"It's nothing I haven't seen before. Now come back to bed. I want you to do that thing again."

What thing? What the fuck did I do? I didn't remember anything. "You...you..."

"I what?" she said and lowered her other strap.

I didn't know. I didn't know what the fuck had happened.

"Seduced my *husband?*"

I dry heaved again. "Put your clothes back on," I said.

She frowned. "That's not what you were saying last night. Let me give you a massage to make you feel all better." She pushed the sheets down. "I know how much you love my hands all over you."

I shook my head. The buzzing started up again and I glanced at my phone on the nightstand. Ian was calling. And pieces of last night started to fall back into place. Ian had driven me to New York to talk to Isabella's father. But she'd answered the door instead. And then she'd handed me a drink and that…that was all I could remember.

"Oh, I know what you need." Her fingers traced the inside of her thigh, pushing up her nightgown.

I definitely did not need that. "You drugged me last night."

She laughed. "Nonsense. We spent the whole night talking. Reminiscing about happy times. Until our yearning for each other turned into a night full of passion. The things you did to me in this bed…"

"I didn't sleep with you!"

"Of course you did."

"I think I'd remember fucking the devil."

She laughed again. "You're hilarious."

"I didn't fuck you, Isabella."

"James, you're naked."

I looked back down at myself again. That didn't necessarily mean… *Fuck!*

"Why else would you be naked in my childhood bed other than to ravish my body?"

I ignored her as I found my discarded sweatpants on the floor. I pulled them on, not taking the time to look for my boxers. I grabbed my t-shirt too. "I didn't sleep with you," I said again. I couldn't have. I wouldn't have done that.

"Then what on earth do you think happened?"

I pulled my t-shirt on.

"Really, James. What do you think happened?"

"I think you drugged me!"

"And then what? Stripped you naked? Put you in my bed? Just to set up an elaborate scene?"

"That sounds exactly like something you'd do."

She pouted. "I didn't rape you, James."

"I didn't say that."

"Didn't you though?"

My heart started racing.

She crawled toward me on the bed. "You think I slipped something in your drink? And then fucked you without your consent? You think I raped you?"

The word echoed around in my head. I was seconds away from hurling all over her pink comforter.

"I have a different scenario that you might like better. You insisted on taking me to bed to have your way with me. And I graciously let you."

Not in a million years. "You're psychotic."

"Would you stop saying that!" Her calm façade finally cracked.

I didn't remember saying it to her before. But clearly she remembered. Which meant I'd said it to her multiple times last night. When she...what? Fucked me when I was barely conscious? I was definitely going to throw up.

The banging noise resumed somewhere in the distance when my phone stopped buzzing. I had a feeling Ian was seconds away from breaking into the apartment.

But I felt frozen in place. This couldn't have happened. I couldn't have let this happen. "You're lying."

"Nope."

"Yes you are." I didn't care if she did drug me. I wouldn't have slept with her. I wouldn't have ruined my chances with Penny. Thinking about her felt like a knife in my chest. I wouldn't have fucking done this. I came here to fix my relationship with Penny, not light it on fucking fire.

"I have proof," Isabella said as she finally pulled her nightgown back up. She climbed off the bed and over to a little trashcan by her desk. She lifted up a condom that was filled and tied off. "The only proof I need, really."

I shook my head. "That isn't necessarily mine."

She laughed. "You think I'd fuck someone else and steal their disgusting condom?" She threw it back in the trash. "I don't think so, darling."

I just stood there. *I didn't do this.*

"I only made you sheath up because you've been parading around fucking your students."

She couldn't possibly know about me and Penny. Like an idiot, I just continued to stand there.

"Don't look so surprised. What kind of wife would I be if I didn't have eyes on my husband at all times? I know all about Penny Taylor."

Fuck.

"Your little whore."

"Don't."

"Don't what? Talk about the trollop you're cheating on your wife with?"

"We're divorced!"

"No. As we both know, I haven't signed the papers yet. And after last night, I see no reason to. Clearly you're still infatuated with me."

Isabella had lost her damned mind. I grabbed my phone and walked past her.

Her fake nails dug into my forearm before I could open the door. "I bet you love that she calls you Professor Hunter. You've always loved what you can't have."

I pulled my arm out of her grip.

"You're sick, James. You just like the chase. We both know the truth. You're addicted to her."

I wasn't.

"You need help."

"The only thing I need is to be as far away as fucking possible from *you*."

"That's not true."

"You just…you…"

"You can't even say it. Because it isn't true."

No, I couldn't say it because I couldn't even wrap my head around the fact that she'd do that to me. I didn't want to believe it. I didn't want to believe I let it happen.

"Now how about we get back into bed?" she said.

"Go to hell, Isabella."

"If you keep pursuing this divorce, I'm going to tell the whole world what kind of man you are. I hope you don't get arrested for preying on young girls."

"She's 20." *Almost.*

Isabella laughed. "Not when you started fucking her. And her age doesn't even matter. It's the fact that she's *your* student. In one of *your* classes. It breaks all sorts of ethical guidelines at whatever shitty university you're teaching at."

"Actually, it doesn't."

"It doesn't mean you won't be fired to prevent a scandal. I mean…cheating on your doting wife with a student? I'll ruin you, James. I'll take every cent to your name. Everything you care about. And I'll ruin her life too. You know I will."

I didn't care about what slander she spread about me. I didn't care about the money. All I cared about was Penny. And I'd do whatever it took to protect her from Isabella's wrath.

"Forget about her. And come back home."

This wasn't my home.

"Come back to me." She put her hand on my chest.

She wasn't my home.

I took a deep breath. "This is the last time I'm going to ask nicely," I said. "Sign the damn papers."

"That was hardly asking nicely. How about we get back into bed and…"

"Get your filthy hands off me." I pushed her hand off my chest.

"You didn't say that last night," she said with a smile.

"I didn't say anything last night because you made me black out!"

"Right. And then I had my wicked way with you without your permission." She winked at me. "As if anyone would ever believe that. I bet Penny won't. She'll see right through all your lies. All your secrets. Does she even know you're an addict?"

There was a small part of me that wanted to wrap my hands around Isabella's neck. Wring the life out of her.

"I can't wait to see what she'll say when you tell her you fucked your wife. While the two of you were on a break."

How the fuck did she know we were on a break?

"And if I find out that you tell Penny some fabricated fib about what happened last night, I'll make sure she knows the truth. That you couldn't keep your hands off your *wife*. And I will find out if you tell her otherwise. Maybe I'll stop by the class you have together to tell her. It's at 8 a.m. on Monday, yes?"

How did she know anything about my life in Delaware? I'd taken every precaution…

Except when it came to Penny. The beach trip. The country club under my name. Anyone could have seen us. And I'd let my guard down because I was so wrapped up in her. So preoccupied. *Addicted.*

"Checkmate," Isabella said. She opened up her bedroom door. "I'll let all my friends know you're coming back to the city. Say hi to Daddy on the way out."

Chapter 2

Saturday

I hurried out of Isabella's bedroom. The light in the hallway was blinding. My stomach churned again and the pain behind my eyes grew tenfold. What the fuck had Isabella slipped into my drink last night?

My hand paused on the railing at the top of the stairs. The pounding on the door downstairs grew louder. My phone buzzing in my pocket was never-ending. I wanted to run out of this hellish house. But I'd come here for a reason. And that reason was standing at the bottom of the stairs staring at me. Isabella's father. It had been a long time since I'd seen him. But he looked the same as I remembered. The same evil glint in his eyes as Isabella's.

"James," Mr. Pruitt said.

"Mr. Pruitt," I replied. I walked down the stairs, trying to look composed even though I knew I was anything but. He was the key to getting me out of this sham of a marriage.

"I was surprised to hear that you spent the night," he said. "When you called last night, I was under the impression that your intentions with my daughter were different."

I could barely focus on his words. The pounding in my head intensified. Or maybe it was the pounding on the door.

"Aren't you going to answer that?" I asked.

"I figured it was best to keep your lap dog outside."

"Don't call Ian that."

Mr. Pruitt raised his eyebrows at me. "I'll call him whatever I please in my own home."

I'd come here last night to have a reasonable conversation with him. Even though I hadn't said why I needed to speak with him on the phone, he knew I was here about the divorce. Why else would I have come by? And he'd set me up. He'd told Isabella I'd be here. He never had any intention of speaking to me.

But he was here right now. This was my chance at freedom. But this was not a good start. Sneaking down from his daughter's room. Telling him to shut up. I ran my hand down my face. *Breathe.* What had I planned to say last night? My headache seemed to grow by the second. I'd just cut to the chase. "I need Isabella to sign the papers."

"Are you sure about that?" His eyes wandered back up the stairs.

Isabella had followed me out. She made a show of pulling her robe over her ridiculously short nightgown and running her fingers through her hair. Sex hair. I was definitely going to throw up.

"Daddy!" She hurried down the stairs. "James and I have decided to give it another go. Haven't we, darling?"

I shook my head. "No. She…"

"I what? I did *what?*" she said.

She was right. No one would ever believe that she'd taken advantage of me. It was her word against mine. And I didn't even know what had happened. If anything.

I glanced into the dining room at the Pruitt family mural. One person was noticeably missing. Isabella used to have a sister. She'd passed away in high school. Where Isabella was cruel, her sister was sweet. Innocent. I'd had a crush on her, I think because of that. Because she never belonged in our world. And even though she was never mine, I really wished I could have married her instead of Isabella. I'd thought about that a lot over the years. How different my life would have been.

And they'd just erased her from existence. Some days I thought I was the only one who still missed her. What would she think of how my life turned out? I didn't need to dwell on it. I knew the answer. She'd be furious with me for marrying Isabella. And I was done being manipulated by this toxic family.

Isabella could mess with my head all she wanted.

But I wouldn't let her ruin my life again.

"We're not giving it another go," I said. "Sign the papers, Isabella. And if there's a problem with them, I'll alter whatever you'd like. Just call me with any changes, Mr. Pruitt."

Mr. Pruitt lowered his eyebrows as he looked at me.

"That's not the deal," Isabella said. "Come home or I'll tell everyone, James. I'm being serious."

"You're right, that's not the deal. I'll be adding a new clause too. If you say one word about Penny to anyone, you won't get a cent from me."

"Daddy!" Isabella yelled. "He can't do that. He's cheating on me with that teenage slut."

God, I wanted to hit her for calling Penny that. Instead, I clenched my hand into a fist and kept it by my side. *Breathe.*

Mr. Pruitt wasn't an idiot. He knew the truth as well as I did. Isabella was the cheat, not me. And I'd said my piece. "Not a cent," I said. I knew the Pruitts didn't need the money. But the fact that Isabella wouldn't get to stay in our apartment would hurt her public image enough. It was the only threat I needed. Isabella only cared about how she looked.

Mr. Pruitt cleared his throat. "Princess, I think it's best if we take another look at the papers."

"But, Daddy!"

It was really gross that she still called him Daddy. She was a grown woman. Even if she was currently acting like a deranged toddler.

I ignored Isabella's protests as I walked over to the front door and opened it. Ian practically fell into the apartment.

"What the fuck, man," Ian said. But his anger quickly turned to confusion as he looked at Isabela and then back at me. Specifically, he was looking down at my shirt.

I followed his gaze. I'd put my t-shirt on inside out. *Damn it.* I closed the Pruitt's door before Ian had a chance to say anything else.

"Are you kidding me right now? I called you a hundred times. I thought you'd be twenty minutes tops."

I ignored him. Each step farther away from Isabella felt better.

"You really spent the night with her?"

I stepped onto the elevator and tried my best not to dry heave again. I would have let the doors close in Ian's face, but he stepped on next to me before they slid shut.

"What about Penny?" Ian asked.

I shook my head. Just hearing her name made my heart start racing. I'd fucked it all up. There was no coming back from this.

"You said you were in love with her, and then you pull this shit because of one dumb argument?"

I ignored him.

"I can't believe you slept with Isabella. What were you thinking?"

The doors slid open and I stepped out.

"Really, what were you thinking, man?"

I walked outside into the stale city air. I'd figure everything out when I got home. Back to Delaware. Where the air was cleaner. Where Penny was. I climbed into the car and slammed the door shut.

Ian got into the driver's seat but didn't start the car. "I'm not driving until you tell me why the hell you'd sleep with Isabella when you're trying to start over with…"

"I didn't fucking sleep with her!"

"I'm not blind, James."

"I didn't! She…I…"

Ian just stared at me.

"She drugged me."

He kept staring at me.

"I woke up naked next to her. But I think she stripped me after I passed out and just slept beside me."

"You think?"

"Or maybe we fucked. I don't know!"

"You don't remember sleeping with her?"

"No. I wouldn't have done that. I wouldn't have…" my voice trailed off.

Now it was Ian's turn to give me the silent treatment.

"Can we please just go home?"

"I think maybe we should go to the police," he said.

I exhaled and looked up at the roof of the car. I hadn't even wanted to tell him. I didn't want to tell anyone. But he kept pushing it.

"Don't worry about it," I said. "It was nothing."

"It wasn't nothing…"

"I'm not going to the police." What the hell would I even say? No one would ever believe my side. *Penny* would never believe my side. I felt like I was going to be sick. "It's Isabella's word against mine. And I don't exactly have a glowing record when it comes to law enforcement."

"James."

"All I need is a doctor's appointment to make sure I didn't catch whatever disgusting STDs she has."

"If that's what you want to do." Ian finally started the car and pulled onto the busy city street.

We were both quiet as the scenery slowly changed from tall skyscrapers to green trees.

Last night I'd finally had hope again. Hope that I might actually deserve Penny.

But today? Isabella had made sure I lost all of it.

I couldn't look Penny in the eye after last night.

I expected to feel better when Ian pulled onto Main Street. To feel lighter somehow at being closer to Penny. But I didn't feel closer to her. I felt farther away than ever.

I'd wanted to win her back. That's what I'd been try-ing to do. And I'd fucked it all up just like I fucked up everything in my life.

What was I supposed to do now? Try to win her back by telling her that I maybe cheated on her? That I'd been too shit-faced to even remember?

And I didn't even really have a choice. It didn't matter if I told Penny what actually happened. Or…what I re-membered. Isabella had said she'd tell Penny that I'd cheated on her. She probably took pictures of the condom that I wasn't even sure was mine. Hell, she might even have pictures on her phone that were even worse. I had no idea.

I'd told Isabella she wouldn't get a cent from me if she talked about Penny to anyone. And yes, Isabella cared about her own image. But it was possible she cared more about destroying Penny's image. And I wouldn't risk any-thing when it came to Penny. My hands were tied.

It didn't matter that I didn't remember.

It didn't matter that I didn't know the truth.

Ian parked the car under my apartment complex. And we both just sat there.

"What are you going to tell her?" he asked.

He didn't need to specify who. I knew he was talking about Penny. "I'm not going to tell her anything."

"You can't just not tell her."

"Yes I can. Because Penny and I are done."

"Are you serious right now?"

"She deserves better than someone like me." I'd known it all along. I'd just been grasping at straws because I was obsessed with her. And that was part of the whole problem. My addiction. Isabella was right. I just wanted what I couldn't have.

"So you're just giving up on your fresh start?"

"I need a drink," I said and climbed out of the car.

Ian got out of the car just as fast as me. "You don't just get to walk away."

"It's what's best for her."

"Or is it just easier for you? To give up and drink your life away? Or…worse."

"You're right. I could be snorting cocaine off a hooker's ass right now."

Ian didn't laugh, even though my joke was clearly hilarious.

"It's just one drink."

"You never stop at one drink, James."

Fuck him. I could stop at one drink if I wanted to. I walked toward the exit and out onto Main Street. It had started drizzling. I didn't have an umbrella or a jacket with a hood. But I didn't even care.

I sighed and stared up at the clouds.

I didn't want a drink.

I just wanted to sit here and drown in my sorrows.

I sat down on the closest bench as the rain picked up. I put my face in my hands.

I'd lost Penny. I'd fucking lost her. And Isabella made sure I could never get her back.

It had been torture seeing Penny in class the past week. Like what we had meant nothing. How was I supposed to keep going like that? How was I supposed to actually give her up?

I wasn't sure there were rehab facilities for broken hearts. I lay down on the bench and let the rain fall on my face.

"Here," Ian said. I opened my eyes and saw him handing me a beer. "It's a better alternative than the cocaine thing."

I laughed, even though it was forced. "I was just joking."

"Well, I wasn't sure."

I sat up and grabbed the beer. Yeah, I wasn't entirely sure either. I took a sip of the beer as we both sat there in the pouring rain.

It felt like life kept taking shots at me. Like I wasn't supposed to win this game. I took another sip. "This is disgusting."

"What? It's the good stuff. Cheap college beer. It's nostalgic."

"It's disgusting," I said again, but I still took another swig.

"I think you should tell Penny the truth," Ian said.

"I don't know what the truth is."

"Then tell her that."

"It doesn't matter what I tell her. Isabella said she'd tell Penny I slept with her." Penny and I already had trust issues. She had a bad habit of believing tabloids instead of me. And if she was hearing directly from my ex instead of some article? I wouldn't trust me either.

"Isabella's the fucking worst," Ian said.

"Cheers to that." I tapped my can against his. "Penny really is better off without me," I said.

"I don't know about that."

"You can't seriously sit here and tell me I'm a catch."

Ian laughed. "I wasn't going to call you a catch, you weirdo. You're a mess. But you're a lot less of a mess when you're with her. She makes you better."

"It's not really fair to put that pressure on her."

"It's also not really fair for you to cut her out for no reason."

"She's 19, Ian. She's just a kid. And I'm a..."

"A monster? Yeah, Ellen told me you said that. I don't think you're a monster, James."

"Because I pay you to not think of me that way."

"Ellen also told me that you gave her the exact same lame reasoning." He shook his head as he stared at me. "I saw monsters while I was overseas. Real ones. And you're not like them."

"She's 19."

"I'm the one that dug up the information about her. So I know her birthday is on Thursday. If you're so caught up on the fact that she's a teenager, that'll change before the end of next week. So your excuse is moot."

"It doesn't matter. She probably won't forgive me for kicking her out. And she definitely won't forgive me for what I did last night."

"You said you didn't do anything. And I believe you. But regardless of what you choose to tell her, the worst that can happen is that she tells you to fuck off and leave her alone."

"Which she should," I said.

"But the best thing that can happen? She forgives you. For all your very many flaws."

I laughed.

"And then you live happily ever after."

I laughed again. Happily ever afters were meant for princes. Penny had said I made her feel like a Disney princess. But I was no prince. I was pretty sure that I was the villain.

Chapter 3

Wednesday

Each day was worse than the last. When I found out that Penny was only 19, I'd told myself that she was better off without me. But for a few hours when I'd had the plan to see Mr. Pruitt, I'd had hope that I could win Penny back. That I could be enough. That I could be better. But now?

I'd been right the first time.

Penny was better off without me.

And I was in hell.

I couldn't seem to focus in class. My lectures were all over the place. And they were always greeted by confused looks on my students' faces. If I didn't get my act together, I knew the dean would be calling me. I could kiss my fresh start goodbye. Not that it felt like a fresh start anymore. It was more like torture.

But I couldn't think about the students I was letting down or about getting fired right now. Because today was Wednesday. I got to see Penny three times a week. And on those days all I could think about was her.

Ian said that we could live happily ever after. But I knew the truth. I'd been so determined to win her back. But I'd fucked everything up.

I wasn't a knight in shining armor. And Penny was better off without me. There was only one answer here. One painful answer that I'd let settle around me.

I was going to let her go. I had to let her go.

But on Mondays, Wednesdays, and Fridays we still got to breathe the same air. I still got to stare at her in class.

We could still be close. I'd give anything to be closer. Just one touch…

Stop.

Fucking stop it.

I walked into the coffee shop where Penny and I first met. I made a habit of coming here every morning, hoping to run into her. I wasn't sure for what purpose. Maybe seeing her outside of class would feel more like us. Maybe I'd be able to find the strength to figure out a way to bring us back together.

But every day I went to the coffee shop, she wasn't there. It almost seemed like she was avoiding it. Trying to get over what we had.

I should have been grateful.

But it just made everything worse.

I had to let her go. But I didn't want to.

Someone behind me cleared their throat.

I blinked. I hadn't realized the line in front of me had dissipated. Everyone was waiting for me to order. But I didn't actually want coffee. I just wanted Penny. I stepped out of the line. God, I just needed Penny.

My hand shook as I reached out to push open the door back to Main Street. For a second I just stared at my hand.

I thought I loved Penny. But it was so much more sinister than just that.

My hand continued to shake.

If I needed any confirmation that I was addicted to Penny, this was it. I was literally feeling some of the symptoms of withdrawal. I desperately just wanted one more fix. And I wasn't sure how much longer I could actually go without succumbing to the temptation.

I was obsessed with Penny. I was addicted to her.

I pushed open the door and stepped onto Main Street. I took a deep breath, but it didn't quite reach my lungs.

I just needed one more fix.

And that didn't mean watching the footage of her on her knees worshipping my cock at the country club. Which just further proved my obsession. Every day I wrapped my hand around my cock and pretended it was her lips. And it wasn't enough. I needed Penny. I fucking needed her. All I could think about was devouring every inch of her one more time.

Dr. Clark thought what I needed was to delete the footage.

But he was an idiot. That's why I'd fired him. I was fucked up in the head and it was his fault. I paid him to help me and he hadn't helped at all.

So I'd watch the video whenever I damn well pleased and at least wallow after finding a fucking release.

And I'd keep watching the surveillance feed of her coming and going from her dorm too.

Honestly it made sense that I'd turned into a stalker. Fitting, really. Another thing to add to the list of reasons why I should be alone. *Monster.*

But it would be a hell of a lot better to have Penny's lips actually wrapped around my cock. Just one more time.

God, just one more fix.

***

I stood outside of class and took a deep breath.

Penny is better off without me in her life. She's good. She's pure. She's perfect. She deserves more.

I'd ruin her life. I'm sick. I'm twisted. I'm fucked up in the head. I deserve to be alone.

Those words had settled into my head when I stared at the ceiling at night. Tossing and turning in my sheets that still smelled like her. Until I got up and went to my office to try to distract myself with work.

I needed those words now. When my hands were shaking. And I was desperate. I felt like if I told myself those words enough, that I could find the strength to leave Penny alone.

I wondered if Dr. Clark would be proud of me for making myself a mantra. Probably not. Nothing I did seemed to please anyone recently. But I'd have to rehire him and show up to appointments in order to see his disdain. And I decided I didn't need therapy. *I'm sick. I'm twisted. I'm fucked up in the head. I deserve to be alone.*

I think I summed it up pretty nicely.

I reached down and snapped the rubber band around my wrist for the millionth time this morning. I wasn't seeing Dr. Clark anymore, but I remembered he'd made me do this. To help control my wandering thoughts. To make me focus on the present.

But what was the present other than hell?

I snapped the rubber band again, but nothing happened. I looked down at my red wrist. The skin was raw and the rubber band was broken on the floor.

Wishful thinking that the rubber band would help. If something so simple worked, I wouldn't have wasted thousands of dollars on therapy. *Fuck.* I picked the broken rubber band up off the floor.

No, it didn't work. But I liked the feeling of pain. I needed a new rubber band. I needed to be doing anything other than walking into this classroom. *Breathe.*

I tried to plaster a fake smile on my face, but even that felt exhausting. Instead I just opened the door to my Comm classroom and walked in. It used to feel like walking into fresh air. Fresh cherry-scented air. I used to stare over at Penny with a hidden smile. Whenever I was around her, it made it easier to breathe.

But today? The room was stifling. And staring at Penny felt like a punch in my gut. I tried to focus on putting down my satchel and organizing my papers. But I kept glancing at her out of the corner of my eye.

I could tell she wasn't eating. Her cheeks looked hollow. And the dark circles under her eyes meant she wasn't sleeping either. But she was still gorgeous. Her wavy red hair made her rosy cheeks look rosier. Her full lips were still begging to be kissed. I wanted them wrapped around my cock and my fingers buried in her hair. *Stop.*

Did she lie awake at night thinking of the same things I did? Of my body pressed against hers? Before repeating some fucked up mantra?

Definitely not the last part. That was a special kind of torment just for me.

I'm sick. I'm twisted. I'm fucked up in the head. I deserve to be alone.

I'd worn one of my sweaters that I knew she liked. Actually, it was identical to the one I'd given her. I wasn't trying to play a game with her head. I just...wanted to see if she noticed. I wanted some kind of realization in her eyes.

Had she even kept that sweater?

Did she still think of me too?

I glanced at her once more before turning to the board. She was sitting with that prick Tyler Stevens. He was leaning over discussing something with her. The chalk almost broke in my hand as I started writing on the board. And I realized all I'd drawn was a straight vertical line. I couldn't even write a word I was so distracted. Just the letter "I" staring back at me. Where the fuck was I going with this? I kept staring at it. The more I stared the less it even looked like an "I." My hand was too shaky.

I'd come here for a fresh start, but I wasn't fooling anyone. Once a monster, always a monster.

How long have I been staring at the chalkboard?

I heard a shuffling of feet and glanced over my shoulder.

Penny was walking out of the classroom with Tyler. Ditching my class with another guy? Right in front of me? I turned back to the board.

It's what I wanted, right? For her to move on? To be happy with someone else?

But not Tyler Stevens. *Fuck that guy.*

Chapter 4

Thursday

Today was Penny's birthday. She was 20 years old. She wasn't a teenager anymore.

Sick fuck.

I raked my fingers through my hair.

I'd had a whole thing planned.

It was stupid.

All of this was so fucking stupid.

Penny looked physically ill in class this week. I could tell she wasn't eating or sleeping. How was her current behavior better than when we were together? Yes, I was a piece of shit. But maybe I at least made her happy. Healthy. *Maybe.* Fuck, I didn't know.

I climbed into my car and started the engine.

Usually it was a little easier to not obsess over Penny on the days I didn't see her in class. But today was a different kind of hell. I couldn't stop thinking about her. And how I should be beside her on her birthday. I couldn't really explain it. It was like I could feel that she needed me. I pulled out my phone for the hundredth time and stared at it, trying to think of something to say.

But no matter what I typed…it would always end in the same way. I'd played the situation in my head over and over again. I'd tell her I loved her. And then I'd have to confess that I slept with Isabella while we were on a break. And then Penny would punch me square in the nose and walk away from me.

I tossed my phone onto the passenger's seat and put the car in reverse.

I was probably going to regret this. But Ellen had been bugging me nonstop when I decided to lie in bed all day on Sunday instead of going to therapy. She threatened to leave a couple times this week if I didn't go see Dr. Clark. I didn't believe her. But maybe talking all this out with Dr. Clark would help.

Wishful thinking.

As I drove down Main Street, I wondered if Penny was opening presents right now. Surrounded by her friends. People her own age. I knew she was having a party on Friday night. A joint birthday with her and Melissa. It was Halloween themed. I could easily blend in…

Stop.

I parked outside of Dr. Clark's office. I already knew what he was going to say. That I was spiraling. That I needed to get my act together before I slipped. But I'd already slipped. I stared longingly at the bar down the street. It would be a lot more bearable if I just blacked out for the rest of Penny's birthday. But the last time I blacked out I wound up naked next to Isabella.

Fuck my life. I climbed out of the car and went into Dr. Clark's office.

The receptionist looked up at me. "Oh. Mr. Hunter. I don't have you on the schedule today." She started flipping through some papers on her desk, like she'd made some kind of clerical error.

"I don't have an appointment. I just need to talk to him real quick. Is he in?" I started walking toward the door.

"Mr. Hunter, wait! He's with another patient right now."

I stopped even though I wanted to just storm in. "I really need to see him."

She nodded. "Okay. But do you mind taking a seat and when his current session is over I can let him know you're here?"

"How long will it be?"

"Um..." she looked at the clock behind her on the wall. "His session just started. It'll be at least 50 minutes."

Seriously? There was no way whatever whack job was in there was paying him more than I was. I sighed when I'd realized I'd basically just called myself a whack job too.

"There's some magazines," the receptionist said. "To keep you occupied."

"Okay," I said and sat down, when really I just wanted to storm through the door. But it's not like I had anything better to do anyway. I picked up one of the worn magazines and flipped through a few pages before discarding it on the table.

I leaned back and closed my eyes.

Ellen was the worst.

No, *I* was the worst.

But it was her fault I was sitting in this shitty waiting room.

***

Someone cleared their throat.

I sat up with a start. Dr. Clark was standing in front of me.

"You requested a word?" He continued to just stand there staring at me.

"Yeah," I said with a yawn. "Just real quick."

"It doesn't have to be quick now. My last patient for the day just left."

The last one for the day? I glanced over at the clock behind the receptionist's head. It was after six. Had I seriously been asleep for three hours? And no one thought it was a good idea to wake me up?

"Come with me," Dr. Clark said. He turned on his heel and went back toward his office.

I grabbed my phone and looked at it quickly before following him in. Penny still hadn't texted. Because of course she hadn't. I was the one that told her I needed time to think about things. The ball was in my court and I was seriously fucking it up.

I sat down in the chair across from Dr. Clark.

"Have you been sleeping well at night, James?"

Was that a serious question? Because I was pretty sure the fact that I'd just fallen asleep in the waiting room was answer enough. I glared at him.

"You came here because you wanted to talk. If all you can do is stare at me, I think I'll call it a day."

I'd just waited three fucking hours for him in the waiting room.

He closed his notebook and looked like he was going to stand up.

"Wait," I said. "I…" I didn't know what I wanted to say. "You have my undivided attention."

Dr. Clark sighed. "We've been over this, James. It's not about you giving me your undivided attention. It's about you wanting to be here. You wanting to make progress. You showing up for yourself."

"I just waited three hours to speak with you."

"No, you slept for three hours because you're sleep deprived. And I want to discuss why that is."

"I don't want to talk about my sleeping habits."

"Then what would you like to discuss with me? Because I was under the impression that you fired me."

"I didn't fire you." Not exactly in those words, anyway.

He opened his notebook back up again. "And I quote: You can cancel the rest of my appointments on your calendar. I won't be returning."

"Well, I barely remember saying that." It had been in the heat of the moment, of course I hadn't really meant it.

"Because you'd been drinking. Heavily I presume. Returning to old vices. Why do you think that is?"

Dr. Clark always did some kind of voodoo magic to make me talk about whatever he wanted to talk about. But it wasn't working today. I'd come here for only one reason. "I don't think Penny has been eating. Or sleeping. So I think that maybe not being with me is bad for her. Worse than actually being with me."

He jotted down a few notes. "Are you asking me? Or telling me?"

"I'm…telling you. I think maybe she's better off with me."

"Better off how exactly?"

Was it just me, or was Dr. Clark being extra saucy with me today? "Well…she was eating when we were dating. And I think we both slept better when we shared a bed."

"Is that why you haven't been sleeping? Because you don't like to be alone at night?"

He was acting like I was scared of the dark or something. "I'm here to talk about Penny."

"And I'm here to talk about you," Dr. Clark said. "James, *you* made the decision to date one of your students. *You* made the decision to break up with her. This is all about *you*."

"I didn't break up with her. I told her I needed some space to think."

"So you've taken that time to ponder your relationship and you've come to the conclusion that she's better with you than without you. Because when you two dated she ate and slept? Is that correct?"

Seriously, so saucy. "Yes, that's correct."

"I don't think her eating and sleeping habits should be the reason you get back together with her. You should be in a relationship because of the connection you two have. The love that you share."

"I didn't say I wanted to get back together with her so she'd eat more." Although, I would definitely like to eat her. I'd really missed that.

He looked down at his notes. "And I quote - I don't think Penny has been eating. Or sleeping. So I think that maybe not being with me is bad for her. Worse than actually being with me."

"That's just one piece of it."

"And the other piece? How have you been coping without her?"

He knew that I wasn't doing well. "I miss her."

"So why are you telling me that? You should be telling that to her."

"I'm trying to do the right thing."

"James, you came here in hopes that I'd agree with you, yes? To give you peace of mind that Penny is better off with you than without you? But I can't decide that. That's a choice you have to make. And if you make it, I hope you believe it. I hope you'll stay clean for her sake, but most importantly for your sake."

"So you think I should speak with her again?"

Dr. Clark sighed. "That's not at all what I just said, and you know it. James, how does being with Penny make you feel?"

"Right now? Seeing her feels like shit. But when we were together…she made me feel better. She made me feel like I wasn't so fucked up. I don't…I don't need anything else when I'm with her."

"And by anything else you mean drugs?"

I pressed my lips together.

"James, you are not addicted to Penny." It was like he knew exactly where my thoughts had wandered. "She makes you happy. She makes you not turn to vices because you're happy when you're together. That's love. Not addiction."

I nodded. "So it is a good idea to try and fix things?"

"Do you think it's a good idea?"

"Dr. Clark, it's a simple question."

He adjusted his glasses. "It is. So answer it."

"Are you acting this way because I tried to fire you?"

"How am I acting? I'm simply trying to get to the root of your problem. You haven't been showing up for appointments. I've been getting worried voicemails from Ellen at all hours."

So…he *was* being purposely rude? "I don't think you realize how your behavior affects others, James."

I felt bad for worrying Ellen. I truly did. That's why I was here. Well, partially. I was mostly here to get Dr. Clark to tell me it was a good idea to continue my relationship with Penny. But he clearly wasn't taking the bait.

"You've seen this all first hand before. The path you're going down is destructive."

"I have control over it this time."

"Do you?"

"Yeah." *Not really.*

"Okay. I believe you."

It didn't really sound like he believed me. I was pretty sure he was just pissed about me getting shitfaced and firing him. "So about Penny…"

"I'm not going to give you an answer, James. You have to find that within yourself. But do you know what I think will help?"

"What?" I was desperate. I just wanted to know I was making the right choice.

"Write Penny a letter. Tell her everything you're feeling. Everything you wish you could say to her. Sometimes it's easier to express yourself in the written word. And then once you write it, you can either send the letter…or you can throw it out and never think about it again. It'll bring you some semblance of closure, whatever you decide."

That sounded as dumb as yoga.

"Just try it," he said. "Now what else is bothering you? Ellen told me you were in a good mood, went to New York, and returned rather ornery."

"How much do you and Ellen talk?"

"I think the important question here is what happened in New York?"

No, the important question was that my housekeeper was talking to my therapist about me. Didn't that cross some kind of ethical line?

"James, answer the question."

This seemed like a good practice run for how the conversation with Penny would go. The way it had to go. "I slept with Isabella." Just saying the lie out loud made me feel sick to my stomach. *God I hope it's a lie.* But it didn't matter what the truth was if I couldn't remember it. I'd woken up naked in Isabella's bed. And I couldn't explain that. I couldn't. Isabella's words echoed around in my head. *Rape.* Yeah, I was definitely going to be sick. *Breathe.*

He raised his eyebrows. "You slept with Isabella?"

I stared at the expression on his face. It was about what I expected. "Yup," I said. I'd had a drink when I shouldn't have. Yes, Isabella had slipped something into it.

But it was a hell of a lot easier coping with this if it was partially my fault. I was used to fucking up every good thing in my life.

"Why?" It was the most normal he'd ever sounded. Like he just genuinely wanted to know. For his own sake. I'd perplexed him.

"I…don't know. I was depressed." More lies. I'd been hopeful that night. So hopeful that I could be worthy of Penny. Until it all came crashing down.

Dr. Clark wrote more down in his notebook. "And after you slept with Isabella? Did you feel better?"

"No. I regretted it." If it had happened…I fucking hated myself for it. But I hoped it wasn't true. I hoped I wouldn't do that. I still hoped I hadn't. At least all my STD tests had come back negative.

"Do you still have feelings for Isabella?"

"No. We've been over this…"

"And yet you slept with her?"

I gritted my teeth together. *I don't fucking know!* "Yup."

"It really feels like you're holding something back here. Do you care to elaborate on your feelings over this matter?"

"No." *Breathe.* He wouldn't believe me. Just like Penny wouldn't believe me.

"One word responses don't help either of us, James."

"It was a mistake. End of story."

He didn't shake his head, or nod. He just stared back at me, waiting for me to elaborate.

But I had nothing else to say. So I just stared back at him.

"Well…" Dr. Clark's voice trailed off. He was finally at a loss for words. "How did it feel to be back in New York after so many months away?"

I pictured the portrait of the Pruitt family hanging in the dining room. "It felt suffocating."

"How so?"

"Like I was being judged."

"By whom?"

I ran my fingers along the arm of the chair.

"Your friend who passed away in high school? She was Isabella's sister, right?"

I seriously never should have told him about her. I don't know why I'd come here. Dr. Clark was annoying.

He skipped through a few pages of his notebook. "You've never mentioned her name to me. Why is that?"

I'd made a pact in high school with my friends. That we'd never speak about her. Being here with Dr. Clark was breaking that promise. But I'd never mentioned her name. Not just because of the promise though. It was hard for me to talk about her. I hadn't said her name out loud in years. Not since the last time I tried to talk to Matt. Before I was sober.

"What was her name, James?"

I cleared my throat. "Lyn." That wasn't her name. Just a piece of it. But if he was going to make me talk about this, a fake name would be easier. It made it feel like less of a betrayal to my friends.

"You said Lyn was originally from Delaware. It's rather curious that you ended up here of all places when you wanted to leave the city. Isn't it?"

"Are you asking me if it was a coincidence?"

"I'm just wondering if you wanted to teach in Delaware because of her."

"Lyn said something to me once." I thought the fake name would help, but it still stung. I could still see her tearstained face as I'd held her close. I cleared my throat. "She saw firsthand how much I struggled in high school.

And she said something about how people here were nicer than the people in the city." *People like me.* I hadn't been nice to her when I first met her. She made me want to be better. Be different.

"Whenever we talk about Lyn, you're adamant that you didn't love her. Are you sure about that?"

I'd just been thinking about how different my life would have been if she'd lived. But it was all ridiculous. Because she was dead. And she'd been dating one of my best friends. She'd never belonged to me. "We never would have ended up together."

"That definitely was not my question."

"I don't see the point of this conversation. I want your advice about Penny."

"Do you think Penny reminds you of her?"

I swallowed hard. "I…" I hadn't really thought of that before. I closed my eyes and pictured Lyn's blonde hair blowing across her face in the autumn breeze. Forever frozen at 16. She was a breath of fresh air. She made it easier to breathe. Just the way Penny did. "They were both sweet." They both made me want to be a better man.

"You're referring to Penny in the past tense, James. Lyn is gone. But Penny is very much alive. And you can still pursue her if you want to. You just have to make the choice for yourself."

"But if I make it for myself it's selfish."

"Not if you're planning on being the best version of yourself for her."

"You mean sober."

"Yes. I also mean being honest with her. Because alas, we've finally come to the root of the problem. You're worried about what happens when you tell Penny that you slept with Isabella?"

"She won't take me back." Why couldn't I remember what happened that night? I felt cursed. Like I wasn't supposed to remember for a reason. Like I was supposed to be miserable.

I'm sick. I'm twisted. I'm fucked up in the head. I deserve to be alone.

"And there's the truth," Dr. Clark said.

"What?"

Dr. Clark was good, but he wasn't a mind reader. He wasn't agreeing with the mantra running through my head. "You're not really worried about whether or not you're a suitable match for Penny. You're worried that she'll reject you."

"I'm not scared of rejection. If I was scared of rejection I never could have started a billion dollar tech company."

"Do you want to know what I think, James?"

"That's why I'm paying you."

"That is not what you're paying me for. But we'll circle back to that another time. I think you did care deeply for Lyn. I think you cared about your ex Rachel as well. I think you even cared enough about your wedding vows to Isabella that you remained loyal despite the lack of connection. But you didn't love any of those women. You *love* Penny. You've told me as much. And you're scared she'll reject you."

"She *should* reject me."

"You said making the choice to speak to her again is selfish on your part. But you're only one part of this relationship. She's allowed to make her own decisions too. So write the letter. Tell her the truth. Tell her how you feel. And once it's done, take a good look in the mirror and decide if you want to give it to her or throw it out. But just write the letter, James."

Chapter 5

Thursday

This time tomorrow, Penny would be getting ready for her birthday party. Or maybe she was going out tonight too. Getting drunk somewhere with her friends. I looked at my phone for the hundredth time. I hoped she was safe. I hoped that she knew she could still call me if she needed a ride home.

But she wouldn't call me. Not until I fixed things.

That had been my plan when I went to New York. To finalize my divorce and prove to Penny that I was all in. And I was still all in. Nothing had changed. I could think about this for a million years and I'd always come back to the same conclusion. I was bad for her. But I still wanted her. And I'd never stop wanting her.

Addict.

I ignored the voice in my head. Dr. Clark said it wasn't addiction. He said it was love. And for once, I was choosing to believe him. Even though I feared he was wrong.

I grabbed a sheet of paper and tried not to think about anything. I just lifted up a pen, ignoring my shaking hand, and started writing.

Penny,

I woke up late the first morning that classes started. I wouldn't have come into the coffee shop at that moment unless I had forgotten to set my alarm. Who knew that such a small thing could change the rest of my life? You've captivated me from the very start. You're timid, yet bold. You're humorous, yet sincere. You're young, yet wise.

You're gorgeous and you don't know it. You're contradictory, and challenging, and passionate. And I love you. I love you with all I am.

These past few weeks have been the hardest of my life. Because you have captivated me, body and soul. I eat, breathe, and dream you. And when you're not beside me, I feel such loss. When I see you in class, I can no longer breathe. When I think about you, I can no longer eat. And only nightmares of losing you accompany me in slumber.

I thought I knew what love was. But I was wrong. The love I have for you is something that I have never known. It is constant and all consuming and it terrifies me. The only thing scarier than realizing what my love for you is, is the fact that I have lost that love.

I wanted to protect you. I didn't want to drag you into my darkness. But I realize that when I am with you, I am not the man I once was. When you look at me, I can feel the way you see me, and I become something better. I want to be the man that you need. And I feel like I can be everything you want.

But you need to know that I have many flaws. And one of them is weakness. When I realized my feelings for you, I left. I left you, and I have never regretted anything so much in my life. Because without you, I am not living. Only with you am I strong. Only with you am I good. Only with you am I whole.

And I am selfish. Because I want you to be with me despite my demons. I want to kiss you every morning when you wake up in my arms. I want to whisper I love you in your ear before we fall asleep at night. I want my days to be consumed by your love. And I want you to love me back even though I am telling you that I am not good for you. Because it is your choice. I tried to stay away from you and I cannot. I am not a good man. But if you choose me I will not push you away again. I will trust your judgment. And every ounce of me hopes that you'll make a mistake and come back to me. Every fiber of my being wants you to make the wrong choice. And if you do, I promise to be the best that I can be for you.

I don't care that you lied to me. I don't care that you only just turned 20. I don't care that you are a student in my class. All I care about is you, Penny. My greatest love.

I put my pen down.

Dr. Clark was right. That did feel good.

I hadn't mentioned what happened with Isabella, but that seemed like a better thing to confess in person. For Penny's birthday, I just wanted her to know how much I loved her. And that I was going to fight for her forgiveness.

I grabbed a copy of my divorce papers that showed my signature. I couldn't give her the finalized papers. But I could show her that I was serious. I folded the two sheets and slid them into an envelope.

I also added the VIP tickets I'd had Ian order for the Macy's Thanksgiving Day Parade.

There.

It was done.

I stared at the envelope. Now I just needed to figure out if I was actually going to give it to her. Or tear it in half and throw it in the trash.

I stared at the envelope for hours. Literally hours. I looked at it almost as much as I did my phone.

Students partaking in Thirsty Thursday were already getting rowdy outside. I could hear the laughter from Main Street.

And I kept sitting at my desk, staring at the envelope. Penny was officially 20 years old now. She wasn't a teenager. That made everything better, right? I could give her this letter today. We were both adults. She could form her own decision.

But I still didn't move.

I'd stayed away from her. It had taken every ounce of restraint I possessed, but I still did it. Because a part of me felt like that was the right thing here. To give her the space to move on. To find someone her own age. Someone good for her. Not that dickhead Tyler.

So...had she? For some reason I was expecting her to call. Or text. Or...something.

But she was probably thinking the same of me. It was her birthday for Christ's sake and I was sitting in my apartment alone instead of with her.

I'd resisted for days, but I turned on my computer. I opened up the camera footage from outside her dorm. And I just stared at it. But everyone that was going out for the night had probably already left.

So I rewound the footage. Back to this morning to see her leave for her first class of the day. Maybe seeing her would be the answer I needed. If I could just see her smile...I'd stay away. For her. I'd do it for her. I just needed to see one tiny smile.

A few students came in and out of the dorm, but none of them were Penny.

Was she lying in bed this morning as depressed as me?

I continued to stare at the screen. I just stared and stared until finally, she emerged.

For just a second, it was a little easier to breathe.

She was walking next to Melissa. Melissa was smiling and laughing about something. But Penny wasn't. I zoomed in on her face and froze the frame.

It was her birthday. And she looked even sadder than she had in class yesterday.

She should have been smiling and laughing and screaming my name with my cock deep inside of her.

Fuck.

I slammed the lid of my laptop shut. What the hell was I supposed to do if this was a lose-lose situation for her?

***

I ran to her dormitory.

Then I ran back to my apartment.

Then back to her dorm.

Then back to my apartment.

I literally ran back and forth, with the envelope in my hoodie pocket, trying to decide what the fuck to do. Until I realized that the best thing to do was try to run the idea of seeing her out of my system.

So I ran farther. Faster. I ran until it hurt more than usual to breathe. Until my lungs ached. Until I knew it was past midnight.

I'd missed her birthday.

I hadn't said a fucking word.

And I regretted it. But at the same time…I didn't. Because Penny was strong. She'd move on. She'd find someone new. Someone who wasn't so fucked up in the head. And then…she'd be happy. Way happier than she would be if she stayed with me.

I collapsed on a bench on Main Street to try to catch my breath.

My phone buzzed in my pocket and I pulled it out.

I had a message from Penny. After days of praying she'd speak to me, now I didn't even want to read it. But her name lit up on my screen was too much of a temptation to resist. I clicked on the message.

"I had a great birthday. Thanks for remembering, Professor Hunter. I assume you had something super fancy and prestigious to do tonight. Sorry I wasted so much of your precious time. I hope you have a great life."

I'd remembered.

I'd been tormented for days.

And every second I'd spent with her were the best moments I'd had in a long time.

My time wasn't precious. My time felt endless. That's what days without her were…an endless hell.

I hope you have a great life.

She was done. She was ready to move on. It's what I wanted and yet…I just wanted to scream.

I had my answer.

And I didn't want it. I didn't want any fucking piece of it. I just wanted her.

I put my face in my hands and leaned forward. I buried my fingers in my hair and just stared at the ground. And stared. And stared.

I hope you have a great life.

How the fuck was I supposed to do that without her in it?

But it wasn't about me.

None of this was about me.

It was about her. And what was best for her. And I certainly wasn't it. I was a washed up drunk. I'd fucked a teenager. I'd fucked a student. I was a piece of shit.

I pulled the envelope out of my pocket. I went to rip it in half. But my hands froze again. I couldn't do it. I couldn't even do this one thing.

I tossed the envelope onto the bench and put my face in my hands.

Penny was ready to move on.

And I already knew I was going to fuck it all up for her. I was going to ruin her life. And I knew I didn't have enough self-control to stop myself from doing it.

I wanted to be a good man for Penny.

But at the same time, I knew that a good man would walk away.

None of that mattered. I couldn't stop. I didn't know how to stop. What mattered was that when I wanted something I got it. I worked my ass off for every single thing in my life. And I could put all that energy into getting Penny back.

I swallowed hard. But what if Penny said no? What if she told me to fuck off?

I'd have to walk away for good. I'd have to live the rest of my life in hell.

But sitting here doing nothing was just delaying the inevitable.

Shit. For once, was Dr. Clark actually right? Was I seriously scared of rejection?

That wasn't me. *Fuck no.*

It was time I won my girl back.

Chapter 6

Friday

A part of me hoped that I could still talk myself out of it. That the next time I looked at the letter I'd be compelled to tear it in half.

I even canceled my classes today in the hope that by not seeing Penny…I'd resist.

But if that was true, I wouldn't be standing in this Halloween store looking for a costume for her birthday party tonight. I'd already made up my mind here. Penny was mine.

It hadn't taken me much research to realize that the party was being thrown at Tyler Stevens' frat house. If there was one thing I knew…I was at least better than that douche.

I wasn't a good man.

I was terrible for Penny.

But I couldn't stay away from her for one more day. I just couldn't. I couldn't stand here and be happy for her with someone else. Not when I needed her. I couldn't watch her get over me with someone new. I just couldn't do it. She said she hoped I had a great life. So I was going to do that. But I needed her to be a part of it.

I knew I was a monster. But tonight it was okay for me to be a monster. Because it was a Halloween party. I could literally be whoever the fuck I wanted. I picked up a horrifying green mask off the shelf in front of me. Yeah, that seemed fitting. But it smelled like cheap plastic. No aftershave in the world could cover that up. And I wasn't putting that anywhere near my face.

I tossed it back onto the shelf next to an axe. A pretty real looking axe. I lifted it up and spun it around. *This'll work.*

***

"James," Ellen said as I stepped out of my room. She was standing at the stove stirring something that smelled amazing.

"What are you still doing here?"

She squinted her eyes at me. "Is that any way to greet me?"

"Sorry. I just figured you'd be gone for the weekend."

"And I figured you'd be grading papers. Not..." her eyes scanned me from head to toe. "...cutting down a tree?"

I laughed and looked down at my lumberjack outfit. I was wearing a flannel shirt and old jeans tucked into a pair of work boots. My knit hat was pulled low to hopefully help hide my identity a bit. I didn't want someone to recognize me from class. But the beard I'd been growing out from a lack of caring over the last few days definitely helped. If it wasn't for the axe, I probably would have just looked like a college hipster. I'd blend in just fine.

"I'm going to Penny's birthday party. It's Halloween themed." I shrugged. I knew that wasn't exactly enough of an explanation. But I didn't really feel like explaining myself. Because I didn't have any reasons to do this except for selfish ones.

"Were you invited to this party?"

"I...*was.*"

"So that means you were invited a while ago, but she has no idea you're coming tonight?"

"That's about right."

Ellen laughed. "Good."

"Good?"

"It's about time you stopped moping around and actually did something about it."

I smiled.

"And James?"

"Yeah?"

"Maybe grovel a bit."

I didn't really do groveling. I'd much rather just hit someone with my axe. "I'm planning on apologizing."

"Splendid. And will there be drinking at this party?"

I laughed. She was acting like I was in high school. Which was hilarious. Because I'd been drunk and high throughout most of that. And my actual mother hadn't cared in the slightest.

"I'm serious, James."

"It's at a frat house. Of course there will be drinking."

"Are you sure that's a wise idea? Given…everything?"

I wasn't sure if by everything she was talking about the abundance of cheap beer or the fact that I'd be surrounded by my students. Probably both. "I've already decided to go." It was an answer she of all people could understand. She knew that once I set my mind on something I was rather relentless.

"And will you be partaking? I think maybe Ian should drive…"

"I'm going to walk." I was trying to blend in. Bringing my bodyguard and rolling up in a Tesla kind of went against my plan here. "And I'm not going to drink, Ellen." I hadn't had a drink since Ian handed me a beer on that park bench. I felt so out of control the morning I woke up next to Isabella. I didn't want to feel that way again. I didn't want to put my relationship with Penny in jeopardy any more than I already had. It didn't matter that I couldn't remember what happened. Unlike Isabella, I had no idea and no way to figure it out. And I really hated feeling out of control.

"Do you promise?" Ellen asked. She pointed her spoon at me like she was tempted to hit me with it.

"You're not my mother, Ellen."

"I'm very aware. Your mother and I couldn't be more different. Now I'll ask you again. Are you going to be drinking tonight? Because if you are...I...I...won't be coming back on Monday." She started stirring whatever was in the pot again as she stared at me.

Yeah, she was definitely different than my mom. My mom didn't give a shit about me. And Ellen did. "I'm sorry, Ellen. I'm sorry about all of it. I promise I won't have a drink tonight."

She nodded. "I'm holding you to that."

"I know."

"I'll be gone before you get back. I just wanted to stay late and make a few extra meals in case Rob comes this weekend. You still don't know exactly when he'll arrive?"

"No, he didn't say."

"Well, I for one am excited. He always brings cheer."

"That he does." Her subtext was that I *didn't* bring cheer. I knew the past couple weeks had been rough on all of us. And I wanted to be better. For Penny. For Ellen and Ian. I just needed to be better. I stopped as I walked through the kitchen and awkwardly gave Ellen a hug.

At first she seemed surprised, but then she hugged me back.

"These things have a way of working out, James."

"I know."

She leaned back and grabbed both sides of my face. "Go get her back."

I nodded. That was the plan. Penny was mine. There were no ifs ands or buts about it. She was made for me and only me. And I was going to get her back.

***

I pulled my knit hat even lower as I walked up to the frat house.

It was ridiculous to walk into this party surrounded by my students. But I'd come late. They'd all be shitfaced by now. And I certainly wasn't dressed the same as I was in class.

As I walked through the doors, not a soul even looked at me. It was pretty dark and the music was blaring. I remembered parties like this. Not vividly though. I'd been an even bigger mess in college than I was in high school.

Penny wasn't on the first floor. And I couldn't make myself go up to the second story and open up all those doors. If I saw her behind one of them with some prick, I...I'd behave like I used to in high school. I wouldn't be able to control myself. Once I started punching someone, it was like I had no control.

No control.

That seemed to be an issue in a lot of areas in my life. I hadn't talked about this specific thing with Dr. Clark yet though. He didn't know how much I loved getting in fist fights until my knuckles were raw and bloody.

It was a rush. The same kind of high as actually getting high.

I clenched my hands into fists for a second and then released them. I didn't need a fix. I just needed Penny. I just needed to focus.

I walked past the stairs. No, I definitely wouldn't be going up there. The last thing I needed was a scene. I took one last look in the kitchen, just in case I'd missed her. But she was nowhere in sight. And Penny wasn't exactly easy to miss. Her red hair was always easy to spot in a crowd. I walked back toward the stairs and looked up.

She wouldn't be up there.

She wouldn't have done that.

We were just on a break.

Hypocrite.

I rubbed my temple. I hadn't slept with Isabella. I know I hadn't. I…*fuck.* I wasn't sure. I put my hand on the railing. If Penny was up there with Tyler, I'd hurt him. I wouldn't be able to stop myself. I just stood there staring up the stairs. *Breathe.* But it didn't matter how many times I told myself to breathe. If Penny had slept with that piece of shit, I'd kill him. *God, breathe.* I gripped the railing so hard that my knuckles started to turn white.

The music blasting from somewhere suddenly stopped.

And then I heard people singing happy birthday.

I saw a few people hurrying down the basement stairs and followed them. The singing was louder down here. The smell of stale beer stronger.

And there she was.

Standing with Melissa in front of a huge cake. A smile on her beautiful face.

I felt the corners of my mouth turn up too. It had been a long time since I'd seen her smile.

I stood in the corner like the stalker I was and stared at her. She was dressed in all green, ivy wrapping up her arms and legs. She'd teased her hair to make it stand out even more. She was Poison Ivy. A very sexy Poison Ivy.

The song ended and the two of them blew out the candles.

"Best. Birthday. Ever!" Melissa yelled as she cut each of them a slice of cake.

Penny said something and turned her attention to the right.

My stomach dropped. She was smiling over at Tyler.

Tyler who was dressed like some kind of lame pirate. I wasn't concerned about his stupid costume though. I was more concerned about the state of disarray it was in. The top few buttons were undone. His hair was a tussled mess.

Penny appeared by his side holding a plate of cake for him.

I watched them talk.

I watched the way they laughed.

I stared back at the buttons undone on his shirt.

And suddenly I couldn't breathe. All I saw was red. This pounding in the back of my head. My hands forming into fists.

They'd fucked.

I knew they'd fucked.

The music picked back up through the speakers. But all I could hear was my heartbeat pulsing in my head.

He'd touched her.

She'd *let* him.

They laughed about something and I couldn't look away. Penny had done what I'd hoped. She'd moved on.

I watched in horror as Penny wrapped her fingers around the back of his neck, stood up on her tiptoes, and kissed him.

I was used to feeling betrayed. But this was worse. It was like she'd physically wounded me. Like she'd stabbed a knife into my chest and was slowly twisting it.

She'd actually moved on. With someone else. Would she still be kissing him if she knew I was here? I could easily imagine her kissing him while staring directly at me, rubbing salt into the wound.

Breathe.

I blinked. Penny wasn't like that. She wasn't evil. That was the kind of fucked up shit I would do. But not her.

She finally pulled back and whispered something in his ear. Tyler laughed and stared down at her like she was his.

Not a chance in hell.

I was going to be sick.

I was going to kill him.

Penny didn't belong to Tyler. She belonged to me.

He said something else to her and she kissed him on the cheek. He unwound himself from her arms and walked through the crowd.

I watched him walk up the basement steps. I was tempted to follow him, but I was more curious about why she hadn't. Was she just finishing her cake before joining him for round two?

Tyler fucking Stevens was going to die before I gave him a chance to take what was mine again.

I didn't even realize I'd moved until I was leaning against the wall where Tyler had once stood. Penny was finishing a bite of cake. She smiled over at Melissa on the dance floor, not a care in the world.

While I was busy drowning. Did she know she was torturing me? Had she really forgotten about me so easily?

I took a deep breath, her cherry scented perfume invading my senses. The scent usually made it easier for me to breath. But it felt like I was choking.

"Have a great life?" I said.

She turned and just stared at me.

Her pupils were dilated. And by the way she was staring, it seemed like she wasn't even registering that I was standing right in front of her.

And suddenly it all made sense.

She was drunk out of her mind.

And that shithead had taken advantage of her. *Again.* What the hell was wrong with that kid?

She blinked and finally it seemed like she realized I was really there. But she wasn't staring at me like she used to. There was no adoration in her eyes. She looked...pissed. "Yeah. Have a great life." She turned her attention back to the dance floor.

"Are you done?" I needed to get us out of here before Tyler reappeared. Because I was going to kill him. I wouldn't even be able to stop myself.

She looked back up at me. "Done what?"

"Done here? Let's go." I reached out and brushed my fingers along her wrist. The feeling of her skin against mine made me feel warm for the first time in weeks. I was honestly surprised I'd lasted this long away from her.

She didn't seem to feel the same way though. Because she took a step back from me. "No, I'm not done. This is my birthday party. I'm not leaving. And I'm definitely not leaving with *you.*"

Yes you are, Penny. I wasn't really asking her. This wasn't up for negotiation. And if we didn't leave right this second, I was going to kill her new fuck boy.

Chapter 7

Friday

She was staring at me like I'd lost my mind. But for the first time in weeks I was finally seeing everything clearly. And I was pretty sure she'd be seeing things a lot more clearly if Tyler hadn't gotten her wasted.

"You're drunk," I said.

"I'm not drunk!" she yelled. Pretty much confessing to me that she was indeed drunk out of her mind.

"Penny, we need to talk. And I don't want to do it here." I tried to lower my voice. A few people were already staring over at us.

"You've had weeks to talk to me. You don't just get to show up tonight and ruin my birthday party. Why tonight of all nights?"

"I thought you'd be happy to see me." Honestly, it was the truth. I thought she would be. I never even considered the fact that she'd actually move on. I'd hoped she would have, but it was all a lie in my head. I couldn't bear the thought. I was selfish and I'd always be selfish when it came to wanting her.

And I'd seen her face in class. I'd seen her pain. But she'd just done a complete 180. I came here tonight thinking I'd be making her smile again. That she'd be leaning on me. Kissing me. Not someone else. She was supposed to be jumping back in my arms, not glaring at me like I was a monster. Which was fitting. Because she was finally seeing me for exactly what I was. I swallowed hard.

"I'm not," she said. "Please just go."

I shook my head. "I'm not leaving here unless it's with you."

"You forgot my birthday." She started blinking faster and bit her lip, like that would somehow make the tears stop from forming.

God, I'd give anything to bite her lip for her. And now that I was thinking about her lips, I was picturing them wrapped around my cock. I tried to focus. "I didn't forget." How could I possibly forget her birthday? She was the most important person in my life. I just needed a few minutes to tell her that. *I'm sorry. I'm so fucking sorry.*

She shook her head. "Fine. You ignored my birthday then."

I winced.

"I feel like that's even worse."

That did sound worse. "Please just let me explain."

"There's nothing to explain. You're my boyfriend, you should have at least wished me a happy birthday. Sorry, ex-boyfriend." She crossed her arms in front of her chest.

Ex-boyfriend. The words echoed around in my head. "Well that explains a lot."

She looked up at me. "What are you talking about?"

"You and Mr. Stevens don't seem to be acting like just friends anymore."

She glared at me. "That's really none of your business."

"Everything you do is my business." I clenched my jaw. Every single thing she did or said was my business. Everyone she talked to. Everyone she even looked at. It was all my business.

"Nothing I do is your business. We're done. You've made that very clear."

"We are not done." Maybe she could quit me. But I couldn't so easily quit her.

"Yes we are. You ignored me for weeks. And now you finally show up. Apparently just to make me feel like shit because I don't hear you offering an apology."

"I told you that I wanted to talk." Somewhere other than here. Anywhere other than here.

"Then talk. Tell me why you acted like I didn't exist. Do you have any idea how hard it was to go to class and feel invisible?"

"Yes, I do." Every time I saw her in class I felt like death. I couldn't eat. I couldn't sleep. I could barely breathe.

"No, you don't." She looked down at the ground and started blinking faster.

I wanted to pull her into my arms and tell her it was going to be okay now. That I'd make it all better. But everything about her body language screamed that she'd rather slap me. And I really couldn't afford to make a scene here. I didn't want anyone else staring at us.

"It's too late to talk," she said. "You waited too long. I can't. I don't want to. Not anymore."

No. It wasn't too late. It couldn't be. I just needed one minute. One minute to fix this mess. "Penny, come on, let's go." I reached out for her hand.

"Stop." She pulled away like my touch repulsed her.

And shouldn't it? *Penny is better off without me in her life. She's good. She's pure. She's perfect. She deserves more. I'd ruin her life. I'm sick. I'm twisted. I'm fucked up in the head. I deserve to be alone.*

Stop. She wasn't better off alone. Tyler had taken advantage of her. And if I'd been here, I could have stopped it. I could have protected her. I could be better for her. And I would be.

Tears finally formed in the corners of her eyes and she just stared at me. Completely lost.

I just needed a second to explain. I'd give her the letter. It was just sitting in my back pocket waiting for her. It would explain everything better than I could in this crowded room. "Penny." I put my hand on her elbow.

"Don't touch me." She took another step back.

Every step she took back felt like my heart was breaking in two. I wasn't going to let her run away from us. I'd seen what my life was like without her in it. And I couldn't do it. I couldn't. The darkness would swallow me whole without her. "Penny." I closed the gap between us.

"She said stop." Tyler put his hand on my chest and lightly shoved me back.

I looked down at my chest and then back at him. He did not just shove me. He did not just put his hands on me because I was talking to *my* girlfriend. When he'd had the audacity to get her drunk and take advantage of her. I wasn't in the wrong here. He was. This guy had a death wish.

"Tyler," I said and nodded my head at him. I hoped he realized that what I was actually saying was, "If you don't step back I'm going to kill you."

"James, is it?" he said sarcastically.

Fuck off. Seriously. It's for your own good. "Look, she's drunk. I'm just going to take her home." My home. Because she belonged with me.

"Jesus, I'm not drunk," Penny said.

Yes, she most definitely was drunk. And this dick was to blame. Was I the only one looking out for her? Where the hell was Melissa right now? She was surrounded by immature idiots. It had never been more clear that she needed me. And I wasn't going anywhere this time.

"She can spend the night if she wants to," Tyler said. "Don't worry about it."

Yeah, he definitely wanted to die. "That's exactly what I'm worried about. Penny, let's go. Now."

It looked like she wanted to come with me. But she hesitated again. And her feet stayed firmly rooted in place.

Tyler put his arm out in front of Penny even though she didn't move. "She's not going anywhere with you. Why are you even here?"

I swear, if he touched her or me one more time, he wouldn't be walking tomorrow. "Because my girlfriend invited me."

"She's definitely not your girlfriend. Get the fuck out of my house."

Penny wouldn't have rubbed this in my face. But Tyler clearly had no problem doing it. I wanted to hear it from him. I wanted him to tell me he fucked my girlfriend right to my face. And then I'd be in the right when I punched him. "What is that supposed to mean?" I looked over at Penny. I wanted to hear it from her too. I wanted her to confess that she cheated on me with this imbecile.

"You know what it means," Tyler said.

What a pussy. He couldn't even look me in the eyes and tell me. "Tyler. Get out of my way." I took a deep breath. I knew I was seconds away from snapping.

Tyler just stared at me. "Or what?"

I took another step toward Penny, but Tyler shoved me in the chest again. Harder this time. I took a few steps back to steady myself. *Don't do it. Don't do it.* I said the words over and over again in my head. But no mantra was calming me down tonight. I shook my head back and forth like I could knock the idea of murdering him out of my head. But it wasn't going anywhere. It was as frozen in place as Penny.

"Tyler," Penny said quietly. She reached out and touched his shoulder.

I stared down at her hand on Tyler's shoulder.

Her hands were mine to hold. No one else's.

But Penny was trying to calm *him* down. She was going to *him*. She was choosing *him*.

And I finally snapped. I balled my hand into a fist and cocked my arm.

"James!" Penny screamed.

But she was too late. *I* was too late. I didn't care about making a scene. I didn't care that I was probably about to be fired. It felt like I'd lost Penny. And nothing else mattered. All I could feel was this pounding in my head. And I just needed a release. Tyler's face was just begging to be rearranged.

So I punched him. Square in the nose. *God that felt good.*

Tyler cursed and stumbled backward. His nose immediately started gushing blood.

I smiled. I'd been dying to do that ever since he'd given her a "friendship rose." *Friendship rose my ass.*

"Oh my God, are you okay?" Penny touched the side of Tyler's face. "Oh my God, Tyler."

She was about to be a hell of a lot more worried about Tyler. Because I'd only just started.

Tyler wiped his nose with the back of his hand. "Hold this for me," he said and handed her something before charging toward me.

"What the hell are you doing?!" Penny yelled after him. *Asking to be killed.*

Tyler dropped his shoulder at the last second, slamming into my stomach. It was a cheap shot. He knocked me into a few couples dancing as we fell to the floor.

I punched the side of his face again before my back hit the hard cement. I groaned. I was too old for this shit.

"I said get the fuck out of my house!" Tyler yelled.

"Not without Penny." The music was so loud that it didn't matter what I said. No one could hear me but him.

People started screaming around us as we rolled and almost knocked into more people.

I grabbed the collar of Tyler's shirt. "I will kill you if you ever even think about touching my girlfriend again."

He punched me square in the jaw. And I didn't even care. I just tightened my hands on his shirt. *You think that hurts me? You think anything hurts me anymore?* I loved the taste of blood in my mouth. *Hit me again you prick.* That was my secret weapon for winning a fight. Let my idiot opponent get worn out with a few cheap shots. Because I didn't feel anything. And once he was tired I'd beat the shit out of him.

"I didn't just touch her," Tyler said.

I tightened my hands even more. Did he know how easily I could snap his neck? "You're messing with the wrong person." It was my final warning. He was a student. Hitting him with a few punches was bad. But making him unrecognizable was another thing entirely. And I was losing control. Slowly. I felt myself slipping.

Tyler landed another shot across my jaw. "Am I? You're the one that's about to be fired."

"I'll set your dick on fire if you ever put it anywhere near Penny again." Now I was an arsonist? That seemed like a good progression from stalker.

The dance music suddenly stopped.

"I'll fuck whoever I want to fuck," Tyler snarled as he landed another punch across my face.

The basement was eerily silent.

Everyone had heard it. Everyone knew what Tyler had done. And if I thought I was seeing red before? It was definitely all I could see now.

The room was quiet for another second and then people started yelling, "Fight, fight, fight!"

"Stop it!" Penny yelled. "Both of you, stop!"

I didn't want her to be worried about both of us. I wanted her to choose me. Right here, right now.

She tried to grab Tyler's arm before he landed another punch across my face. But I didn't even care when his knuckles collided with my jaw. It didn't faze me one bit. I was doing my best to show restraint, but when I'd bought my axe prop, I'd thought about how fun it would be to hit someone with it. And I didn't want to miss my chance. So I grabbed it from the floor beside me, and whacked Tyler on the side of the head. *If only it had been a real axe.*

He teetered slightly. *Lightweight.* This was barely even a fight.

I grabbed Tyler's collar again and pulled him close to my face. "If you know what's good for you, you'll stay the hell away from her."

"I can end you," Tyler said.

Didn't he see? I didn't fucking care. I was nothing without Penny. He was fighting a losing game here. "Then do it." I let go of his collar and pushed him back down to the floor.

I stood up. I knew I was probably sporting a black eye. And the taste of blood wasn't going away, so I probably had a busted lip. I looked over at Penny. *Come with me. Now.*

But instead of understanding my silent demand, she looked over my shoulder as Tyler stood up.

"Please stop fighting," she said. "James, please just go. We can talk tomorrow, okay? Please."

And leave you here with Tyler? Not a chance in hell. "Penny, do not make me carry you out of here," I said.

"Hey, asshole! She asked you to leave." Something hit the back of my head.

I looked down at Tyler's pirate sword. He'd literally just stabbed me in the back. I bet his dick was as weak as his plastic sword.

I rubbed the back of my head. But I didn't break eye contact with Penny. *Come with me. Now.* I knew she knew what I was thinking.

But she still didn't budge.

Suddenly the blood in my mouth tasted sour. The pounding in my head eased. The high of wanting to pulverize Tyler's face subsided. And I was just…numb.

Penny didn't want me here.

She didn't want me at all.

I'd waited too long.

I'd missed my chance.

All the endorphins I was feeling from the fight evaporated. My high was gone.

Everyone was staring at us. I wasn't sure if anyone could recognize me. Especially with all the blood on my face. But I'd made a scene. I'd punched a fucking student. And I don't think the dean would care that the student was a dipshit. The longer I stayed here, letting people stare, the worse my odds were of going unrecognized.

"Okay," I said. I stared at Penny, waiting for her to change her mind, but she didn't. I'd lost control. And she was staring at me like the monster I was.

This was what I'd wanted.

This was what I'd asked for.

No. I wanted her. I needed her. And I'd fucked everything up.

"Okay," I said again. I couldn't stand her staring at me like that. I wanted to remember when she stared at me with stars in her eyes. I wanted to drown in that memory. I would drown in that. I turned away from her and walked toward the stairs. I needed out of this dingy basement. I needed to somehow get the image of Penny kissing Tyler out of my head. I needed to wake up from this nightmare. I couldn't have lost her. I couldn't have.

I passed by Tyler on my way to the stairs.

"You should have heard her screaming my name," he whispered.

And suddenly I wasn't numb anymore. I'd tried to hold back during our fight. I really had. But he was just begging for me to beat his ass.

I tackled him. We fell onto the table they were using as a makeshift bar. Glass shattered everywhere, but I didn't even feel it digging into my skin. I only had one train of thought. I punched Tyler across the face. Again and again. I was blinded by my own rage.

"What is wrong with you?!" Penny screamed. She tried to grab my arm, but she wasn't strong enough to stop me. She kept screaming at the top of her lungs.

I landed one more punch and stood up before I knocked Tyler unconscious. As much as I wanted to kill him…I didn't want to add homicide to the reasons Penny shouldn't be with me.

Tyler slowly stood up.

He was like a parasite that just wouldn't stop.

He took a swing and I stepped to the side to avoid it.

And a second too late I realized my mistake.

Penny had been right behind me. And Tyler's fist landed on her stomach.

Penny bent over, gasping for air. She stepped backwards and slipped on some of the spilled alcohol. I tried to put my hands out to catch her, but I wasn't quick enough. And her reaction time was too slow from the alcohol coursing through her veins.

Her head slammed against the concrete floor and her eyes rolled into the back of her head.

Chapter 8

All my anger dissipated. Penny was lying there lifeless. The "fight, fight, fight" chants died away.

Everyone was frozen in place now.

Except for me.

I crouched down next to her, cradling her face in my hands. "Penny?"

She didn't respond.

"Penny?"

I heard Melissa sobbing. "Someone call 911!"

No. Penny was drinking underage. She'd be expelled. This would ruin everything she was working toward.

"She slipped," someone said. I looked up. A girl was already on the phone with the 911 operator. I needed to get Penny out of here. I'd get her home and have a doctor come to us.

"Is she okay?" Tyler said.

No, she's not okay. You punched her, you fucking idiot. I kept my eyes trained on Penny so I wouldn't punch Tyler again. "I've got her," I said. I gently picked Penny up, cradling her in my arms. Being extra careful to support her neck.

"I'm so sorry…I didn't mean to," Tyler said. "What should we do?"

We? There was no *we* here. "I've got her," I said again.

Tyler didn't try to stop me as I walked toward the stairs.

"She needs to go to the hospital," Melissa said as she ran beside me.

"I've got her," I said again. I didn't trust Melissa. This was as much her fault as it was Tyler's. She was supposed to be Penny's best friend. So why was Penny so drunk? Why was no one looking out for her?

"James, please, the ambulance is on the way." She followed me up the stairs.

"I'll have a doctor come to us," I said as I carried Penny out of the house. "Penny," I said as I stared down at her unconscious body. "Penny can you hear me?"

She didn't even stir.

Panic laced around my heart. She needed to wake up. She needed to look up at me.

I'd forgotten how light she was when she was in my arms. I remembered thinking that she'd be so easy to break. Since I was so broken.

I shook my head. I wasn't going to break her. I wasn't. This wasn't my fault. But I was lying to myself. All of this was my fault. "Penny," I whispered. "Please."

"James, stop!"

I turned around on the grass. "Melissa, would you just listen to me for two seconds?" I snapped.

For the first time I realized she was crying.

"Take a deep breath," I said.

I wasn't sure if she followed my instructions, but she didn't keep talking, so that was good.

"Now grab my phone out of my pocket." I gestured to my back pocket.

She pulled out my phone.

"Dial number 2."

She hit the number on the phone.

"Tell Ian to pick us up immediately and have him call Steven." I shook my head. "I mean Dr. Ridge. He'll know who I'm talking about."

"Ian?" Melissa said on the phone. "There's been an accident with Penny. Can you please call Dr. Ridge and come pick up Penny and James?"

She looked up at me. "He hung up!"

"He's just doing his job."

She nodded and grabbed Penny's hand. "Penny? Wake up. Please wake up."

I heard the ambulance in the distance.

Come on, Ian. Come on. If Ian didn't arrive first, Penny wouldn't be the only one in trouble. Not that I cared about the fact that I was a professor crashing a college party with underage drinking. I'm pretty sure everything I'd done with Penny was worse than that. And I didn't care about any of it. I just wanted her to wake up. "Penny," I whispered as I stared down at her lifeless face.

It only took another minute before Ian sped up to the curb outside the frat house.

Melissa was reluctant to let go of Penny's hand.

"It's okay, I've got her," I said. "I promise." And I meant it. I was never letting Penny go again. Not even for a second.

Melissa blinked back her tears. "I'm so sorry. I…"

"It's not your fault." I'd put blame on her. And on Tyler. But none of this was their fault. It was mine. I would have stayed there and consoled her more. But there wasn't time.

"What the fuck happened?" Ian said as he climbed out of the car.

"Open the back door." I didn't have time to explain.

He opened the door and helped me get Penny into the back seat. I climbed in next to her, cradling her face in my hands. "Penny, I need you to wake up."

She didn't stir.

The car started moving. I moved my hand from the side of Penny's head and realized my palm was covered with blood. Her hair was matted with it. Where was she cut? I tried to inspect the wound but there was too much blood.

"James, what the fuck?!" Ian yelled.

"Just get us home." A drop of blood landed on her forehead. And I realized some of it was dripping from my face onto her. *Please let it just be my blood. Please.*

"Is she breathing?" Ian asked.

I smoothed her hair out of her face and put my fingers along her throat, smearing more blood along her neck. Her heart was beating steadily. "Yes, she's just unconscious. She hit her head pretty hard."

"What did you do?"

I finally looked up from Penny. "I didn't hurt her, Ian," I said. But it was a lie. I had hurt her. This all happened because I didn't speak to her for weeks. All I'd done was hurt her.

The tires squealed as Ian took a sharp right into the parking garage beneath my apartment. He tried to help me lift Penny but I held her closer. "I've got her."

The elevator ride felt excruciatingly long.

"Seriously, James what the hell happened?"

I ignored him and stepped out of the elevator. "Get some water and some towels." I carried Penny into my bedroom and placed her gently on my bed. I knelt down next to her. "Baby, wake up. Please wake up."

Ian came in with some towels and a glass of water. I grabbed one of the towels and wiped some of the blood off her neck and face. I gently blotted the spot along her hairline. There was so much blood. Why was there so much fucking blood?

"What happened to your face?" Ian said.

"Get out."

"James…"

"Get out," I said more firmly. I didn't mean to snap at him, but I wasn't worried about myself right now.

Ian shook his head and left the room.

I wiped more of the blood away from her pale skin. "Penny," I said. "Penny? God, Penny open your eyes."

But she didn't respond.

"I'm so sorry. Please, just wake up. I'll be better. I'll be better for you." I promise. I can be better for you.

Penny just laid there.

I felt the wetness on my cheeks.

I needed to do something. Anything. Or I'd lose my fucking mind. I stared down at the costume she was wearing. A costume that no one should have ever seen her in but me. And I wondered if she'd bought it when we were still together. If it had been meant for me. But all I could think about was Tyler peeling it from her skin. *Fuck that guy.*

I grabbed a t-shirt from my closet and slowly undressed her. For just a second my eyes fell to her exposed tits. God, I'd missed those. Seeing them in person was so much better than the videos. All I wanted to do was lean forward and pull one of her nipples into my mouth. It felt like a lifetime since I'd tasted her skin. *Stop.* I was such a sick fuck. I quickly pulled the t-shirt down over her.

"I'll be better," I said again.

She looked so young in just my shirt. My eyes fell to her nipples pressing against the fabric. And I heard that voice in the back of my head. *Monster.*

I shook away the thought. "I'll never let anything happen to you again. Just wake up, baby."

She gasped and sat up.

I felt like I exhaled for the first time in an hour.

She cringed at the light and touched her head. When she brought her hand back down she stared in horror at the blood.

"Penny?" I said gently. *It's okay. I'm right here.*

Her eyes focused on my face. "I thought you weren't talking to me?" she mumbled. She reached up and touched her forehead again. "What happened?"

I just stared at her. What did she mean by what happened? "You fell." I searched her eyes for some kind of recollection, but there was none there. "Don't you remember?"

"What?" She looked down at the bloody cloth in my hand.

This wasn't good. How did she not know what happened? "Penny, what is the last thing you remember?"

She just blinked up at me. "I don't know. You weren't talking to me."

Baby, I'm so sorry.

She looked around my bedroom. "Why am I here? How did I get here?"

"I carried you." I stared down at her. How much had she forgotten? "Penny, tell me the last thing you remember."

"I don't know." She started to cry. "I don't know why I'm here. I can't remember. Am I okay?"

"You're going to be fine. The doctor is on the way." I tried to keep my voice even. But I was internally freaking out. She'd hit her head pretty hard. She'd been unconscious for a while. This wasn't good. I lightly pressed the cloth in my hand against her forehead.

She put her hand over her mouth and tried to climb out of bed. But she seemed disoriented and started to fall.

What the hell was she doing? I caught her in my arms before she fell off the bed. I kept my arms firmly around her as I set her back down. "Penny, stay still. The doctor will be here any second. You're going to be fine." *Please be okay.* I sat down on the bed next to her and rubbed her back.

She immediately threw up down the front of my shirt. I tried not to flinch. I just kept rubbing her back. This was probably good. To get all the alcohol out of her system. *Let it all out.*

"I'm so sorry," she groaned.

"It's okay." I held my breath. "It's okay." But I did need to get out of this shirt or I was pretty sure I'd start throwing up too. "Stay right there. I'll be right back." I hurried out of the room, tore off my shirt, and chucked it in the trash. I took a deep breath of clean air as I grabbed a bottle of ginger ale out of the fridge. I took another deep breath. She was awake. She was going to be okay. She had to be. I'd never be able to forgive myself if she wasn't okay.

I walked back into the room. And for the first time since seeing her at the party tonight, I felt a little more relaxed. Because her eyes still trailed down my abs the same way they always did. I climbed back on the bed beside her and handed her the ginger ale. "Drink this."

"I'm so sorry," she repeated.

"Please stop apologizing. All of this is my fault." I looked down at my watch. What was taking Dr. Ridge so long? "Where the hell is he? He should have been here by now."

Penny reached up and grabbed my chin, slowly turning my face to hers. "You're hurt."

"I'm fine, baby. I'm fine." I removed her hand from my face and kissed her palm. The last thing she should be doing was worrying about me. I just wanted to take away her pain. I brought her hand to my lap and stroked my thumb along her palm.

"No." Tears started to stream down her cheeks again as she stared at my face.

I must have looked pretty rough. "You should see the other guy." I tried to smile, but I could tell it looked forced. And I was pretty sure she could tell too.

"Was this my fault?" she asked.

Not in the slightest. I continued to rub my thumb against her palm. "No. It's mine."

A buzz sounded through the apartment. "Finally." I climbed off the bed. "Don't move." Not that I was worried she'd try to after almost falling a minute ago. I walked over to the elevator just as the doors dinged open.

"James," Dr. Ridge said. "What is going on? Ian said that some girl was unconscious?"

Some girl? Penny wasn't just some girl. But I was relieved that Ian hadn't gone into too much detail. I tried to keep my voice low so Penny couldn't hear. "Thanks for coming, Steven. She's awake now. But she just threw up."

"Has she been drinking?"

"Yes. But that's not why I'm worried."

"How much?"

I didn't think the alcohol was why she couldn't remember what happened. But maybe she'd had even more to drink than I realized. "I don't know."

"Let me see her."

"Steven, she fell. She hit her head hard. She's disoriented. She doesn't even remember what happened."

"Where is she?"

"In my bedroom."

He raised his eyebrows, but didn't say anything about it. "And what's her name?"

"Penny Taylor."

He nodded and walked past me toward my bedroom. "Miss Taylor, I'm Dr. Ridge."

"Hello," she said. Her voice was so quiet and scared.

It's going to be okay, baby.

"Can you tell me what happened tonight?" Dr. Ridge asked.

She shook her head.

"How did you hit your head?"

Penny looked up at me. "I...fell?"

That's what I'd told her. But she clearly didn't remember. She was just repeating what I'd told her.

"Do you remember falling?" he asked.

"No."

"Have you been drinking?"

"I don't...I don't know." She looked so confused. "Yes. I think so."

"How much alcohol have you consumed?" His tone was accusatory, but I bit my tongue. I was just as curious about the answer.

"I don't know. I don't remember." She started blinking fast like she was going to cry again.

Dr. Ridge walked around the bed and put his bag down on the floor. He pulled out a small flashlight and pointed it to her eyes. "Follow the light with your eyes," he instructed.

She did what she was told.

"Please stand for me."

I stepped closer in case she fell again.

Penny slid off the bed and onto her feet. But her legs were definitely wobbly. Dr. Ridge put his hands on her arms and helped her back onto the bed.

"You have a concussion. Sit back for me."

I swear I stopped breathing. She had a concussion. Because of me. I clenched my jaw.

Penny leaned back against the pillows as Dr. Ridge grabbed something else from his bag. He blotted her forehead.

"You need stitches," he said.

She had a concussion and needed stitches? It felt like there was a knife in my chest. Ian was right to accuse me of hurting her. I had. This was all my fault.

"Shouldn't I go to a hospital?" Penny asked.

"I'll fix you up better than any emergency room doctor at this hour. Close your eyes. This is going to sting, but then you won't be able to feel anything."

I ignored the look on Dr. Ridge's face as I climbed onto the bed beside Penny and grabbed her hand.

Penny closed her eyes as Dr. Ridge pulled a syringe out of his bag. But I kept my eyes open the whole time. I needed to see this. I needed to see the pain I'd caused her.

It was easy to forget that my actions had consequences when I was drowning. When all I could think about was coming up for air. But I'd done this. I'd caused it.

Penny squeezed my hand as the needle jabbed her forehead.

"Keep your eyes closed, Penny," I whispered. I stroked her palm with my thumb, hoping I could distract her from the pain.

I watched each stitch that Dr. Ridge made.

And I vowed to never hurt her again.

Not in a million years.

I'd protect her. I'd put her first. I'd be better. *I'll be a better man for you. I will, I swear.*

"You're all set," Dr. Ridge said when he finally finished.

Penny slowly opened her eyes.

"Take it easy for a few days."

"Thank you," she murmured.

Dr. Ridge nodded and gave her a small smile. But I could tell there was a lot more he wanted to say. I squeezed Penny's hand one more time before following him out of my bedroom.

"What about her memory?" I asked when we were out of earshot.

"She's just in shock. She should be fine in the morning. Call me if she's still having trouble with her memory."

I nodded. "Thank you for coming out, Steven."

There was an awkward pause. "Did you want to tell me what happened tonight?"

Not really. And I knew that wasn't really the question he wanted to ask me. "A sequence of unfortunate events is all."

"I see." Another awkward pause. "How old is she?"

And there it was. I didn't need to defend my relationship with her to him. "Old enough."

"Does Isabella know?"

For Christ's sake. I walked him closer to the elevator, further away from Penny. "Isabella and I are divorced, Steven." *Almost.*

"That's not what I've heard. I thought the two of you were giving it another go?"

What the hell was Isabella telling people? "It's over. And you shouldn't believe anything you read in tabloids." I hit the button for the elevator and the doors dinged open. I was grateful for him coming out in the middle of the night. But I was seconds away from shoving him onto the elevator.

He shrugged. And instead of stepping onto the elevator he opened his bag. "Put this on her forehead." He lifted up a Ziplock bag full of bandages. "And have her take these. They'll help with the pain." He handed me a container of pills and the Ziplock. "I'm assuming you don't want anything?"

"No, I'm good." I knew better than to take any pills. I'd taken enough in college for five lifetimes.

"Put some ice on that eye, James." He stepped onto the elevator.

"I'd appreciate your discretion with this."

"You already have my signature, James."

The doors slid closed behind him and I exhaled slowly. I honestly didn't even know when I'd made him sign an NDA. Probably one of the many times I was high out of my mind.

I sighed and stared down at my wrist. It was still red from my rubber band.

I needed to take my sessions with Dr. Clark more seriously. I'd do whatever he told me to do. I just wanted to be better. I didn't want to be sick anymore.

Chapter 9

Friday

I walked back into my bedroom. The smell of cherries was everywhere. I hadn't realized how much it had faded since Penny had last been here.

And even though Penny was hurt and scared, she still looked beautiful. I'd never stood a chance when I was trying to stay away from her.

I sat down on the edge of the bed and opened the Ziplock bag Dr. Ridge had given me. "Stay still," I said. I gently dotted some of the salve onto her forehead.

I'd told myself I could protect her. And the first thing that happened when I showed back up in her life was this? *I'm so sorry, baby.* My heart ached as I touched the stitches. I'd been so scared of breaking her. And here she was. Sitting in my bed...broken.

Tears started falling down her cheeks.

I pulled my hand back. "Why are you crying? Does it hurt?" I was trying to be gentle.

She shook her head.

It wasn't convincing. But I needed to finish this up. I placed a white bandage over her stitches. I tried to be gentler as I applied the medical tape to keep it in place. I didn't want to keep hurting her. It was like it was all I was capable of.

Her bottom lip trembled. "I want to go home."

"Penny, you are home." I cupped her chin in my hand. "Please, Professor Hunter."

"I'm not letting you out of my sight." *Not ever again.* Yes, this happened tonight when I showed back up. But

- 75 -

she'd been drinking. She'd been hanging out with a piece of shit.

Breathe. From here on out I was going to keep her safe. I pulled her head onto my chest.

"I need to go home." She sniffed. "Please."

I kissed her forehead. Her scent calmed the ache in my chest. I heard her words, but I couldn't do it. *I can't.* It wasn't just that I wanted to keep her safe. It was that I finally had her back in my arms. And I couldn't let go. I'd stayed away from her for so long. I'd never be strong enough to do that again. "You need rest."

She looked down at her lap. "Why am I wearing one of your shirts?"

"I didn't want Dr. Ridge to see you in the outfit you were wearing earlier." The costume was sexy as hell. No one should have ever seen her in that but me.

"You undressed me?"

"Yes."

"You shouldn't have done that."

"Penny, I've seen you naked plenty of times."

She looked up at me. "You're not allowed to see people naked that you've ignored for two weeks. That's not how things work. You've got everything backwards."

She was rambling. It reminded me of when we first met and she kept losing her words around me. I still found it incredibly endearing. "In that case, I'm sorry."

"Good."

I kissed her forehead next to her bandage.

A rumble of thunder sounded outside. A moment later I could hear the patter of rain against the window. I breathed in Penny's perfume and closed my eyes, remembering our first kiss. It was a stormy night just like this.

"It's raining," she mumbled.

I kissed her forehead again.

"Whenever it rains I think about you. It's when I missed you the most."

There was a lump in my throat that wouldn't go away. *Me too, Penny.*

"You promised you wouldn't be mad at me. You promised."

I had nothing to say to that. I did break my promise to her. I knew I was a disappointment. I knew I was a fucking mess. But couldn't she already see all that? So instead of answering her, I kissed her forehead again.

She looked up at me. "You should put ice on your eye."

"Don't worry about me, Penny." Why was she always worried about me? She was too good for me. Too kind. Too sweet. Too perfect.

"You're very worrisome," she sighed into my chest. "You never talk to me. You won't let me in."

I ran my fingers through her hair. I didn't know what to say to that either. I swallowed hard. "I'm trying." *I promise that I'm trying.*

She yawned. "It's normal to worry about the people you love."

I started blinking fast. But I couldn't stop it. I felt a tear slide down my cheek.

No one worried about me.

My parents never cared.

And I'd lost all my friends.

All I had was her. And she loved me despite my flaws. This was real. We were real.

It felt really good to know that someone cared. But even as I thought it, I felt guilty. Ellen cared. Ian cared. Rob cared. But this was different. I paid Ellen and Ian to stick by me. And Rob was family.

Penny didn't have to care about me. She was choosing to.

She lightly snored in my arms. I reached out and ran my fingers through her hair. Being a better man for her meant not making her worry. I'd get my shit together.

I slowly unwound my arms from around her, being careful not to wake her. And then I texted her friends to let them know she was okay. I let Ian know too. I showered. I ignored the cut on my lip and my eye turning more purple by the minute. And then I climbed back into bed where I belonged. Next to her.

***

The sound of the shower woke me up. I slowly opened my eyes and yawned. I hadn't slept that well since the last time Penny was in this bed with me.

Last night had not gone at all how I'd planned. But it had been a wakeup call. From here on out, I was going to be the man Penny needed me to be.

I climbed out of bed and walked into my closet. I pulled on a pair of sweatpants, grabbed a clean outfit for Penny, and set it down outside the bathroom door for her. Penny needed carbs to soak up the rest of the alcohol in her system. A hangover combined with her concussion...she was not going to be feeling good this morning. And I was going to make her feel better.

The shower turned off just as I got the waffles in the toaster. I put the box back in the freezer. Not that I was hiding the fact that these weren't homemade.

Penny emerged out of my bedroom a moment later. Her eyes raked over my body. But unlike last night, when it seemed like she'd savored staring...today she looked pissed. She stopped at the counter.

"How are you feeling?" I asked.

"I'm fine," she said.

That couldn't be true. I was sure her head was pounding.

"I'm going to get going."

I raised my left eyebrow. Was she joking? I pushed a plate of waffles in front of her.

"I thought you didn't cook."

"I don't. They were frozen."

She looked down at her plate. "I'm not hungry."

"You've lost weight. You need to eat."

"So now you suddenly care about me again?"

"I never stopped caring about you." I couldn't prevent the scowl from forming on my face. She had this all wrong. "I see that you have your memory back."

She defiantly pushed the plate away.

I walked over and placed two pills down on the counter. "You need to eat with these." I pushed the plate back toward her.

"I'm not taking those."

Yes. You are. "Dr. Ridge left them for you. They're for the pain."

"I'm okay. Actually, I'm used to dealing with pain now. Where is my phone?"

I clenched my jaw. "Penny, take the pills. Eat the waffles. I'll give you your phone when you're done."

"I need to tell Melissa where I am."

"Your friends know where you are." I emphasized the word friends. Because I'd even texted limp dick Tyler Stevens. And that prick would never be anything more than her friend ever again.

She huffed and sat down.

Well, if I hadn't known she was a teenager a few days ago, I would have guessed it now. I was withholding her phone privileges because she was being petulant. My hand was itching to spank her. And I knew she'd like it. She liked that I was older than her. She liked when I punished her. *Breathe.*

She downed the pills with some water. "How do you know Dr. Ridge?" She cut up the waffles and poured syrup over them.

"He's an old friend." I clenched my hand into a fist so I wouldn't actually be tempted to spank her. That's not what she needed right now. She needed to eat every piece of that waffle and drink the rest of her water.

"A friend of Isabella's too?"

Fuck me. "No." I put my elbows on the counter and buried my fingers in my hair. *Stop pushing my buttons and eat your food.*

She took another bite and then pushed the plate away. "I can't eat anymore."

Forcing this wasn't working. I needed to make her feel comfortable here. To calm her down. I walked over and sat down on the stool beside her.

"Look, thank you for taking care of me last night," she said. "You didn't need to do that..."

"I did need to." I put my hand on her thigh, savoring how warm she felt even through her yoga pants.

She immediately swiveled her chair to remove my hand. "You didn't. But I do appreciate it. I'm fine now, though. And I need to go. Please give me my phone."

Absolutely not. "I can't let you leave. You have a concussion."

"I can take care of myself."

I forced myself not to laugh. "You certainly didn't take care of yourself last night."

"I was fine before you showed up," she snapped.

"You haven't been taking care of yourself these past few weeks either."

She stood up, her stool squeaking against the floor. "How dare you throw that in my face? I tried. How can you sit there and judge me for feeling? I loved you. I loved you so much."

Past tense. The knife was back in my chest, slowly twisting.

"And it meant nothing to you. *I* meant nothing to you. You're completely fine. It's so hard to see you that way when I'm falling apart."

She couldn't be more wrong. "Penny..." I reached out for her.

"Don't touch me. Don't you dare touch me." She glared at me. "I couldn't eat. I couldn't sleep. Because of you! Because you left me!"

The words seemed to echo in my apartment. And maybe I needed to hear them over and over again. To remind me of my mistakes. So I wouldn't be tempted to make them again. But this wasn't all on me. We'd had a fight because of her. "That's not fair, Penny. You can't put all the blame on me."

"Yes I can. You're the one that left. You're the one that refused to talk to me. You shut me out. You didn't even give me a chance. I made one mistake and you left. You left me."

"Only because you lied to me!"

"Yes. Because I wanted to be with you. I didn't think you'd want me if you knew how young I was. And I hate that I lied to you."

I tried to take a deep breath. Did she need me to harbor all the blame? Is that what she wanted? Because I already felt like shit every fucking day. I didn't know how much more weight I could hold on my shoulders. "I know," I gritted out.

"No. Not because it made you leave me. But because it made us get together in the first place."

The knife in my chest twisted again. "You wish we had never started fucking?" I knew that she wouldn't have used those words. But I was seconds away from snapping.

"And that's it, isn't it? Just fucking? See, that's the problem. I thought it was more than that. I want someone to love me. Unconditionally."

"And that's what Tyler does? Because last time I checked, taking advantage of someone when they're drunk isn't love." I gripped the side of the counter. I needed it to ground me before I completely lost it.

"And what do you know about love? You're fucking married to a woman that you don't love. You didn't even love her when you got married. And instead of facing it and getting divorced, you just go around screwing students like it means nothing."

"I don't go around screwing students. You're the exception. You know that."

"Do I? Because I don't think I know you at all."

"You know me." I stood up. My fingers gripped the side of the counter harder. "You'll never forget what it feels like to have my rock hard cock deep inside of you. You'll never be able to stop screaming my name."

She glared at me. "I was already forgetting you. Tyler didn't take advantage of me. I told him that I wanted him. I asked him to fuck me."

All I could see was red. "Because you were drunk."

"No! It was because you left me! Because I was numb! You ruined me." Her voice cracked. She turned around like she couldn't even bear to look at me. "You ruined me."

No. I'd promised myself I wouldn't do that. The knife in my heart twisted again. *Breathe.* I didn't ruin her. She was fine. We were going to be fine. I grabbed her arm and pulled her into my chest. But then I looked down at her lips. The same lips she'd let Tyler kiss. "So it's my fault that you're loose?"

"I'm not loose." She shoved my chest and took a step back from me. "You broke up with me. I was trying to get over you."

"I never broke up with you. I said I needed time."

"I gave you time. Weeks! In order to work things out, normal people usually talk. What was I supposed to think?"

I'm not a normal person. I'm a fucking mess! "That's not how I work through things."

"That's not an excuse. Keep my phone. I'm leaving. I don't want to hear anything else you have to say." She stormed off toward the elevator doors.

"What is wrong with you?" I yelled after her.

She turned back around. "What is wrong with me? What is wrong with you?!"

I got it. This was my fault. Because everything was always my fault. But I'd tried to stay away from her for *her sake.* And she wasn't giving me a second to explain. I walked toward her. I was trying to have a conversation with her and she just wanted to run away. *Again.* "Stop acting like a child."

"I'm not acting like a child. Get over yourself."

"I'm trying to talk to you now. Which is exactly what you wanted. You're being immature."

"And you're being an asshole!"

I lowered my eyebrows at the rash comment. We both stood still, staring at each other. And I couldn't help it. My anger shifted. I didn't want to look at her lips for one more second and be haunted by her kissing Tyler. I wanted to erase the memory. I needed her beneath me screaming my name.

I was done with this conversation. She was mine. We both knew it. And it was about time I reminded her. "You're infuriating, Penny."

She stared back at me.

Exactly the way she'd stared at me in my office when I'd said those words to her the first time.

"Then punish me, Professor Hunter."

Chapter 10

Saturday

There was nothing hotter than my name on her lips. It felt like I'd been waiting for her to say my name like that again for years. And I knew exactly what she was asking.

I closed the distance between us and pressed her back against the wall. I needed her. Yes, *needed*. She was my drug and I just needed more. I pushed her tank top up her torso.

Penny lifted her arms in the air and let me pull her shirt the rest of the way off.

I grabbed her jaw and turned her face toward me. I knew my fingers were digging into her skin. And I didn't care. I needed her to give me her full attention. "I will never share you again. Do you understand me?"

"Yes." Her voice was shaky, but filled with desire.

I shoved her yoga pants down her thighs. As she stepped out of them, I put my hands on the wall on either side of her face. I knew she was angry. But I also knew she was as desperate for me as I was for her. And I wanted to hear her say the words. "I want to fuck you. Hard. Is that what you want?"

"Yes." The word fell from her lips as a gasp even though I wasn't even touching her yet.

Her pupils were dilated. And she was staring at me like she used to. Like I was a fucking god. Because only I could give her what she liked.

I pushed my sweatpants down, grabbed her ass, and lifted her legs around me. I didn't bother warming her up. I knew she'd be soaked. She was as turned on by our fight as I was. She loved driving me crazy. I'd show her how crazy I was for her. I sunk my cock deep inside of her tight pussy and stifled a groan. *Fuck.*

She closed her eyes at the sensation of me filling her.

Baby, I'm just getting started. I'm giving you what you deserve after torturing me. I thrust in and out of her, pressing her ass against the wall.

She buried her fingers in my hair, pulling my lips down to her neck. I'd missed the feeling of her fingers in my hair. I missed her always pulling me closer, like she could never get enough of me. I kissed her collarbone as my hands gripped her ass tighter. I missed the weight of her ass in my hands too.

She moaned.

But that's what I missed the most. Right there. The sound she made while I fucked her senseless.

Usually fucking her calmed me down. But I could still feel the anger coursing through my veins. I slammed into her harder. Faster. My breath was ragged against her neck. "You think I ruined you?" I whispered into her ear. I thrust my cock even deeper.

She moaned again.

I bit down on her earlobe. "I'll show you what it's like to be ruined." I pulled out of her and set her feet back down on the ground. I turned her so that she was facing the wall. My erection pressed into the small of her back as I grabbed her hands and placed them against the wall.

She was practically panting.

"You asked me to punish you." I grabbed her hips and pulled them until she was arching her back. Her hands were still pressed against the wall. I loved her just like this. Completely at my mercy. "And I intend to." I let my eyes trail from her tiny waist, past the dimples at the bottom of her spine, and down to her pale ass. I swallowed hard.

"Don't move out of this position." *This is going to sting. And you deserve it, you dirty girl.* I lifted my palm and slapped her ass hard.

She gasped in surprise.

I needed her to stop acting like a child. And as long as she did, I was going to scold her like one. Just the way she liked. Because my girl loved being a little slut for me. I was starting to wonder if I'd like her calling me Daddy as much as I liked her calling me Professor Hunter. "When I tell you it's time to go, you will not make me ask twice. Do you understand?"

"Yes," she said breathlessly.

I spanked her again. "You will not jeopardize your safety on purpose."

"I didn't..."

I spanked her even harder. The time for conversations was over. I was the one in control, and she was going to agree to every fucking thing I said. "Do you understand?"

"Yes."

Good girl. I cradled her red ass cheek in my hand, caressing it gently. I wasn't done with my demands, but she was finally behaving. And good behavior meant a reward. So I slipped my other hand between her thighs. *You're dripping, baby. My perfect little slut.* I slid one finger inside of her wetness, teasing her.

"Professor Hunter," she panted.

She wasn't going to distract me by using my title. I spanked her harder still. "And you will not lie to me." I slipped another finger inside of her.

"Never."

I slapped her ass again. "Tell me that you need me as much as I need you." Because I did need her. Like a drug in my veins. I'd never stop needing her.

"I need you," she moaned. "I need you, Professor Hunter."

Baby, if only you knew what need really is. What obsession really is. I grabbed her hips and thrust back inside of her from behind. *Fuck yes.* My fingers dug into her skin. Even though she'd agreed to everything I'd said, I was still angry. I grabbed her long red hair and pulled her head back. And I fucked her harder than I ever had before. So that she'd never be able to forget who was in control here.

"Professor Hunter," she moaned.

Fuck. "Come for me, Penny." I tugged her hair again. I was close. Each time I slid into her tight pussy, she drove me closer and closer to the edge.

"Professor Hunter," she panted again as her pussy clenched around me.

I felt the pull in my stomach. I pushed myself deeper, all the way to my hilt, and exploded inside of her. There was no better feeling than her gripping my cock.

I exhaled and slowly pulled out of her. I stared down at the red mark my palm had left on her ass. It felt like something inside me broke. I knelt down and placed a kiss against where I'd spanked her. And I just kept staring at my handprint. It had been someone else's hands on her last night.

Tyler's words echoed around in my head: *You should have heard her screaming my name.* I had Penny back. But I didn't think I'd ever stop thinking about her with someone else. I didn't think it would ever stop hurting. "The thought of you screaming his name haunts me. Never again. You're mine." I kissed the mark again.

Penny turned to face me.

I stayed on my knees. I couldn't look at her. Yes, I'd always be haunted by what she'd done with Tyler. But I was also a hypocrite. I'd woken up naked in Isabella's bed.

And it didn't matter that I didn't remember what happened. What mattered was that if I didn't know how to forgive her...how could she forgive me? And I really needed her to forgive me. I leaned forward and kissed the bruise on her stomach. *I'm so sorry that I am the way I am.*

I just wanted to stay down here and beg her not to leave me.

Penny knelt down beside me. "I didn't scream his name."

My eyes finally found hers. *What?*

"Actually, I screamed yours." She shrugged her shoulders.

I couldn't help but smile. *Fucking Tyler.* I imagined his reaction when Penny had moaned my name instead of his. Certainly that had hurt his pride as much as my fist. No wonder he'd lied to me. "I'm not as easy to forget as you implied?"

"No. I've tried."

We were finally at the point where I could talk about what really happened. The conversation that we'd needed for weeks. But now I was scared to have it. I'd been tormented without her. Dr. Clark was partially right, no matter how badly I wanted him to be wrong. No, I wasn't scared of rejection. I was just scared of Penny rejecting me. Penny was all I cared about. All I thought about. "I wanted you to."

Her eyes searched mine. "What? What do you mean?"

"I wanted you to forget about me. That's why I haven't been talking to you."

"Why? I told you that I loved you."

"I know. But I'm no good for you. You deserve someone without so much...without so many issues."

"What issues?"

I swallowed hard. "You were right. You don't know me as well as you should."

"I do."

"You don't," I said. She was probably expecting me to elaborate. But I'd never been good at offering information freely.

She just stared at me. "So if you wanted me to forget about you, why did you come to the party last night?"

"When you sent me that text about having a nice life it made me realize that I couldn't. Not unless you were in it."

"That's a selfish reason." She repeated the words back to me that I'd used. When she told me her excuse for lying about her age.

"It is. But I've seen you disappearing these past few weeks. Not eating. Drinking too much. Not focusing in class. I may be bad for you, but I'm better than the alternative."

"So I get to be with you by default?"

"I need you, Penny. I'm addicted to you." She wanted the truth. And that was the truth. Despite what Dr. Clark said, I knew myself. And I knew this feeling. I loved Penny. I did. But my love was intertwined with something much more sinister. All I could offer her was my promise to try and be better. "I want what's best for you. And I'm going to try hard to be that for you."

"You know that I'm addicted to you too."

You're not. Not like I am with you.

"Or else our argument wouldn't have just turned into sex. But you left me. I've never felt so broken before. Tyler was there to help try and pick up the pieces. And if I'm being honest, I didn't just sleep with him because I was drunk."

"I know." I gritted my teeth. Even though I kept telling myself otherwise, I knew. I'd seen the two of them together. He made her laugh. He made her smile. And all I seemed to do was make her cry.

"I have feelings for him too."

Breathe. "Here is where I should tell you to go to him. Where I should be unselfish. Please don't make me do that."

"I know you said you needed time, but you waited so long. You made it seem like you wanted nothing to do with me. You wouldn't even look at me in class. I thought...I thought..." She put her face in her hands. "I made a mess of everything."

"No, I did." I hated seeing her hurting. It made me feel physically sick. And this wasn't her fault. It was mine. I grabbed her face in my hands. "I never should have walked out on you that night. I understand why you lied. And I did exactly what you feared. But I need you to know that the age difference means nothing to me." It should have. But I was a sick fuck and that wasn't exactly groundbreaking news.

"When you were in high school, I was in elementary school."

I laughed. "It doesn't matter."

"You're my professor."

"It doesn't matter." *It's never fucking mattered.* I leaned forward and kissed her, ignoring the sting of the cut on my lip. I grabbed the back of her head and leaned into her until her back hit the floor. "I'm sorry." I kissed the top of her bandage, then the side of her neck. I trailed kisses between her breasts and down her stomach, tasting every inch of her skin.

"Mmm."

I kissed the inside of her thigh. "I missed you." *I missed this.*

"I missed you too."

I kissed the inside of her other thigh. "I want you again," I whispered against her skin. I'd never stop wanting her. *Needing her.* I lightly brushed my fingers against her clit. She was still aroused. Still soaking wet. She'd been without me for so long and her pussy was always greedy for me.

Penny grabbed the bottom of my chin and tilted my head toward her. "I want you too."

I leaned forward and pressed my lips against hers. Gently this time. Lovingly. I needed her to know that this was more than fucking.

Penny wrapped her legs around me and I slowly entered her warmth.

Fuck. I swear my cock was made for her pussy.

She ran her fingers down the muscles of my back, savoring this moment just as much as me. I loved punishing her. But I loved this too. The contrast between the two didn't seem possible. I needed that raw passion just as much as I needed this right here. Penny possessed everything I needed. She was made for me. *Just me.*

I reached down and massaged her clit.

Her moan of pleasure making my hips move faster, thrusting my cock deeper.

"Professor Hunter," she gasped.

My perfect dirty girl. I ran my hand up the side of her torso. I swear it felt like her warmth was seeping back into my cold soul. I felt lighter than I had in weeks. And I was never letting go. I intertwined my fingers with hers, lifted her hands above her head, and pinned them against the floor. I moved my hips faster and her legs wrapped tighter around my waist.

"Promise that you'll remember that you're mine," I said.

"I promise," she moaned as her pussy clenched around me.

I squeezed her hands as I emptied every last drop of my cum inside of her. Right where it belonged. I stared down at her as I tried to catch my breath. I rubbed the tip of my nose down the length of hers and gave her another kiss.

I had her back. *Finally*. My thoughts immediately stopped.

I didn't have her back.

I hadn't told her what I'd done. Or...hadn't done.

Fuck. I pulled out of her and stood up. I grabbed my sweatpants off the floor and pulled them on as I stared down at her naked on my floor. And I kept staring. Because I wanted to imprint this in my mind. If I was lucky, the cameras Ian had installed in my apartment had captured the perfect angle of her. Just in case I had to play this scene on repeat while I was alone again.

Because I'd told Penny we were on a break. I'd been adamant about that. About how she shouldn't have slept with Tyler because we were technically still together.

And I'd done worse. I'd slept with the devil.

Chapter 11

Saturday

Penny was never going to forgive me. I didn't even forgive me. I didn't want it to be true, but I couldn't change what had happened. *Or hadn't happened. Fuck.*

I cleared my throat. The only move I had was to at least cushion the blow. "I have a present for you."

She sat up. "So you did remember my birthday?"

"I told you I remembered." I forced a smile onto my face. But it felt more like a grimace. I turned away so she couldn't see my face, and walked out of the kitchen. When I reached my office I took a deep breath.

How was I going to explain what happened? I pictured Dr. Clark's face when I told him that I'd slept with Isabella. He was just…confused.

Penny would be confused too. And angry. And hurt.

I looked out the window at Main Street below. Why couldn't I remember? How had I let this happen? Isabella's words echoed around in my head. *Rape.* I raked my fingers through my hair. Just thinking about it made me feel out of control. And when I felt out of control…I slipped.

Breathe.

I wanted to believe that nothing happened, but I'd never know. All I had was a blank memory. But Isabella has her version of events. And she'd tell them to Penny no matter what I said. If there was one thing I believed, it was a threat made by Isabella.

Breathe.

Penny slept with Tyler. She'd have to understand. She had to. But she thought we'd broken up. Me on the other hand? I knew better. And it didn't matter that I didn't mean for it to happen. It didn't matter that I didn't want it.

Breathe.

My heart was beating funny in my chest. Penny was the best person to calm me down. All I wanted was to curl up with her in bed and sleep the rest of the day away.

But if I didn't get this off my chest now, I knew I never would.

I grabbed the envelope off my desk and walked back down the hall and into the living room. Penny was no longer in the kitchen. For a second I thought maybe she'd run off again, but then I heard her in my bedroom. She was probably just putting on some clothes.

I sat down on the couch and stared at the worn envelope in my hands. I'd tried so many times to rip it in half. I'd tried so hard to keep my distance.

Penny walked out of my bedroom fully dressed. She was even wearing a jacket and sneakers. Like she was getting ready to walk away. She was beautiful, but she was definitely a flight risk.

Breathe.

Penny closed the distance between us and sat down next to me.

"What is it?" She sounded so excited. But she wouldn't in a moment.

"I wanted you to get over me." I couldn't even look at her. I kept my gaze glued to the envelope.

"You already told me that."

"Before you open this I need to tell you something."

"Okay."

"I did something I regret. But I can't take it back."

She didn't respond.

If I was going to lean into this. I had to make it make sense. I didn't want her to ask a million questions like Dr.

Clark had. I just needed her to accept what happened and we could try to move on. "I thought I needed to get over you. I thought it was best for you."

"And for you?"

"No." I shook my head. "I always knew it wasn't best for me." I finally let my eyes move from the envelope and fall on her. "You said that it didn't look like I was in pain. But I was. I felt numb. My days dragged on. Without you there's nothing for me here. It sounds like I'm trying to make excuses but I'm not. I can own up to my mistakes. I just needed you to know that I was in pain too. I need you to understand the place I was in."

"I don't want to know what you did."

"Penny..."

"Please don't tell me."

"I want you to be honest with me. How can I expect you to be if I'm not honest with you?"

It already looked like she wanted to cry. "Is it going to hurt me?"

I took a deep breath and ran my hand through my hair. "Yes."

She bit her lip. "You kept my clothes in your closet. Why?"

I didn't mind a second of delaying this. "I felt like if I got rid of them then what we had really would be dead." I honestly hadn't even considered getting rid of them.

"So this thing that you did didn't make it feel like what we had was over?"

"No. I thought it would, but it didn't." I wanted to cringe at my own words. I hated saying that I'd wanted it. That I wanted any of this.

"I wish you would have talked to me. I wish you would have told me that you thought you weren't good for me. I would have convinced you otherwise."

"You've convinced me otherwise the whole time we were together."

"You still should have talked to me."

I know. "I can't take that back either."

She nodded. "I kissed some guy that lives in your apartment."

What the fuck?! "Who?"

"Does it matter?"

"Yes." I tried to keep my voice even, but I'm pretty sure it came out icy. *I'm such a hypocrite.*

"His name is Brendan."

Breathe. "Okay. Just one kiss?"

"Yes. And he gave me some advice. About how if things are so hard between us maybe we're not meant to work things out."

Fucking Brendan. "It's not bad advice."

"Clearly I didn't take it."

"I know." We were both silent for a moment. I knew I should just rip the Band-Aid off, but I didn't want to. I wished I could be honest and tell Penny I couldn't remember what happened with Isabella. But doing that would mean I accepted what Isabella had done. I already felt weak. Believing that she'd raped me? I wasn't sure I could live with that. I tried to shake the thought away. It didn't matter that I couldn't remember. It didn't matter what Isabella was threatening. I just needed to fucking man up to what I did.

"Is what you did worse than that?" she asked.

"Yes." I looked down at the envelope. I was holding it so tightly that I almost ripped it.

"Is it worse than the fact that I slept with Tyler?"

I closed my eyes. "I left you. You thought I had broken up with you. You weren't in the wrong."

"Is it worse?"

"By default, yes."

"So you had sex with someone else?"

I leaned forward and put my elbows on my knees. *No.* "I did." I felt like I was going to throw up.

She stood up from the couch. "A stranger?"

Breathe. "No."

She was staring at me like she already knew the truth. And she so easily believed it.

I'd made the right choice here. By not telling her I'd blacked out. She would have believed Isabella's lies anyway. I wasn't exactly trustworthy.

"Did you enjoy it?" she spat.

I don't remember it. But I wouldn't have. It wasn't Penny. "It was just sex. It didn't mean anything. It wasn't like it is with you."

"So you did enjoy it?"

"Penny..."

"When we were arguing earlier you said all we were doing was fucking."

"I didn't mean it. I was upset." I really felt like I was going to be sick now.

"I shouldn't be upset with you. I slept with someone else too. But I am. I don't know what you want me to say."

"You're allowed to be upset with me." I was upset with her for sleeping with Tyler. Were we just doomed to always be mad at each other?

"It was her, wasn't it?"

I looked up at her. *Don't make me say it. I can't.*

"Isabella? Your wife?"

"Yes." *Breathe.*

"Okay."

"Penny, I didn't go to New York with the intention of sleeping with her." I didn't even want to see her. I never wanted to see her again.

"Okay."

"It just happened." *Maybe.*

"Okay."

"Please stop saying okay. It's not okay. And I'm sorry. I'm so, so sorry, Penny."

"You don't have to explain it to me. She's your wife."

Her words were like a slap across my face. *My wife.* I wanted to laugh. I wanted to cry. "I needed you to know."

"I need some air."

"Okay. Let's take a walk."

"I want to be alone."

"Penny, you have a concussion..."

"I'm okay. Please. I just need some air."

Maybe it would be better for us to have a few minutes apart. To try to calm down. She wasn't saying she was leaving for good. She just needed a moment. This wasn't goodbye. "Take this." I lifted up the envelope.

She shook her head.

I stood up, folded the envelope in half, and slipped it into the pocket of her jacket. I added her phone next to the envelope. Every inch of me wanted to get back on my knees and beg her to stay. But she had the whole story now. She had to make her own choice. "Please be careful."

"I promised you I would be." She gave me one last disheartened glance and then walked over to the elevator.

And my heart started beating funny in my chest. What if one minute to calm down truly did turn into a goodbye? What is she never came back? What if she walked away for good? *Breathe.* But thinking the words didn't help. It was like the air wasn't reaching my chest. When I was little, I used to get panic attacks. But I hadn't had one since I was a kid. I'd never forget the feeling though, as it wrapped around my chest. "Please stay."

"I can't."

"I'm begging you, please."

"I can't look at you right now." The elevator dinged as the doors slid open. She stepped on.

"Penny." My voice broke as I stood there staring at her. *I can't breathe.*

"Professor Hunter."

The doors closed and she was gone.

Breathe.

I needed to go after her.

Breathe.

I took a step forward and then stopped. I needed to give her time.

Breathe.

I just stood there like a fucking idiot, gasping for air. Penny's cherry perfume was the only scent I wanted to inhale. But she wasn't here. And I didn't know what to do.

Breathe.

I'd told her Isabella's story about what happened and I felt out of control anyway. Why did I always feel out of control? Why couldn't I get a grip?

I wanted a drink.

I wanted to search my whole building and find a guy named Brendan and break his nose.

I wanted to be someone other than myself. Anyone else.

I fell to my knees as I gasped for air. When I was a kid, Rob had always helped me when I lost my breath. What had he always said? Fuck, he just told me to breathe. And that wasn't fucking helping right now.

I grabbed my chest as I stared at the metal doors.

Come back, Penny.

Please come back to me.

I don't know how to live without you.

Please, I'll be better. I swear.

I closed my eyes and pictured being back at my childhood home. It was like I could feel Rob's hands on my shoulders as he made me stare back at him. *"Breathe, James."* Picturing the scene made it even harder to breathe. Rob was younger than me and he was always taking care of me. Because I'd always been a fucking mess.

I felt a tear run down my cheek.

I'd always been weak.

I can't fucking breathe.

I felt that familiar pain in my chest. The pain that made me reach for vices. I'd always known that the pain would one day devour me whole.

I just wanted to be better. I wanted someone to fix me. I was just so tired. So fucking tired of living this way. The thought settled around me as the pain in my lungs eased. I closed my eyes. You shouldn't be able to break the broken. But here I was, broken on the floor.

I'd been so worried about hurting Penny. But she was the one that ruined me. I literally couldn't breathe unless she was beside me. I laughed out loud, the sound echoing around my empty apartment. It sounded sad and lifeless.

The elevator dinged.

I opened my eyes as the doors slid open.

And standing there was...Ian. I just stared at him. I had nothing to say.

He stepped out of the elevator. "Get up." He put his hand out for me.

No.

"James, if there's one thing I've learned in the past few years, it's that you always need to get up."

No.

"Get up. Now."

"Go to hell."

"Not before you." He grabbed my arm and hauled me to my feet.

I groaned. Everything hurt.

He slapped me on the back. "There. Much better. I ordered pizza for lunch. It'll be here any minute."

"I'm not hungry."

"I don't care."

Ian was the worst employee in the history of employees. "Are you even going to ask me why I was hunched over on the floor?"

"I saw."

I just stared at him. "You saw all of it?"

"And I heard it too."

I narrowed my eyes at him. I didn't really care that he was aware of my kink of Penny calling me Professor Hunter. But I didn't love the fact that he was watching me so closely. Not when my life was unraveling around me. I pictured him eating popcorn and laughing at the footage. Or masturbating to it. Yeah, I didn't like that at all.

"You lied to her," Ian said. "Penny left because you lied. So don't sit here and feel sorry for yourself."

"I didn't lie."

Ian put his hands on my shoulders. And it reminded me so much of when Rob used to do it. I was glad Rob was visiting soon. I missed him. I missed the way we used to be. I thought about Mason and Matt too. I missed the way we all used to be. Before everything broke.

"James, we both know you didn't willingly sleep with Isabella. She…"

I pushed him off me before he could finish his sentence.

Ian sighed. "You can't keep lying to yourself. Who is it helping?"

"Me. It's helping me."

He shook his head. "You have a visitor arriving in just a minute."

"The pizza guy?" That was a weird way to describe him.

"No."

"Oh. Rob's finally here?" *Perfect timing.* We could go out and get drunk. I would have asked Ian to go to a bar with me, but he'd seen me at my worst the past couple weeks. And he'd stopped being fun. Day drinking wasn't going to be on his approved list of activities. He was acting more like a father than a friend. And he definitely wasn't acting like an employee. Or else he'd listen to me more.

"No, Rob's not here yet. At least, not that I know of."

Really, when was Rob coming? I hated when things were up in the air. Why did he insist on spontaneity when I needed structure? "Well, I don't know anyone else."

Ian folded his arms across his chest. "You're going to want to fire me. But you'll thank me later."

I lowered my eyebrows as I stared at him. "What did you do?"

"What's best for you."

"What did you do?" I repeated. But I had a sinking feeling. *Please don't say Dr. Clark is on his way here.*

Chapter 12

Saturday

"James you were there for me when I needed you," Ian said. "I don't care if you want to sit on the floor for the rest of the day. But you will get back up. And you will keep going. Because that's the only option."

That wasn't the only option. I could hurl myself out the window and onto Main Street below. It would make the pain stop.

"And I already know what you're thinking. That's why you have a visitor coming."

I glared at Ian. "You did *not* invite Dr. Clark to my home."

"You need help, James."

"And you need a new job."

"You don't mean that. And we both know it." He slapped me on the back. "You'll thank me later. And I hope Rob does get here soon because you're exhausting."

"You're exhausting."

"You're definitely not thinking clearly. Because that was the lamest comeback ever. Do you want to put a shirt on or something?"

"Dr. Clark coming to my apartment is equally inappropriate to him seeing me in just sweatpants. Call him and tell him I'm fine."

"You're not fine."

"What am I paying you for?"

Ian smiled. "To keep you safe. Which is what I'm doing."

He was interpreting that differently than I wanted him to. I'd never hired him to protect me from myself.

"I'm fine," I said again. "Call Dr. Clark and tell him to abort whatever mission you two are on."

"No."

"Ian, I'm only going to ask you one more time."

"Ask as many times as you want. The answer's still no." He looked down at his phone. "Besides, it's too late."

The elevator dinged and the doors slid open. Dr. Clark and a pizza boy were both standing there. They each looked a little confused by the other's presence.

I glared at both of them.

Ian paid the pizza boy and then welcomed Dr. Clark inside.

"James," Dr. Clark said. "Ian said you had something very important to discuss. And that it couldn't wait."

I do not. Last night, I'd promised myself I'd take these sessions more seriously. But this wasn't technically one of my sessions. "Well, Ian is misinformed and currently looking for a new job."

Ian laughed from the kitchen.

"Is this about your black eye?" Dr. Clark asked. "How did you get it?"

Fuck, I'd forgotten I looked like I'd just been in a boxing match. I smiled, thinking about how Tyler probably looked similar. I really hated that kid. "I was in a fight."

"With...whom?"

I didn't want to talk about this. I didn't want him here at all.

"Are you hungry, Doc?" Ian asked.

"I could eat," Dr. Clark said. He walked into the kitchen and sat down at the counter like he'd been here a million times.

Why were they both in my home right now? I followed them into the kitchen.

Ian handed me a plate. He put his elbows on the counter and stared at me. "So are we going to talk about this now?"

"This isn't group therapy, Ian," I said.

"But you're not going to tell him the truth unless I'm here."

"Ian can stay if you want," Dr. Clark said and took a bite of pizza. "Maybe having a friend here will help you open up."

I sighed. I liked it better when Dr. Clark just thought Ian was an employee. I stared at the two of them eating pizza. Like this was the most normal thing in the world. An addict, a bodyguard, and a therapist... It sounded like the start of a bad joke.

"How are you feeling, James?" Dr. Clark asked.

"I feel like shit. I always feel like shit." *No thanks to you.*

Dr. Clark's eyes softened. "I see that your wrist is red."

I looked down at where I'd snapped a rubber band so many times that it broke and made my skin raw. I folded my arms across my chest.

"Having a hard time staying present again?"

Yes. Because my present was a dumpster fire. I'd just had a panic attack for the first time in years, and my bodyguard had to piece me back together. I glanced at Ian. He looked...so worried. About me.

I took a deep breath. I'd just been on the floor, desperate for someone to help me. Ian had done the right thing by calling Dr. Clark. No, I didn't love him in my home. This was definitely an invasion of privacy. But I needed him here.

"I had a panic attack," I said. I sat down in one of the stools and slid Penny's barely eaten waffles to the side. I took a bite of pizza. If they were going to act like this was normal, so was I.

"You've never mentioned those before," Dr. Clark said.

"I haven't gotten them since I was a kid." I'm sure I would have while I was living with Isabella, but I'd been too high to realize that my life was shit.

"So why did you get one today?"

"I told Penny that I slept with Isabella. And then she left."

"Did she break up with you?"

I shook my head. "She said she needed some air. And that she couldn't even look at me." Which was fitting. Most days I couldn't bear to look at myself either.

"And how does that make you feel?"

I shrugged my shoulders. "I think it'll be fine. She slept with someone else while we were on a break too." And kissed someone else. "So we're even."

"Even? This isn't a game, James. Relationships aren't about getting even."

"And they're not even," Ian said. "Because of that thing that James wants to talk to you about."

"Are you ready to talk about that?" Dr. Clark asked.

I sighed. "There's nothing to talk about." I never should have even told Ian about this. It was a moment of weakness. All of it.

"James, not telling me what's hurting you isn't helping anyone."

"No one hurt me."

Dr. Clark lowered his eyebrows. "That's not what I said. But your black eye begs to differ."

"This isn't about that."

"Then it is about something," he said.

For Christ's sake. "Ian thinks Isabella raped me." The words settled around me. And I felt like I was back in Isabella's room. My stomach churned.

"Are you talking about when you slept with her last weekend?"

"He doesn't remember what happened," Ian said. "He woke up naked in her bed. But Isabella drugged him. She said they had sex, but he doesn't remember."

"Is that true, James?" Dr. Clark asked. "Why did you tell me that you slept with her willingly?"

"Because I...I..." my voice cracked.

"Because it made you feel out of control. And when you feel out of control you reach for vices."

I stared at him. "Yeah. That."

"So to feel better...you got in a fist fight with some-one?"

"Honestly that did make me feel better." I laughed but no one else did. "Look, I just want to keep the past in the past. None of this matters."

"James, what do we talk about in almost every session? The past is a part of who you are. And if you ever want a healthy relationship, your partner deserves to know your past. All of it. Every sordid detail."

"I've blacked out before. It's not a big deal," I said, even though I didn't believe the words.

"James, you usually black out when you *choose* to over-indulge. This is different."

"Well I still don't fucking remember anything."

"Because you were drugged. By saying you blacked out, you're putting the blame on yourself instead of where it really belongs...on Isabella."

"It doesn't matter."

"It does...."

"It doesn't," I said again, cutting him off. "None of it. I don't fucking remember what happened. And I'm not telling Penny that I don't remember sleeping with Isabella."

"Why not?"

"Because I already told her otherwise. It's done."

Dr. Clark sighed like I was exhausting him. "I'll ask you again. Why won't you tell Penny the truth?"

Ian cut in. "Isabella insists James slept with her willingly. And that she'll leak her side of what happened to Penny if James says otherwise."

"So she's blackmailing him?" Dr. Clark asked. He turned back to me. "Surely Penny will believe your side."

"It wouldn't be the first time she believed someone else's word over mine. Isabella is a sore subject because she won't sign the damned papers. I don't want her to ruin this one good thing in my life. I just want to move forward."

"With Penny?"

"If she'll have me."

Dr. Clark finished his last bite of pizza. "And you're building your relationship on half truths and flat out lies. That's not a strong foundation. It's bound to crumble, if it hasn't already."

"It hasn't. Penny will come back." She had to.

"But she can barely even look at you."

"Well, she can't eat or sleep without me. She needs me just as much as I need her. She was letting herself waste away when we were apart."

"So being with you will save her?"

"Yeah."

"You don't sound convinced about that," Dr. Clark said. "Is that what you want here…to save her?"

"Maybe. Or maybe she needs saving *from* me."

"James, do you blame yourself for Lyn's death?"

It felt like there was a knife in my chest again, slowly twisting. Ian couldn't be here for this. I'd already betrayed my friends' trust by talking to Dr. Clark about her. "Ian, we need a moment."

Ian nodded. "You got it, boss."

So now he was listening to me?

He tossed us each another slice of pizza, grabbed the box, and left the two of us alone.

"This isn't about Lyn," I said.

"I think maybe it has more to do with her than you realize. I'll ask you again, do you blame yourself for her death?"

There was a lump in my throat that wouldn't go away. "Partially. Yes." My mind was numb. I wouldn't let myself picture that day.

"You never told me how she died."

I shook my head. "I can't."

"But you think it was partially your fault?"

Probably more than partially. Rob, Mason, Matt. Isabella. Her father. We all played a roll. Every single one of us.

"I think that maybe you're projecting," Dr. Clark said. "You couldn't save Lyn, so you want to save Penny."

"I never thought that Lyn needed me. Not in that way."

"Okay. But you think it was partially your fault that Lyn died. So maybe you're worried about your role in that. And you don't want to hurt Penny. You're worried that if you're together you might...what?"

Penny's words swirled around in my head. "I don't want to ruin her."

"Ah. The heart of the matter. James, you've told me yourself that you're better when you're with her. And she's better when she's with you. So how are you going to ruin her?"

"She already told me that I did. Before she walked out today. You should have seen her face."

"Well, she's upset, just like your upset. You both need to move forward."

"Or we can just be miserable together." The words fell out of my mouth. And I instantly remembered saying them before.

"Miserable together? No, James. That's not what I was saying. I was saying that if the two of you can have an honest discussion and move forward, you can be happy together."

I barely registered Dr. Clark's words. Because I was stuck on that line. *Let's be miserable together.* I closed my eyes remembering the first time I'd proposed. To *Lyn*. The fake name still made the knife in my chest twist. I'd proposed to a girl that wasn't mine, one who'd forever be frozen at 16. *Let's be miserable together.* That's what I'd said to her. And it wasn't the first time I'd said it to her either. I remembered holding her while she cried in the shower. If I closed my eyes tight enough, it was like I was still there.

I remembered feeling hopeful when I'd proposed. Just like Penny made me feel hopeful. An escape from the life I was currently living.

There was just one key difference. I was in a good place when I'd met Penny. The circumstances were different. And maybe, just maybe, this could work out. I'd reached out to Lyn as a lifeline. But I didn't need Penny to save me. I just needed…her. Because she made me happy. She made me feel young again. She made me feel…like a better version of myself.

I took a deep breath.

"What are you thinking?" Dr. Clark asked.

"That I'm sick of torturing myself for my past." That's exactly what I'd been doing since Lyn's death. Torturing myself. Because Dr. Clark was right, I felt guilty for what happened to her. I'd always partially blame myself. But I'd already done my penance by marrying Isabella. "I'm allowed to be happy."

Dr. Clark nodded. "So what now?"

"I'm ready to move forward. With Penny. And not just because she eats and sleeps when she's with me."

He smiled. "Show her the real you, James. And be happy."

I hoped it was that easy. Hell, sometimes the princess did choose the villain. *Right?*

Chapter 13

Saturday

Penny needed time to think through things. And that was fine. I'd give her time. As much time as she needed. A few hours, days, weeks. It didn't matter. Because we were meant to be. I'd waited this long for happiness. I could wait a little longer if that's what she needed.

I felt eerily calm as I grabbed my phone and hit Rob's name.

The phone rang a few times and then Rob answered. "What's up?" he asked.

What did he mean, "What's up?" He'd told me he'd be visiting but never told me when. I took a deep breath and exhaled slowly. It didn't matter. I was excited to see him whenever he got here. "I'm just checking in. Are you back in the states yet?"

"You sound weird. What's wrong?"

I laughed. "Nothing."

There was a long paused. "Are you dying or something?"

"What? No."

"Well, good. But you still sound strange. You're sure everything is good?"

I was pretty sure I was just…happy. And I felt bad that Rob couldn't even recognize me with that emotion. I hoped Penny would be back in my arms by the time Rob visited. I wanted him to know that I was good. That he didn't have to worry about me so much anymore. "Yeah, everything is good. I'll have a surprise for you when you get here." He was going to love Penny.

"Oooh what kind of surprise?"

"It's a surprise."

"Can I get a hint?" he asked.

"No, that kind of defeats the purpose of a surprise."

"Boo you whore."

I laughed. "I know you mean that lovingly."

"Unless you're suddenly whoring around town with all the hot, single co-eds."

I definitely wouldn't word dating Penny that way. "No."

"Boo…"

"Don't call me a whore again."

Rob laughed.

"So," I said. "When are you coming?"

"I figured that's why you were calling. Tell Ellen I'll be there by next weekend at the latest."

"And why am I telling Ellen?"

"Because I want her to make me all my favorites. Tell her exactly that. She'll know what I mean."

"She's not your chef, Rob." But Ellen would of course be excited. She loved Rob. She'd just been telling me this.

"I know. She's yours. But she likes me better."

Probably true. "So next weekend? And how long will you be staying for exactly?"

"Indefinitely?"

I pressed my lips together. Penny could be calling me any minute. Or she could take a while. I was hoping on sooner rather than later though.

"That's okay, right?" Rob asked. "I figured when you invited me to stay that it was an open ended invitation. It'll be fun. Like old times."

Old times. "Have you spoken to Matt recently?"

"Nah, not for a few months. I talked to Mason the other day though. Mr. and Mrs. Caldwell are cutting him off."

"Why?"

"Because he won't take over the family business. He has…other interests."

"The marketing firm he wants to start?"

"What marketing firm?" Rob asked.

"The one he talks about sometimes." I don't know. It had been a while since I'd spoken to my childhood best friend.

Rob laughed. "No, man. I heard he's starting a sex club."

Wait, what? "You're joking."

"And since when do I joke around?"

"Um…always?"

Rob laughed again. "I would never joke about a sex club."

"Fair."

"Speaking of the Caldwells, I should go visit. If they're disowning Mason, maybe they'll adopt me. Pretty sure I'm their favorite son anyway."

Honestly, he was probably partially right about that too. We'd basically grown up at the Caldwells' house. We were practically family. The Caldwells had been through a lot and everyone always welcomed the laughter that came along with Rob. "So does that mean you're staying with them instead of me?"

"Slow your roll. I was kidding. I'm not made to take over MAC International. I'm more made to…sleep on your couch."

"You'll have your own room."

"Score. I gotta go. But I'll see you soonish."

"You said next weekend."

"Yeah. Next weekend-ish."

"I'm telling Ellen you're coming next weekend, so if you're not here I'll be eating all your favorites."

"I hate schedules. But fine. I'll be there. Later, man. I'm excited for my surprise!" He hung up.

I hoped he wasn't expecting a car or something. I stared down at my phone. There was still no new message or call from Penny. I forced myself to click on Matt's name in my phone.

"Hey, man," Matt said.

I wasn't sure why, but hearing his voice made tears pool in the corners of my eyes. When would this stop hurting? When could we go back to just being us again?

"I'm a little busy right now," he said. "Can you maybe call back later?"

He did that a lot. Avoided talking to me. But I needed to have this conversation. I think we both did.

I cleared my throat. "What are you doing?"

"Fixing up an apartment."

"Your apartment? Or someone else's?"

"Mine I guess. I'm living here right now. But I'm not staying."

"Why?"

There was a long pause before he responded. "It's...too loud."

It seemed like every time I called Matt, he was moving to a new apartment in New York.

"I've been seeing a therapist," I said. It was a weird segue. But I didn't think there was a good way to bring this up.

Another long pause. "That's good."

We'd grown apart. But I knew he still cared about me. Just like I cared about him. "Sometimes it's good to talk about stuff."

"I'm not going back to therapy," Matt said.

That wasn't what I was saying. "I just meant that if you ever want to talk about her, I'm here." I didn't need to say who. He'd know who I was talking about.

The power drill sounded again. And he didn't respond.

Matt had gone to therapy for a while after her death. I knew this was a sore subject. But… "I just need you to know that I'm here," I said again.

"Last time I checked, you weren't in New York."

"I'm teaching in Delaware now. You could visit. Rob's visiting soon too. Maybe a change of scenery would be good for you. A fresh start somewhere outside the city."

"Her grave is here."

I swallowed hard. I got that. I'd visited it a few times when I moved back to the city after graduating. There were always flowers on her grave. And I knew Matt left them. But if he thought leaving the city meant leaving her, he was wrong. He needed to keep living. But I knew he didn't want to hear that from me.

"Look, James, I really am busy. If there's nothing else…"

It was a Saturday afternoon and he was holed up in some apartment he hated. Missing her. I knew he was missing her. That's why he kept moving. Perpetually searching for a home when he'd never find it. Because she was his home.

"I miss her too," I said.

"Don't."

We'd made a pact not to talk about her until Matt was ready. But if her death ate at me this much, I couldn't imagine what it was doing to him. He couldn't keep living like this.

I took a deep breath. "And I'm sorry. For everything. For the part I played."

"I know." He sighed. "I don't want to talk about this anymore."

He wouldn't talk to me or any of our friends. And he wouldn't talk to a therapist. So who was he going to talk to?

"I'm here when you're ready."

"I know," he said again.

"Matt?"

"Yeah?"

"I miss you too. I know I've been a shit friend. But maybe one day soon the four of us could hang out again. Like old times."

"Like old times," he repeated back to me. Like he couldn't even understand the phrase.

I was ready to move forward. But he wasn't. I got that. But he needed to keep going too. "I'm getting a divorce," I said. "From Isabella." I don't know why I added that last part. Probably because of the silence on the other end.

"Rob told me. I don't know why you ever married her in the first place. After everything she did."

"I thought I deserved her. After everything that happened."

"You worked that out with your therapist, huh?"

"He certainly helped, yeah."

Another long pause. "Well, no one deserves Isabella."

I smiled. "Thanks, man. I was also really high."

Matt laughed. "Yeah. I remember. Do you even remember your wedding day?"

"Barely."

"I guess that's probably a good thing in this case."

Yeah. I wanted to ask him if he still pictured getting married one day. But I was afraid I already knew the answer.

"I'm happy for you," Matt said. "That you're finally walking away from Wizzy. And that you're going to therapy and working through your shit. And all that."

"Thanks." But that wasn't why I was calling. I already knew that deep down Matt still cared about me. Because I cared about him. I was calling to make sure he knew I was sorry. And to make sure he was okay. But I wasn't really sure he accepted my apology. And he didn't sound okay to me.

"Rumor has it that you might be getting to take over MAC International after all," I said.

"We'll see. Things have a way of not working out how I imagine they will."

"I think you're due for a lucky streak." I hoped he did take over his father's company. He'd always wanted it more than Mason.

"I really should go. I have some drywall to put up."

Okay then. I'd said what I'd needed to. He knew I was here for him, whenever he was ready. Our relationship was strained right now. But I was determined to fix it. Whether he wanted me to or not. "Tell Mason I say hi. And your mom and dad."

"Will do." He hung up.

I stared down at my phone. There were still no messages or calls from Penny. I knew she needed time. But I also knew I wasn't going to walk away from us. And I needed to make sure she knew that.

I called her and it went straight to voicemail.

I sighed. Patience had never been one of my virtues.

I needed a distraction. So I ran.

I graded papers.

I went for another run.

I ate cold pizza with Ian.

I showered. Not with Ian.

And I called Penny again before climbing into bed. Again it went to voicemail.

I'd checked the security feed from outside her dorm earlier. She'd never returned to it. I wondered if she was out with friends somewhere. *Drinking.* I really didn't like the idea of that. She was supposed to be taking it easy.

I stared at my ceiling. I knew she'd call when she was ready. I just wished I could fast forward time.

Three hours later, my phone buzzing would have woken me up if I wasn't still wide awake staring at my ceiling. I grabbed it and glanced at the display. It was 2 a.m. But more importantly...I finally had a text from Penny.

"Are you up?"

I texted back. "Yes." *But you shouldn't be.* She needed rest. What the hell was she doing?

My phone buzzed again. "Can we talk?"

Seriously, why the hell was she up right now? Maybe she was having as much trouble sleeping as I was. And I could fix that situation. "I'll come get you. Are you in your dorm?"

"We can talk on the phone. Call me."

I frowned at the text. "I want to see you." *I need to see you.* I needed to make sure she was okay. She'd left more than 12 hours ago.

She didn't text back right away.

Fuck. She was breaking up with me. The thought settled around me. But I immediately pushed it away. That wasn't going to happen. Finally my phone buzzed again.

"Let's just wait until the morning. I'm actually pretty tired."

Of course you are, it's fucking 2 a.m. And I had a sinking feeling in my stomach. It wasn't that she didn't want to talk to me. She said we could talk on the phone. Which meant she just didn't want me to know where she was. "Penny, where are you?"

My phone buzzed again. "Please don't freak out."

If she was with Tyler, I was most definitely going to kill him. I gritted my teeth as I typed out a response. "Where are you?"

"I'm in the hospital."

I stared at her text. For a second, my tired brain refused to understand her words. And then it hit me like a ton of bricks. *What the fuck? What happened?* I pushed the covers off of me. I never should have let her leave. I knew it and I still fucking let her. I almost fell over as I hopped around, pulling on a pair of jeans while balancing my phone. "I'll be there in twenty minutes."

"I think visiting hours are over."

Fuck that. She needed me. And I was always going to show up for her when she needed me now.

Chapter 14

Saturday

The possibilities went around and around in my head on repeat. Dr. Ridge said that Penny had a concussion. But if she was in the hospital...what if it was worse? All I knew was that this was my fault. Her getting hurt in the first place. He roaming around Main Street alone. If something had happened to her... Fear gripped my chest as I pulled into the parking lot and cut the engine.

I hurried inside. Ignoring everyone else in the waiting room, I walked up to the desk. It took less than a minute for the woman to tell me to come back tomorrow. Penny was right, visiting hours were over. But there were some pros to being rich. This woman didn't seem like the one to bribe though.

"What room is she in?" I asked. "For when I come back tomorrow," I added when she gave me a dirty look.

"She's in room 216. I will see you *tomorrow*, sir."

It was like she somehow knew what I was planning.

"Have a good night," I said and walked away. When she wasn't looking, I pushed through a side door and ran right into a male nurse. He probably looked as tired as I did.

"Sorry," he mumbled with a yawn. "Wait, you shouldn't be back here." He stared at my face. "Are you here about that shiner?"

Having a black eye made everything harder. Upstanding citizens didn't get in fist fights. And they also didn't bribe staff members. But this guy was tired and overworked. He would do. I pulled out my wallet. "I need you to escort me to room 216."

"Visiting hours are over."

"I'll make it worth your time." I pulled out all the cash I had and placed it in his hand.

His eyes grew round. He looked at me and then back at the cash. And then back at me. He cleared his throat. "Are you related to the patient?"

"I'm her husband," I lied.

He kept staring at me. And I knew it was because of my black eye.

"We were...mugged," I said. Lies always seemed easier for me than the truth. "I've been at the station describing the incident all night. But I need to make sure she's okay. I can't believe they kept me so long."

"Oh," he said. "That's awful that they made you go all the way to the station." He shook his head. "Come on, follow me."

Well, that was easy. It was a good thing I didn't say I was her professor. I would have been out a thousand bucks and I still wouldn't be any closer to seeing Penny.

I followed him up to the second floor and down an empty hallway. This hospital seemed understaffed. Penny needed the best care for... Fuck, I didn't even know what had happened. I just needed to see her.

"Don't tell anyone that I..."

I cut him off. "You got it." Did I look like a guy that tattled? *I* was bribing *him*. We were in this shit together. I opened up the door to Penny's hospital room.

It felt like my throat was constricting as I stared at Penny. She looked so small lying in the hospital bed. For a second I just stood there. I thought she was asleep, but then she slowly opened her eyes.

I'd been so worried. Angry. Lost. I was lost without her. She didn't say anything, but she didn't need to. I knew when she needed me. I closed the door and made my way over to her bed. I kicked off my shoes, lifted the sheet off her bed, and climbed in next to her.

"James," she whispered. I could hear the emotion in her voice.

I need you too. I wrapped my arms around her. "I shouldn't have let you leave." I kissed her forehead.

"I didn't give you much of a choice."

"No, you didn't." But I still should have insisted. I kissed her forehead again. I was just happy that she seemed okay. I wanted to hold her like this forever. Her being in my arms was my favorite thing in the world. "How long have you been here?"

"We can talk in the morning."

She wasn't getting out of this that easily. "How long, Penny?"

"Since this afternoon I guess. Not long after I left your place. I passed out on Main Street."

My chest ached. She passed out? "And someone found you?"

"Brendan."

I pulled back slightly to look down at her. The same Brendan that she'd confessed to kissing? I clenched my jaw. It was a good thing I hadn't found him earlier and punched him. "I'll have to thank him." Or maybe I'd still slug him. I hadn't decided yet. Had she gone to him after our fight? Why did she keep running to other guys? I just wanted her to run to me.

"How did you get up here?" she asked, trying her best to change the subject.

But Brendan's name was seared into my mind. "Having money has its advantages."

"You bribed the hospital staff?"

The way she said it made me pause. Like she was judging me. "I didn't say that."

"I'm glad that you're here." She was quiet for a moment as she stared at me. "I'm sorry."

"You have nothing to be sorry for. Even though you're not nervous around me anymore, you still like to apologize for things you haven't done." I forced a smile onto my face.

"You still make me nervous."

I lowered my eyebrows as I stared back at her. "Why?"

"You're so hot and cold. I never know how you're going to react to things. It's unsettling. And confusing."

"There's nothing to be confused about anymore. I'm here and I'm not going anywhere." *I promise, Penny.* I placed a gentle kiss against her lips.

"Do I make you nervous too?" she asked.

I glanced down at her hand on my chest. She could probably feel how fast my heart was racing. "Sometimes. I'm nervous right now."

"Why?" She rubbed her hand against the scruff on my cheek.

"You left me today because you needed time to think over things." I pulled her hand away from my face and kissed her palm. "And I can't tell what you're thinking." I turned her hand over and kissed each of her knuckles. "I don't know what you've decided."

"I opened my present."

I swallowed hard. "And?"

"You've never opened up to me like that before."

"I want to be able to give you what you need, Penny."

"Why is it so hard for you to talk to me?"

I took a deep breath. "Most people look at me and judge me in one second. I'm well off. My parents are well off. They think everything has been handed to me. And when I was younger, it was. So I can't correct their opinion. I haven't met anyone who sees more than that."

"Because you refuse to open up. So what else are they supposed to see?"

"You see more."

"That's because I don't care about your money. I care about you."

That was all I'd ever wanted. For someone to care about me and not what I could offer them. "I know. I'm trying, Penny. I'm not used to this."

"This?"

"The way I feel about you." I'd written that I loved her in the letter. But I was having trouble reading her tonight. I was worried that saying the words out loud would just scare her away. She was 20 now, but we were still at very different stages in our lives.

"I've never been in love before," she said.

"I know." I ran my fingers through her red hair. God, I'd missed this. I'd missed us.

"Have you?" she asked.

Dr. Clark and I had beaten this subject to death. And I'd never been more sure of the answer. I stared down at her. "I've never felt like this."

"Does love always hurt this much?"

I don't know. Maybe. "I'm not trying to hurt you. I don't want to ever hurt you again."

"You're not good for me."

Fuck. Who was telling her that? Tyler? Brendan? It didn't matter, because it was true. I sighed and put my arms around her again. "No, I'm not."

"But I love you anyway."

It wasn't the first time she'd said it to me. I pictured her straddled on top of me on my bed, confessing her lies.

Confessing her love. She'd said it in a state of desperation. And now she was saying it again, but I wasn't sure if she'd even remember it in the morning. But it still made my heart feel warm. Like her goodness was seeping into me.

A tear slid down her cheek. "I'm sorry. Geez, I don't know why I'm so emotional today."

"It's a side effect of having a concussion."

"Oh." She laughed and wiped the tears off her cheeks.

No one should look this beautiful when they cried. "You're so gorgeous."

She laughed. "I have a huge bandage on my head."

"You're still gorgeous."

She slowly reached up and traced the bruise around my eye with her index finger. "I love you."

I had no right to be loved by her. And her words haunted me. *Does love always hurt this much?* I was so tired of hurting her. And I was scared that saying it back to her meant she'd be doomed for the rest of her life. A life with me. I tried to push away the thought, but it clung to me. So I didn't say it back.

And I wasn't just scared of hurting her. I'd never truly given my heart to someone before. I didn't like how out of control that made me feel. But I did love her. I'd told her as much in my letter to her. She knew it. I didn't need to say it out loud. I loved her so much I physically ached when we were apart. *I love you.* I ran the tip of my nose down the length of hers. *You know that I love you.*

"I'm actually really tired now." She rolled over so that she was no longer facing me.

Fuck. She was going to keep pressing this, wasn't she? "Hey." I leaned over and grabbed her chin in my hand. "What's wrong?" I asked, even though I already knew.

She sat up so that my hand fell from her skin. "Why won't you say it?"

"Say what?"

"I've told you multiple times that I love you. You never say it back. Why won't you say it?"

"I have said it." I wasn't sure what I was so scared of really. This was what a relationship was. Feeling vulnerable. And when she was staring up at me with tears pooling in the corners of her eyes, it didn't seem so scary to be vulnerable too. I could do this. It didn't mean she'd be doomed. It didn't mean she'd run away. What we had was real.

And I knew this was important. She'd told me once that her ex didn't believe in labels. And she'd just told me she'd never been in love before. This was a big moment. For both of us. And I'd promised her I'd always be better than her shit ex. She deserved someone that would worship her and love her out loud. I took a deep breath. It was time to jump all in.

"No, you haven't."

I tried to hide my smile. "I haven't?"

"No."

I pushed the sheets off of us and straddled her, pinning her in place. "I could have sworn I said it."

"You haven't."

"My mistake." I kissed the freckles on her shoulder. "I love you." I was surprised at how easily the words fell from my lips. I kissed the curve of her neck. "I love you." I pulled down the neckline of her hospital gown and kissed her clavicle. "I love you." I tugged on the string behind her neck and pulled the gown down even more. "I love you," I said as I kissed her between her perky breasts. Once I started saying it, it was like I couldn't stop.

The machine she was hooked up to that monitored her heart rate started beeping like crazy.

I laughed. I loved riling her up. I loved her. I hesitated at her stomach and lightly kissed the bruise on her stomach. "I love you." I pushed the fabric to the side and kissed her hip bone, where I'd bruised her before against my desk. "I love you."

She moaned.

I smiled against her skin. The heart rate monitor kept beeping faster every time my lips touched her skin. My breath lingered between her thighs. "I love you." I pressed my lips against her clit and gently sucked.

She lifted her hips to meet my mouth.

But I was setting the pace tonight. I pushed her hips back down, spread her thighs wider, and licked her delicious pussy. The machine beeped even faster as I slowly swirled my tongue around her wetness. God, I'd missed the taste of her. I'd be perfectly content eating her out for the rest of the night. But I wanted to show her that my words were true. I looked up at her. "I love you. And I want to make love to you."

"Then do it."

I kept my eyes locked with hers as I sat up. I unbuttoned my jeans as I stared at her. She was so beautiful. And I wasn't sure how I'd gotten this lucky. I didn't deserve her. But I wanted to.

Penny reached out and unzipped my hoodie with her hand that wasn't attached to the IV. She stared at my abs in the way that she used to. Like she was staring at a fucking god. And I was glad that I hadn't had time to put on a shirt before grabbing a hoodie and running out the door. I wanted her to keep looking at me like this forever. Like I was her whole world.

I pushed my pants and boxers down. I needed her. Desperately. But this wasn't about what I needed. I slid the rest of her hospital gown to the side and looked down at her naked body. *Perfection.*

I glanced at the monitor. It had started beeping so rapidly that I thought it would break. "Your heart is beating so fast." I leaned down and kissed her left breast. *Oh, I definitely missed these.*

"Because you're torturing me."

"Am I?" I took one of her nipples in my mouth. I swirled my tongue around it and gently bit down with my teeth.

She turned her head and tried to hide the moan in her pillow.

The hallways had been empty. No one was going to hear us. My hands slid to her ass. I lifted her up and slowly entered her. *Fuck yes.* I'd missed this the most.

She moaned into her pillow again.

I leaned into her as I lowered her back down onto the bed. Fuck, she was so tight. I needed to calm down. *Breathe.* I put one of my hands down on the pillow by her face.

She turned to look at me and I captured her lips in a searing kiss. She buried her fingers in my hair, trailing one of her hands to the back of my neck.

I knew she wanted more. My greedy girl. I squeezed her ass cheek as I thrust deeper inside of her.

She moaned into my mouth. I'd really missed that sound too. I wanted to hear it over and over. I bit her lip so that she'd make it again.

The machine started beeping louder.

I pulled back. "Are we going to break that thing?"

"I don't care." She grabbed a handful of my hair and brought my lips back down to hers.

God, I loved when she kissed me like that. Like she was desperate for me.

She wrapped her legs around my waist, trying to make me move faster. But I kept my pace. Slow and relentless. Each time I thrust she gripped me tighter. I'd had it right the first time. Her pussy was made for my cock.

"I love you, Penny."

"I love you, Professor Hunter," she panted.

Dirty girl. She was definitely made just for me.

Her fingers ran down my back and down to my ass. She squeezed it hard as she tried to make me move faster again.

Fuck. I groaned and moved my hand to her thigh. "I'll never get enough of you." If she wanted me to go faster, I would. I buried my cock deep inside of her, all the way to the hilt. Just the way she liked.

She moaned.

"Come for me, my love," I whispered against her lips. I tilted my hips down, hitting her in that spot that I knew always sent her over the edge.

"Professor Hunter," she moaned as her pussy clenched around me.

Just like that, baby. Grip me. "Penny," I groaned. I lightly bit down on her earlobe as I filled her.

Chapter 15

Sunday

Someone tried to nudge me awake. I breathed in the familiar cherry-scented perfume. *Mmm.* "Penny," I mumbled and kissed her shoulder.

She elbowed me hard in the stomach. "Mom, Dad, hi."

"Huh?" I slowly opened my eyes and smiled at her. She had sex hair. And it was just begging for my fingers.

She glared at me.

Wait, what had she said when she elbowed me? I was still half asleep.

Penny pushed me again. "James," she whispered and tilted her head toward the door.

All I wanted to do was pull her closer. But it looked like she was seconds away from shoving me out of her bed. I slowly sat up as she tried to run her fingers through her tangled hair.

I rubbed my eyes and looked over at the door. There were two people standing there that I didn't recognize. And Penny's greeting to them finally registered in my head. *Oh, fuck.* This was really not the way I wanted to meet Penny's parents. Lying next to their daughter in a hospital bed where we'd clearly just slept together.

"Oh," I said, trying to stall. I was about to climb out of bed, but my pants were unzipped. *Screw me.* I pretended to cough as I zipped up my pants. *Please don't have heard that.* "Oh, umm..." I quickly climbed off the bed and laughed awkwardly. Yeah, this definitely wasn't a great first meeting.

I looked down and zipped up my hoodie too. It was fine. I was good with people. I could fix this. "Wow, this is not how I expected to meet you Mr. and Mrs. Taylor." Okay, so I was normally good with people. But for some reason my heart was racing. I was glad I wasn't hooked up to that monitor. This meeting mattered. Because Penny mattered. And I was pretty sure I was fucking it all up. I ran my hand through my hair and looked over at Penny for help.

"Mom, Dad, this is James."

That wasn't much to work with, but at least it was an introduction. I walked over to her parents and held out my hand to her father. "I've heard so much about both of you. It's a pleasure to meet you, sir."

Penny's father looked at Penny and then back at me. He did not look pleased. Actually, he looked a little pissed. Which I totally understood. Because of the whole just sleeping with his daughter thing. *Seriously, fuck.*

"That's quite the shiner," he said dryly and finally shook my hand.

"Oh." I touched my black eye and tried to laugh it off. I'd forgotten about my black eye. *Shit.* I'd thought about meeting Penny's parents. About having to tell them that I was her professor. It never went well in my head. But somehow…this felt worse. "I had forgotten about that. Just a misunderstanding."

I turned toward her mom. "And Mrs. Taylor." I put out my hand and she quickly shook it. I breathed a sigh of relief. She didn't look angry at all. She actually looked ecstatic.

"Excuse my outfit," I said and tugged the zipper on my hoodie all the way up to my neck. "I just rushed over as soon as I heard what happened." I grabbed my shoes off the floor and sat down in a nearby chair. I was stalling.

Trying to think of a way to make her father stop glaring at me. But at least her mom seemed to like me. I laced my shoes and stood back up.

"It's so nice to meet you, James," her mom said. She was smiling from ear to ear. "So how do you know Penny?"

"Oh." At least I could answer this honestly. I smiled over at Penny. "We actually met at a coffee shop on Main Street at the beginning of the semester."

"Is that so?"

"And we ended up having a class together. Comm." I'd got to be honest about a bit of it at least.

"Do you hate it as much she does?" Penny's mom asked.

I laughed. Penny complained to her parents about my class? I wasn't expecting that. "I actually love the class. It's my favorite this semester. Mostly because Penny's in it." I smiled at her. "You know, I didn't actually know she hated it, though. Her speeches are really good. She tends to be too hard on herself."

"That's what I always say," her mom responded. "It's so nice to get to meet Penny's new friends. We got to meet Brendan yesterday. Such a sweetheart. He stayed and waited for hours to see if she was okay. Are you friends with him too?"

Fucking Brendan. Seriously, who the hell was this prick? *Breathe.* "No. And actually, Penny and I aren't just friends. She's my girlfriend."

"Oh?" Her mom looked even happier, if that was possible.

"Yes."

"I'm so sorry, James. Penny didn't tell us she was dating anyone. I'm so embarrassed. Penny, this is kind of a big deal isn't it? Your first boyfriend?"

I'd forgotten about that. Maybe I should have let Penny tell them herself. But I couldn't help but smile when I glanced back at Penny. She looked completely mortified. My parents never tried to embarrass me. They just ignored me completely. And it was weird being in such a normal situation that didn't feel normal at all to me.

"It's still new," Penny said. "I was going to tell you." She had a deer in headlights thing going on and it was absolutely adorable.

I bit the inside of my cheek so I wouldn't start laughing.

"You know what?" her mom said. "James was the first thing she said when she woke up. We had no idea what she was talking about. But I guess she wanted to see you. Isn't that sweet, honey?" She looked over at her husband.

"Mhm," her dad said and crossed his arms.

Penny's mom loved me. But her father hated me. *Maybe I should give them all a moment alone.* "Well, I don't want to interfere with your time, Mr. and Mrs. Taylor. I just spent all night with her." *Fuck, what did I just say?* "Sleeping," I quickly added.

"Excuse me?" her dad said.

I cleared my throat. "Not sleeping with her. I was just in bed with her. Sleeping next to her I mean. Just beside her." I shoved my hands into my pockets. Why the hell had I said that? The man already hated my guts.

Fortunately her mom laughed. "Don't be ridiculous, James. We'd like to get to know you." She walked into the room and sat down in one of the chairs. Penny's dad walked over to the only other chair and sat down. His arms were still crossed.

I half stood, half sat on the edge of Penny's bed. The last thing I needed was for them to picture the two of us in bed together. I usually wasn't easily intimidated. But Penny's father wasn't just some guy I could fight in a bar. This mattered.

Penny reached out and grabbed my hand.

I automatically relaxed. She knew just what I needed. I took a deep breath and squeezed her hand. We were in this together.

An awkward silence settled around the room. And for the life of me, I didn't know how to fill it. Luckily there was a knock on the door and the doctor walked in.

"You look a lot better this morning," she said. Her eyes flit toward me for a second. Hopefully that staff member hadn't ratted me out.

"Do you think I can go home today?" Penny asked.

"Let's see." She pressed a button on the machine that had been monitoring Penny's heartbeat. It started printing out a long chart. "Well that's strange."

"What is it?" Penny's father asked.

"Well, it looks like there was a twenty-minute period of escalated pulse."

I laughed and then turned it into a forced cough. I hadn't thought about the doctor bringing up the fact that we'd fucked last night. *Please don't say anything else about that.* Penny's father already hated me enough. I squeezed Penny's hand and looked down at my shoes.

"How are you feeling?" the doctor asked. "Are you struggling for breath at all? Have you noticed that your heart is racing? Or any palpitations?"

I pressed my lips together. They probably thought she was about to have a heart attack or something.

"No," Penny said. "Not at all. I'm fine."

The doctor flipped a few switches on the monitor. "It could have been a computer malfunction. It seems to be working fine now, though. Strange." She leaned down and unplugged the machine and then plugged it back in.

"Maybe it was just a nightmare or something," Penny said quietly.

Oh, Penny. She wasn't as good of a liar as I was.

"Possibly," the doctor replied. "So the man who brought you in said you had fallen a couple nights ago and hit your head pretty bad. And then you fainted yesterday afternoon. Are you feeling lightheaded at all today?"

"No. I feel a lot better."

"Well you have a moderate concussion. You shouldn't have been walking around by yourself. Plus you had an empty stomach and you were dehydrated. It's no wonder that you fainted."

I winced. That was all my fault. "Will she be okay now?" I asked.

"She needs to rest and build her strength back up."

"Can she leave today?"

"Let's keep the IV in for a few more hours to help with your dehydration. I'll be back to check on you soon. And if everything looks good and your heart rate stays down, you can head home."

"How long should she stay at home?" Penny's mom asked. "She has classes." She looked at her husband. "I can take tomorrow off. I just need to call in."

"I'd recommend taking it easy for a few days. Definitely no classes on Monday. And just see how you feel on Tuesday. Don't push yourself. I'll be back in a few hours to check in." The doctor nodded at Penny's parents and walked out of the room.

"Okay, let me call the office." Penny's mother stood up and grabbed her purse.

"She can come back to my place," I said. I'd only just gotten Penny back. And I wasn't letting her out of my sight again. Honestly, I didn't really want her to be alone with her father. The last thing I needed was for him to spew poison in her ear, when I'd already done enough harm myself the past couple weeks. I wasn't sure how important his approval was to her. "If that's okay with both of you, of course."

"A dorm room isn't the best place to recuperate from this," her father said coolly.

"He actually lives in a nice apartment, Dad. It would be okay with me. I don't want to inconvenience you guys."

"It's never an inconvenience, Penny. Besides, James has classes. We can't ask him to miss them," her mom said.

"I can cancel them," I said. "I mean, skip them. Not a big deal at all."

"Well, if you're sure it's okay, James. And if that's really what you want to do, Penny," her mom said.

Her father lifted his hand. "Nonsense. You'll be coming back with us, Pen." His tone was firm. It seemed like the end of this discussion.

Well, he'd definitely heard me zipper my pants then.

There was a knock on the door and Melissa burst in. She ran over to the bed.

"Oh my God, Penny!" She threw her arms around her. "Have you been here this whole time? I thought you were okay." She turned to me. "Thanks for keeping me in the dark, James."

I was pretty sure Melissa hated me as much as Penny's father. "I didn't know she was here either. I would have told you."

"Then where were you, Penny? I haven't heard from you since Friday night. I can't believe..." she let her voice trail off. "We can talk later." She walked over to Penny's parents. "Thanks for calling me, Mrs. Taylor." She hugged both of them at the same time.

So her parents loved Melissa? Huh. I wondered if they'd feel differently knowing how drunk Penny always got when she went out with her.

"Oh, I have someone I want you to meet," Melissa said when they finally finished hugging. She opened the door and poked her head out. "Hey guys, it's okay, you can come in."

A man I'd never seen before walked in, followed by... *Tyler. What the fuck is he doing here?*

I ignored whatever Melissa and the stranger were talking about. I was too busy staring at Tyler. He was hovering by the door because he clearly wasn't wanted in this room. And he looked like shit. Definitely worse than me even though I'd let him take tons of cheap shots. The inside corners of both his eyes were bruised. I was pretty sure I'd broken his stupid nose.

"And that's our friend Tyler," Melissa said and pointed over to him.

Penny's father frowned as he looked back and forth between me and the idiot kid. His brow furrowed.

"Nice to meet you both." Tyler smiled at them but didn't move.

Penny's parents went back to talking to Melissa.

"Thanks for coming, Tyler," Penny said quietly.

Thanks for coming? It was this shithead's fault that she was here.

Tyler glanced apprehensively at me. But then he walked over to Penny. "Yeah, well, Melissa needed a ride. It's hard to say no to her."

Was he even going to apologize to Penny? He really was a pussy.

"Right." Penny smiled at him. "Well, thanks for bringing her. My parents can take them back. You don't have to stay if you don't want to."

"What? No, that's not what I meant. I wanted to come."

Every word out of his mouth made me grip Penny's hand tighter and tighter. Like I was afraid if I let go I'd break Tyler's nose again.

"How did you end up in here?" Tyler asked.

"I fainted. On Main Street."

"Penny." His voice sounded strained. "I knew I shouldn't have let you leave. You're so stubborn."

Shouldn't have let you leave? What the fuck? I loosened my grip on Penny's hand. She'd went for a walk to see Tyler fucking Stevens?

"I'm okay, Tyler," she said.

"That's what you said yesterday too. So I don't believe you."

Tyler loved asking to be punched. I let go of Penny's hand and stood up. I couldn't listen to any more of this conversation. Penny's father already hated me. Punching this kid again wasn't going to help my case. "Does anyone want some coffee or something to eat?"

No one said anything.

Good. I'd get the full story directly from Penny about why she went to Tyler's yesterday. Until then, I needed a minute alone anyway. "I'll be right back." I raked my fingers through my hair as I walked out the door without looking back.

But I heard footsteps behind me.

I turned around, expecting Tyler to be there pushing my buttons again. But it was Penny's father. And he did not look happy.

Chapter 16

Sunday

"I think the two of us need to go get that coffee," Penny's father said.

"Um. Yes, sir."

He shook his head like he was annoyed with my existence and walked past me.

I still needed a minute to calm down from Tyler popping up like that stupid whack-a-mole game. I really didn't feel like being reprimanded by a complete stranger right now. But I wanted Penny's father to like me. This was important.

I hurried after him. But all I could think to talk about was the weather. And I had a feeling that wasn't what he wanted to discuss.

We stepped onto the elevator without a word.

The doors slid closed and we both still said nothing.

I cleared my throat. But neither of us offered a topic. Why was this so awkward? I wondered if it was because yesterday I'd thought it would be kind of sexy if Penny called me Daddy while I punished her. I'd definitely decided against that now. I didn't want her to think of her father while I fucked her.

I cleared my throat again. "So…fly Eagles fly?" That's what everyone said around here.

"Oh, you're an Eagles fan, James?"

That was a reasonable assumption after what I'd just said. But I was really just trying to start a conversation. *Any* conversation. Why was this so fucking awkward? "No, a Giants fan actually."

"Hmph." He stepped off the elevator.

I had a feeling that was the final nail in my coffin. We silently made our way to the cafeteria and stepped into the long line.

"So you got that shiner fighting that other kid, huh?"

I'm a grown ass man. Tyler was the only kid. But I bit my tongue. "Penny's worth defending."

He raised his eyebrows. "Defending? What happened?"

I probably shouldn't have said that. "I don't want to get in between you and your daughter. It's better if you ask her directly. But I meant what I said. I'll always defend her."

His eyes finally softened. Just a bit. "Good, good," he said.

When we reached the front of the line, he pulled out his wallet for the coffees.

And I let him pay. Because I was supposed to be a poor college student.

"I will admit," he said. "I wish we had Odin Beckman."

Who? What in the hell was he talking about? And in what context? Did he mean like here? Was Odin some guy that he wanted Penny to date or something?

I just stared at him, but it didn't look like he was going to offer any further information. "Odin?" I asked.

"Yeah, your star wide receiver," he said. "Number 13. Beckman. Boy is he great with those catches."

Wow. Okay. He was talking about Odell Beckham? I just stared at him. Was this some kind of joke about how little he cared about the Giants or something? But if that was the case...why had he gotten Beckham's number right? "Mhm," I said. "He is good." I took a sip of my coffee.

Mr. Taylor nodded. "But the little Manning brother is past his prime. Nothing like good old Sam Bradfury. Lucky number 7. He'll be great, just needs more time to get used to the plays."

Sam Bradfury? Who the hell was he talking about now? Did he mean Sam Bradford? And if so…he'd butchered that name just as badly. But also gotten his jersey number somehow correct?

So he wasn't making fun of the Giants. He was just terrible with names? Really, really bad with names. And bad at spotting good players, because Bradford was made of glass. There was no way he'd be able to stay healthy for an entire season. In my opinion, they should have kept Foles.

The Eagles were in a rebuilding phase. Honestly, the Giants probably were too. But I'd choose Eli Manning over Sam Bradfury, as Mr. Taylor put it, any day.

"So you think he'll be your quarterback for a long time?" I asked. I refused to repeat the name wrong. I wanted him to like me, but I just couldn't do it. And correcting him seemed like a bad move too.

He sighed. "No. That Chucky Keller got rid of all our best players. I hope he gets fired."

Chucky who? I tried to wrack my brain. Was he talking about the Eagles' coach, Chip Kelly? I bit the inside of my cheek so I wouldn't laugh.

"At least we got Nelly Agnolotti."

"Who?" Was he talking about a rapper or a delicious Italian pasta dish right now?

"Number 17." He stared at me like I was the one who didn't know anyone's name. "He's going to be one of the greatest wide receivers we've ever had. You just watch. He'll be better than Beckman."

Did he mean Nelson Agholor? If so he was dead wrong…because Agholor had the slipperiest fingers I'd ever witnessed. He was no Odell Beckham. With all the wrong names this conversation was getting more confusing by the second. But I had to hand it to him, he did know all the players' numbers. I guess he was a numbers man.

"So you really think the Eagles can beat the Giants on Monday night?" I asked, trying to steer him away from the names of specific players.

"You betcha."

Wishful thinking. "I guess we'll find out. The Giants are definitely having a better year."

He laughed. "Just you wait and see. Are you into stocks at all?"

That was a pretty strange question to ask a college student. But it did align with the fact that he seemed interested in numbers. I had quite the portfolio, but it didn't really seem like I should know much about this topic. "A little," I lied.

"Have you heard about that Tesller? I think that's a good one right now."

Did he mean Tesla? It really felt like he was fucking with me. "Mhm," I said. This had to be one of the strangest conversations ever. But he was being nice. Unless this was some kind of weird prank. I preferred this over the angry glares though.

We made our way back to Penny's floor as he told me all about Tesller.

I wondered what he'd think of Ian's Tesla.

Penny's doctor was standing outside her room looking at a chart. We approached her and Mr. Taylor started asking her a few questions as we walked back into the room.

"Okay, Penny," the doctor said. She clicked a few buttons on the monitor and read the report. "Everything looks normal now. You all set to get out of here?"

"Absolutely," Penny said. She grimaced as the doctor took the IV out of her hand.

"Take it easy, okay." She handed Penny some forms to fill out. "Release forms."

Penny quickly signed her name and handed the clipboard back to her.

"Nice meeting all of you." The doctor turned to me and smiled.

I nodded at her and she walked out of the room. Penny's parents were discussing something. Probably butchering a bunch of names. I grabbed Penny's clothes and handed them to her.

She slid out of bed, making sure to hold the back of her gown. "I want to come back with you," she whispered.

"I'll see what I can do." I winked at her. I could be very persuasive when I needed to. When Penny disappeared into the bathroom I walked over to her parents. "I really would love if she stayed with me until she felt better. I'll watch over her. And I'll make sure to let her watch the big game tomorrow night."

Her father laughed. "Well…" he turned to his wife. "If you think it's alright."

Penny's mom nodded. "If that's what Penny wants, it's fine with us."

I smiled. It seemed like this meeting had actually gone alright. Even though they knew I was sleeping with their daughter. It honestly could have gone a lot worse. I walked over to Penny when she emerged from the bathroom. "If you want to come back with me, you can." I put my hand on her cheek. "Whatever you want to do."

She nodded and went over to her parents. "Is it okay if I go back with him, Dad?"

"As long as you promise to take it easy, Pen." He leaned down and hugged her. "Don't worry us like that again."

"I'm sorry, Dad."

"Call us once in a while, okay?"

I thought he'd flat out ask her about why Tyler had a black eye too. But honestly, I was relieved he didn't press it. He probably knew that Penny would eventually open up to them about all this.

Penny laughed. "I will. I love you."

"I love you too."

Her mom gave her a hug next. "Don't forget what I told you, Penny," she said. "And when big things happen, call us. No more surprise boyfriends." She laughed. "I love you, sweetie."

"I love you too, Mom."

"Maybe we can come down sometime again soon and take you two out to dinner. Wouldn't that be nice?"

"Sounds wonderful," I said. Hopefully one day we could laugh about the fact that they thought I was a poor college student. "It was really nice meeting you, Mrs. Taylor." I put my hand out for her.

"Don't be ridiculous." She hugged me.

I wasn't really used to being hugged. Honestly, I wasn't used to being touched at all, except by Penny. I didn't really know what to do with my hands, so I awkwardly patted her back.

"And Mr. Taylor." I put my hand out for Penny's father and this time he shook it without hesitation.

"Just because the Eagles season didn't start out well doesn't mean they won't beat the Giants," he said.

I laughed. "We'll see."

Her parents waved to us and walked out of the room.

Penny closed the distance between us and clasped her hands behind my neck. "You seem to have won over my dad."

Maybe. I wanted to ask her about the fact that he couldn't remember anyone's names. But I didn't want to offend her or anything. "You never told me how intimidating your father is."

"I didn't know he had an intimidating bone in his body until today."

I tried to hide my smile. "Maybe it's because I had to zip up my pants when they came in."

"Do you think they heard that?"

"Well if they didn't, the accelerated heart rate may have tipped them off. Or my rambling about sleeping next to you."

"You were so flustered," she said. "It was cute. And mortifying, of course."

"Or I guess they could have just been surprised that you finally had a boyfriend after all these years."

"Shut up and kiss me."

I laughed and placed a kiss against her lips. "I like that I'm your first boyfriend, Penny."

"And I like that you're my first boyfriend. I feel like we're a normal couple right now. It's refreshing."

"Do normal couples usually hang out in hospitals?"

"No. Can we go back to your place now?"

I thought you'd never ask. "Yes." I picked her up in my arms.

She laughed. I'd forgotten what her laughter sounded like. I was so tired of making her cry. We'd fought so much. And I just wanted to make her laugh again and again.

"You don't need to carry me," she said. "My legs work fine."

"I know." I pulled her tighter to my chest. "I want to."

She rested her head against my chest. "You smell really good. Have I ever told you that?"

"No, you haven't." I carried her into the elevator and hit the button with my elbow.

"You can put me down if you need to."

"I don't need to." The elevator doors opened and I stepped out onto the main floor. I carried her through the entrance, but paused when I saw the rain. I slowly set her down on her feet. "I'll pull the car up."

"I like the rain."

"Yeah, you're not getting a cold on top of everything else. I promised your parents I'd take care of you." I pulled my hood up and gave her a quick peck on the lips. "I'll be right back."

I ran into the rain. Penny was right. The rain felt like...us. I hoped that I never had to be apart from her during another rainstorm. By the time I reached my car I was soaked. I climbed in, slammed the door, and started the engine.

The autumn air had really settled in too. I turned on the heat and drove toward Penny. I pulled under the veranda, quickly got out, and opened the door for her.

"You're really handsome," she said.

"Get in the car, Penny."

"You love bossing me around."

"I like when you listen to me."

"I know." She slid into the car and I closed the door behind her.

When I got back in the car, I unzipped my wet hoodie and threw it into the back seat. I smiled when Penny's eyes immediately fell to my abs.

I turned the heat up even higher and pointed one of the vents at her. I waited for her to buckle her seatbelt, and then I sped off.

Once we were on the highway I took a deep breath. I hoped that we never had to step into another hospital again anytime soon. I put my hand on the center console, palm up. She immediately slid her hand into mine.

We were going to be okay. I'd told her about Isabella and she was still staring at me with stars in her eyes. I tried to focus on the road. I just hoped she still looked at me like that after I told her the rest.

Chapter 17

Sunday

I pressed my foot down harder on the gas as I thought about the conversation I needed to have with Penny. About the kind of man I was.

"So you liked my parents okay?" she asked, pulling me out of my thoughts.

"Your parents are fantastic." Even if her father was playing some kind of elaborate, long, strange prank on me. "And I appreciated that they tried to ignore the fact that we're, well...you know."

"Banging?"

I smiled. "You're very eloquent with your words, Miss Taylor."

"Are you going to get in trouble for canceling so many of your classes?"

"I haven't canceled that many classes."

"You cancel class all the time."

I laughed. "Well, no one has said anything to me yet. I doubt any students would complain about having more free time."

"True. But I really do feel better. Maybe we should both go to class tomorrow."

"The doctor specifically said to take tomorrow off."

"I know. But I've been skipping class a lot recently. And when I went I barely paid attention."

"I noticed," I said.

She bit her lip. Normally I liked when she did that. But today she looked…nervous.

What wasn't she telling me?

She turned her gaze away from me and stared out the window. "I'm going to fail statistics. I've never failed a class in my life."

"Then why do you think you're going to fail?"

She looked back at me. "My Stat professor has a really thick accent and it's hard to understand him. I was teaching myself by reading the book but I was so unmotivated recently that I've fallen really far behind. And there's a test next week. And I don't even understand why I'm bad at it. I was great at math in high school. I took A.P. Calculus and I never had a problem."

"It's more business oriented than math oriented."

She laughed. "I guess I suck at business then. That's not great for the major I chose. Either way, I think I need to hire a tutor."

I did not want her hanging out in the library for hours with someone else. "I can tutor you."

"In Stat? You're a marketing professor."

I laughed. "So you really haven't read that much about me online then?"

"Not much, no. Are you secretly a statistics expert?"

I couldn't help but laugh again. "No, I wouldn't say that. But it is your lucky day, because you're dating a genius."

"I know that you're intelligent, but you took Stat ages ago. You're forgetting that you're an old man."

Oh, I was going to spank her later for that. "Do you want my help or not?"

Penny laughed. "Yes."

"Good. You're definitely not going to fail Stat."

"That's very sweet of you to take such an interest in my education, professor."

"I have selfish motivations."

"And what are those?"

"I don't like to see you upset. And I'm pretty sure you'd be upset if you failed a class."

"Yeah, probably." She ran her fingers across the palm of my hand and up the inside of my forearm, sending shivers down my spine. "Any other reason?"

"If you have to retake classes you'll be in school forever."

"And that would bother you?"

"Yes, it would bother me." I didn't want to have to hide our relationship for any longer than necessary. I hit my turn signal and pulled into the parking garage underneath my apartment building. I slid into one of my spots and cut the engine. "When you graduate I can finally have you all to myself."

I grabbed my sweatshirt out of the back seat and climbed out of the car. I opened the door for Penny.

She grabbed my hand, but she looked apprehensive for some reason.

We stepped onto the elevator and the doors slid closed. Silence surrounded us. And I wondered if I'd said something wrong.

"Well after I graduate, I'll get a job," she finally said. "If anything, we'll probably have less time together."

Oh. So that's what this was about? Because I said I'd have her all to myself? I meant it. "Maybe."

"You don't think I'll be able to find a job?"

She was taking this all wrong. "I didn't say that." I dropped her hand and leaned against the wall to stare at her. She had to know what I meant by this. She knew I was wealthy. She wasn't going to be working as an unpaid intern after graduation. Not when she didn't need to.

"Then what do you mean?"

I shrugged. I had a feeling she wasn't going to like what I had to say. "I just meant that you won't really need to work."

"Of course I will."

"Not necessarily." It seemed like this was leading towards an argument. And I was so sick of fighting with her. I lifted her into my arms, hoping it would make her laugh. It did not. But I still carried her into my apartment.

"So that's your master plan for after I graduate? You want me to stay in your apartment all day while you work? I'd be bored out of my mind."

"Well, it would be our apartment, not mine."

"No it wouldn't. I wouldn't have any money to pay for my half of the rent."

This was ridiculous. I couldn't help but laugh as I put her down on the couch. I knelt down on the floor beside her. "I have enough money for both of us, Penny. Besides, I don't rent this apartment. I own it."

"James...I'm getting a job after I graduate. I want to be able to provide for myself. I'm not going to mooch off of you."

Hmm. I lifted up her tank top and kissed her right below her belly button. God, her skin was so soft.

"Hey, stop trying to distract me." She cupped my chin in her hand.

I smiled at her. How could she not see how silly this conversation was?

"It's a good thing I am young. Because now I have extra time to convince you that that's a terrible idea."

"Mhm. It doesn't sound that terrible to me right now," I said.

"Certainly you'd be sick of me by then anyway."

Did she seriously think that? I lifted her legs, sat down on the couch, and put her legs down on my lap. "No, I don't think so." I'd never grow tired of her. I loved every inch of her. I slowly unlaced one of her sneakers, pulled it off her foot, and dropped it on the floor. I repeated the process with her other shoe.

"Are you hungry?" she asked.

I was surprised but relieved by the change of topic. "I'm guessing that means you are?"

"I'm starving."

"What would you like?"

"Can we order a pizza or something?"

"That sounds fantastic." I pulled out my cell phone. "Where do you want it from?"

"Is Grottos okay?"

"Sure. I haven't tried their pizza yet."

"Are you serious? How can you live here and not try that?" She bit her lip, like she could already imagine biting into a slice.

"I'm assuming you like it?" I asked.

"It's the best."

"Grottos it is then." I found their number and pulled my phone to my ear. "What kind of pizza do you like?"

"Plain."

"Is it weird that I didn't know that?" I rubbed my thumb along the inside of her ankle. I should have known her favorite everything by now.

"We've never had pizza together before. How would you know?"

I guess. I kept caressing the inside of her ankle as I ordered. When I hung up I smiled at her. I'd learn her favorite everything in time. Because she was stuck with me. And right now we had all the time in the world. At least until we had to go back to reality on Tuesday. "So what makes their pizza the best? Because I'm from New

York, and I'm pretty sure New York pizza is supposed to be the best."

"You'll just have to wait and see."

"What else don't I know about you?"

"You know me pretty well. Although, we don't do much talking when we're together." She tried to raise her eyebrow at me but failed miserably.

I laughed. "I'm glad you can't give me a scolding look."

"I'm not trying to scold you. I think that being intimate is time well spent." She pressed the sole of one of her feet against the zipper of my jeans.

I grabbed her wandering foot. "Except you're supposed to be taking it easy. Which gives us a perfect opportunity to talk."

"Okay. Let's play a game."

"What did you have in mind?"

"Truth or dare."

I laughed. But then I saw how serious she was. "Wait, really?"

"The idea of playing truth or dare with a guy I liked has always excited me. I don't know, we don't have to. You can just ask me some questions."

I liked that I was that guy. The one and only guy that would give her what she wanted. "No, I'll play."

She smiled up at me. "Okay, truth or dare?"

"Truth."

"What do you usually do in your free time?" She was looking around my very empty apartment.

"I grade papers."

"That can't be all that you do."

I swallowed hard. It wasn't possible that she knew about the cameras. Or that I spent a good chunk of my time jerking off to a really fucking hot tape of us at my country club. No. She definitely didn't know that. "Recently I've been busy thinking about you." I smiled at her.

"So you grade papers and think about me? But what do you do for fun?"

Jerk off to images of you. "Thinking about you is fun when you're not mad at me. But I believe it's my turn now. Truth or dare?"

"Truth."

"Why didn't you tell your parents you were dating someone?"

"I thought our relationship was supposed to be secret."

"At first. But then things changed. You told Melissa."

"I didn't want to lie to them about you being a professor."

Fair. "So are you mad that I met them today?"

"No, not at all. I think they both liked you."

"Only because they don't know that I'm your professor."

"Maybe. My mom thought you were hot."

I laughed.

"Truth or dare?" she asked.

"Truth."

"So back to my original question. What do you do for fun?"

"You."

She playfully kicked my leg. "Seriously, James."

I shrugged. I was worried that maybe she did know about the cameras because she kept pushing this question. Maybe Dr. Clark was right. I should have Ian take them down. "I exercise most days."

"Obviously. What do you do for exercise?"

"There's a gym in the building. And I like to run outside."

"Do you even have a T.V.?" she asked.

"No. I can get one if you want."

"Don't you get bored? Alone in your apartment?"

"I've been toying with the idea of starting a new company. It keeps me busy."

"Another tech company?"

"Yeah. I've been working on some logistics for a while. But it's in the beginning stages. It doesn't make sense financially to start it right now." Fuck, why had I said that last part?

"Do you mean, it's better to wait until after you're divorced?"

I ran my fingers through my hair. "I'm not giving her half of this too." Just thinking about Isabella made me feel sick to my stomach. Mr. Pruitt said they'd have another look at the papers. But I hadn't heard from either of them.

"Truth or dare?" she asked.

"I think it's my turn, Penny."

"Truth or dare?" she said more firmly.

I sighed. "Truth."

"Why did you go to New York while we were broken up?"

"I needed to talk to her." I didn't want to talk about this. It was done. I didn't like picturing Ian's concerned face. Or Dr. Clark's for that matter.

"About what? Why didn't you just talk to her on the phone?"

"I was hoping I could convince her to sign the papers." Actually, I was hoping to convince her father to get it done.

"By having sex with her?"

No. "It wasn't like that."

"So what then? You went to talk about getting divorced and ended up sleeping with her? One step forward, two steps back."

I had nothing to say to that. Isabella had her version of events. And she'd threatened to show up to my Comm class and tell Penny herself if I didn't comply. I'd already made up my mind here. I tried to swallow down the lump in my throat. "I missed you. I was a mess. I'm sorry, Penny." I knew that wasn't good enough. But it was all I could offer her.

"Do you still have feelings for her?"

"No." *Absolutely not.*

"Then why did you sleep with her?"

For fuck's sake, can't we drop this? Penny had slept with someone too. And she fucking remembered it. She'd fucking wanted it. *Breathe.* "It's not like I made love to her. It was just sex."

"And what about the first time we had sex? Did that mean nothing too?"

I sighed. "No. It meant everything. It's different with you. Everything is different with you. I don't know what else I can say. I was upset. I made a mistake. End of story."

"It's not the end of the story because you're still married." Her voice cracked.

I was so tired of hurting her. But I didn't know how to fix this. I hated that I didn't have control over the situation. And I swear I was seconds away from snapping. "Truth or dare?" I asked.

"Dare."

What the fuck? "Penny..."

"Fine, truth."

"And what about Tyler?" I seethed. Okay, I'd already snapped.

Chapter 18

Sunday

Penny stared at me with defiance. But she was in the wrong here too. She'd slept with the prick.

"What about him?" she asked calmly.

"You went to see him yesterday. What did you talk about?" If she thought I was going to let that tidbit of information go, she was dead wrong.

"I went to see him to tell him I wanted to be with you."

"After you read my letter?"

"No, before. I want to be with you. That's all that I want. But you're complicated. The situation is complicated. And I don't mean just because you're my professor. It's because you're still married. How can you sit there and talk about a future with me in this situation?"

"Because I know it's over." Why wouldn't she believe me? Why wouldn't she trust my word? "I'll talk to her again."

"No." Penny pulled her feet off my lap and hugged her knees into her chest.

"I'm not going to sleep with her again." I wasn't even sure I had in the first place. But I definitely wouldn't again. Or have anything to drink around her. But Penny didn't seem to believe any of it. And I had a feeling that Ian was watching us right now. Listening and shaking his head. But I was already too deep into this mess to unwind it. "Penny." I leaned forward and kissed her kneecap. "I'm getting divorced. I've already signed the papers."

"I know."

"So why are you still upset about it?"

"It makes me feel like a bad person. What if she never signs the papers?"

"I'll get her to sign them." I kissed her knee again. "I'm sorry about what happened. Please forgive me."

"I love you," said Penny. "I love you so much. There's a million reasons why I should give you up. But I can't. I don't want to. And we were broken up. So there isn't anything to forgive."

"Penny, Penny, Penny." I leaned over her and placed a kiss against her lips. "I love you."

"I love you, too." Tears started to fall from her eyes. She pushed herself up into a seated position. "Stupid concussion." She forced a laugh as she wiped away her tears.

"Hey." I closed the distance between us and wrapped my arm around her shoulders. It seemed like something else was going on here. We'd already talked about all this shit with Isabella. I'd hoped we'd already moved past it. Was I missing something else here? "What's wrong?"

"If this really is love, then it won't matter if we wait."

Her words felt like a slap across my face. "Wait for what?"

"For your divorce to be final. For me to graduate. For things to be less complicated."

"Is this about Tyler? Or Brendan?"

"No. It has nothing to do with them."

I lowered my eyebrows as I stared down at her. Because it seemed like it had everything to do with them. And I was still itching to bang on everyone's door in this apartment complex looking for Brendan.

"I thought you didn't want me," she said. "I was a mess. I was trying to get over you. But I don't want either of them. I felt so empty when you stopped talking to me. I just didn't want to feel empty anymore."

Her words hung in the air for a long time, settling around me. I got that. I did. And it was my fault because I'd wanted her to move on. I'd stayed away. This was on me. And if I wanted her to forgive me for whatever the fuck happened with Isabella, I needed to forgive her too.

"I felt empty too," I said.

We were silent again as we looked into each other's eyes.

"I choose you," she finally said. "I just want to wait till it's right."

I looked down at her legs and traced a circle around the inside of her knee. I tried to think of the right words to say. Words that wouldn't make her angry. Wouldn't make her cry. And wouldn't make her push me away again. "Penny, I've spent my whole life doing things I didn't want to. I don't want to wait anymore. You make me happy. To me, that's all that matters."

"Am I not worth waiting for?"

"That's not what I meant. Of course you're worth waiting for." I grabbed her hand and rubbed my thumb against her palm. "But I feel like I've been waiting my whole life already. You're young. I get that." I sighed. "But two years is a long time. I don't want to wait anymore."

"Then we can just wait until your divorce is final. What's the point of being together if we can't fully commit to one another?"

"I am committed to you. I've told you I love you. I don't take that lightly."

"But our relationship is a secret and you still have a wife. How happy do you think we can be for the next two years like this?"

What did she want from me here? Was she asking me to throw my career away? Was that the only thing that would show her that I was serious about us? "What if I disclose our relationship to the dean?"

She stared at me. "What?"

"Is that what you want? Will that prove to you how I feel? We won't have to hide our relationship anymore."

"We'll get in trouble."

"Not necessarily. Only if someone complains."

She pressed her lips together. "What about Comm?"

"I'm not sure what will happen with that."

"I don't want to have to take it again."

I swallowed hard. Now that we were having this conversation, it didn't seem that hard. I felt empty without her, just like how she felt without me. I wasn't sure I'd feel empty without teaching. Maybe I would. But the alternative of having to be without her for two years was worse. I knew that. I took a deep breath. "So how about I quit?"

"Teaching?"

"If it's the only way."

"I thought you loved teaching. It's your fresh start."

"*You're* my fresh start. And I don't love teaching nearly as much as I love you." It was the truth. If I had to give one of them up, it wouldn't be her.

She straddled me on the couch.

My hands settled on her waist as she leaned forward and hugged me.

"I don't want any of that," she said.

I breathed a sigh of relief. Because even though my mind told me it would be okay to give up teaching, I worried. I knew what kind of man I was before I changed professions. What if...what if I slipped again? What if I lost teaching *and* her?

"I'm sorry," she said. "I just want your divorce to be official. I don't want you to have to change who you are. I love who you are." She put her forehead against mine. "I don't want to wait. I just don't want to have to feel guilty about not waiting."

"There's nothing to feel guilty about. But I'll have my lawyer figure something out, okay? I'll take care of it." This shit with Isabella ended now.

"Soon?"

"Soon."

***

"Favorite soda?" I asked.

"Cherry Coke."

It was my lucky day. "I had my fridge stocked with a bunch of things when I thought you'd be staying here more often." I pulled out a Cherry Coke and handed it to her.

She grabbed the fridge handle before I closed it. "Let me see." Her eyes wandered the shelves and she grabbed a pack of juice boxes. "Juice boxes? Seriously? How young do you think I am?"

Shit. "Those are actually mine." I grabbed them from her, put them back in the fridge, and closed the door.

"Why don't you just buy a bottle of apple juice if you like it so much?"

I tried to think of something to say. I pressed my lips together. I wasn't sure why my first instinct was to lie. We were trying to get to know each other here. *Breathe.* "I was never allowed to have them when I was a kid." There. The truth wasn't so hard.

But I didn't recognize the way she was staring at me.

I shrugged, trying to play it off.

"Okay," she said and handed the soda back to me. "I actually want one of those."

"You do?"

"Yes, please."

I smiled and opened the fridge back up for her. She grabbed the juice boxes while I grabbed the plates. We sat down at the kitchen counter and I watched her take a huge bite of pizza. It was only a matter of seconds before her first slice was gone.

I knew I was staring, but I couldn't seem to stop. She was ravenous. And I was pretty sure that's exactly how I felt about her. "I'm glad to see that you've gotten your appetite back."

"That's what your love does for me."

I smiled and took a bite. "This is pretty delicious."

"I told you." She put her lips seductively around the straw of her juice box and took a sip.

Okay, so maybe she wasn't purposely being seductive. But whenever she wrapped her lips around anything all I could picture was them wrapped around my cock.

"Why is everything so much better with a straw?" she asked.

"I don't know, but it really is." I took a sip from my juice box too.

And she immediately started laughing.

"What's so funny?" I asked.

"It's just...you look like a model and you're drinking from a juice box. It's like, the sexiest apple juice ad ever."

"Marketing at its finest?"

"Absolutely."

I laughed. I wanted to keep making her smile. "What do you want to do with our day off tomorrow?"

"It's not really a day off. I'm supposed to just recuperate, right?"

"We're both ditching class. So it's kind of a day off. We can do whatever you want."

"I think I'd like to see what a normal day is like for you. The behind the professor's facade special."

"You do like to watch a lot of T.V., huh?"

"I don't think I watch an unusual amount. You're the weird one. Who doesn't have a T.V.?"

I shrugged. "Sometimes I watch stuff on my computer. Speaking of which, I need to send out that email about canceling class." And one other thing. "I'll be right back."

"It really is okay if you need to go to class."

"I don't need to." I kissed her and slid off my stool. I walked into my office and called Ian as I booted up my computer.

"What's up?" he said.

"I need your help with something." I started typing out emails to cancel my classes.

There was a long pause. "Are you going to tell me what this something is?"

I stopped typing. I was assuming Isabella had snapped a few photos of me when I blacked out. Incriminating photos she'd use for…something. I didn't really know her plan here. It seemed like she just didn't want to get divorced. And that wasn't up for negotiation.

Dr. Clark had asked me once if Isabella was on medicine. I'd been thinking a lot about that. How she always took something every night. Maybe she was off her meds. If she was…that was bad. Because I couldn't remember a time when she hadn't taken them. Maybe back in high school, before her father sent her to that facility. If she was reverting back to her younger self, I had to fight fire with fire.

I cleared my throat. "Actually, does Max still have the same number?"

"Why?"

"I need his help with something."

"I thought you said you needed *my* help with something? What are you planning?"

"I need someone to follow Isabella. And you can't tail her. She'll recognize you."

"Follow her?" Ian sighed. "Now I know why you asked for Max. You're planning to blackmail Isabella back? I don't think that's a good idea, man."

"What else am I supposed to do? I need her to sign the papers."

Ian sighed. "Fine. Yeah, Max has the same number. But just for the record…I hate this plan. At least you're not making me do it though."

"Can you also let Ellen know she doesn't need to come in for the next few days?"

"Penny will eventually need to get used to the fact that you have a staff."

"I know. But it's a lot, right? I want to ease her into all this."

"Did you just call me a lot?"

I laughed. "You know what I meant."

"So this means she's staying, right? For good this time?"

"I hope so."

"Me too," Ian said. "I'll let Ellen know to lay low. And I'll do the same. Wait, does this mean I have to watch the game alone tomorrow night?"

"I'll let you know. We might be able to still catch Odin Beckman dominate Sam Bradfury."

"What the fuck did you just say to me?"

"It's a long story. I'll fill you in later."

He laughed. "You got it, boss. Have a good night." He hung up.

I pulled out one of my desk drawers and rifled through the papers until I found Max's number. I called him as I sent off the rest of my emails canceling classes.

Max answered after just a few rings. "Long time no see, James. How's Delaware treating you?"

I wasn't surprised he knew where I'd moved. That was kind of his job to know things. "Great. I have a job for you."

"What kind of job?"

"I need some incriminating photos of my ex with other men. It won't be hard. I'm sure she's seeing someone. Just get it done quickly and quietly."

"You're talking about Isabella?"

"Yes."

"The usual fee?" he asked.

"Of course. Just send the photos when you have them."

"You got it. And just so we're clear, we're not just talking about a dinner date, right? A picture of her on a date is easy, but it will take me a little more time to figure out who she's currently fucking and when and where they're doing it. There's an art to these things."

"That's fine. I just need it done."

"What's the exact time frame?"

"By the end of the week at the latest."

"No problem at all. I'll email you the pictures when I have them."

"No, I'll need it hand delivered. I don't want a cyber footprint on this."

"Will do."

"Thanks, Max."

There was a knock on my office door. *Shit.* I hung up the phone.

"Professor Hunter?" Penny said.

I pushed the papers with phone numbers and details about people that I probably shouldn't have back into the drawer and slammed it shut. Penny didn't need to know *how* I was finally going to finalize the divorce. She'd just care that it was done. I opened the door for her but didn't invite her inside.

"So I'm a pressing personal matter?" She smiled up at me.

I'm glad she knew the cancellation email was about her. Everything I did was always for her. "Yes."

She glanced over her shoulder down the hallway. "Your apartment is a lot bigger than I realized."

"Do you want me to give you a tour?" I stepped out of my office and closed the door behind me. I grabbed her hand to lead her down the hall, but she didn't budge.

"Well, what's in there?" She nodded her head towards my office door.

"It's my office. Nothing fancy."

"I'd like to see that."

"It's kind of messy." I'd been sleeping in there recently. It was the one room in my apartment where her cherry scented perfume hadn't reached. Not that it really kept my mind from wandering to her. Especially because I watched her through the security feed in there.

"Good, because the rest of your apartment is unnervingly clean." She stood up on her tiptoes and clasped her hands behind my neck. "Please?"

How was I supposed to say no to her when she was staring up at me like that? "It's really not much to see." But maybe that wasn't true. It was the only room that had any decorations at all. Dr. Clark would want me to show it to her.

"So it doesn't matter if I see it then."

I smiled down at her. I was trying to be more open with her. And that meant inviting her inside my office. Willingly. "Whatever you want." I opened the door back up. She let go of me and wandered into the room.

I folded my arms across my chest as I tried to see it from her point of view. Mathematical formulas covered my whiteboard. My floor to ceiling bookshelves were packed with books. There were papers scattered about my desk. And some crumbled up papers on the ground that I'd missed when I shot them into the little basketball hoop above the trash can. I wasn't sure what any of that said about me, besides that I was a bad shot.

"You're kind of a hoarder," she said as she walked farther into the room.

"I'm not a hoarder," I said with a laugh. "I actually use all this stuff."

"What on earth do you need this many computers for?"

I looked around at the dozen computers that were spread through the room. I shrugged. They each had their purpose.

"And you do have T.V.s." She stared at the few mounted next to the whiteboard.

"Oh. Well, yes, but I just use them as monitors. They're hooked up to my computers." The only T.V. I ever watched on them was games with Ian.

She glanced at the leather sofa in the corner. Where I still had a pillow and blanket.

She turned back to me. "So the rest of your apartment is immaculate because you spend all your time in here?"

"I spend most of my free time in here, yes."

"Well, you seemed very judgy of my wonderfully comfortable dorm room bed. Yet, you usually sleep on a leather sofa?"

"I've been finding it hard to fall asleep in my bed when you're not in it with me." I pressed my lips together. It was odd being so blatantly honest. Odd but...refreshing.

"Oh." Her cheeks flushed.

I'd forgotten how much I loved when she got flustered. Her rosy cheeks reminded me of the matching color her ass turned when I spanked her.

She walked over to my desk. "So this is where all your personal stuff is?" She lifted up a picture frame off my desk. "Are these your siblings?"

I walked over to her and stared at the picture. "Yeah." I was younger in it. A much better age for Penny. But I'd been a fucking mess back then. I was happy in that picture, but the feeling had been fleeting. I barely even recognized myself with a smile on my face. If I was worried about ruining her now...I definitely would have ruined her then. *Breathe.*

"What are their names?"

"Jennifer and Rob."

"When was this taken?" she asked.

"At the launch party of my company."

"Is that a thing? That's rather extravagant."

"It was a P.R. nightmare."

"How old were you?"

"22." It felt like a lifetime ago.

"Hmm."

"What?" I smiled down at her.

"You look so happy in this picture. Do you miss it?"

Miss what exactly? Living under my parents' thumb? Being high every night? Slowly killing myself? I had a feeling her question wasn't so heavy. I cleared my throat. "Running a company?"

"Yeah."

"You'd think that being a C.E.O. would mean I didn't have to answer to anyone." I sat down on the edge of my desk. "But most of my time was spent doing things I didn't love. I do miss certain parts though."

"Is that why you're thinking about starting a new company?"

"Well, as you have so eloquently pointed out, I've had a lot of free time. I needed something to occupy myself." But that wasn't the only reason. In the back of my head, I was worried my time at this university would be cut short. That Penny and I would be found out. And if I didn't have something else lined up, I was worried what that free time would do to me. I wasn't good at being idle. I needed a routine. I needed structure.

She laughed and moved between my legs. She put her hands down on my thighs. "I had a question about my present."

"And what is that?"

"The tickets to the Thanksgiving Day parade. Is that an invitation to meet your family?"

I smiled down at her. "If you want it to be."

"Do you think they'll like me?"

"Jennifer and Rob will love you."

"What about your parents?"

I tried to not let my smile falter. I wanted her to meet Jen and Rob. But...I wasn't on speaking terms with my parents. Her meeting them wasn't on the agenda for Thanksgiving. If she really wanted to meet them though? I'd let her. I didn't want to hide anything from her any-more. "If you could just laugh off everything they say like they're crazy people, that would be best."

"You don't think they'll like me? Why?"

I pulled her closer, making her hands slide farther up my thighs. "I don't like to try to think like them."

"Maybe they'll love me."

No. I don't think so. They don't even love me. "Isn't my love enough?"

"Yes." She moved one of her hands to the waistline of my jeans. "Speaking of which, it's a shame that I'm supposed to be taking things easy. That probably means no sex."

Rough sex maybe. But I knew how to be gentle with my girl. "I don't think that's what that means."

"I'm pretty sure." She slipped her hand slightly beneath my waistband, running her fingers through my happy trail.

Was she teasing me? I usually liked being in control. But I kind of wanted to see where she was going with this. "I don't consider you to be one to shy away from breaking rules, Penny."

"Me?" She unbuttoned my jeans and slowly unzipped them.

I'd jerked off to images of her while I was alone in this room. Countless times. Never once had I pictured this.

"I'm a stickler for the rules, Professor Hunter."

"So you'd be mad if, for example, I did this?" I leaned forward and pushed her jacket off her shoulders.

She shook it the rest of the way off. "Furious."

"What about this?" I slid my hands up her waist, peeling off her tank top. She didn't say a word as the fabric fell to the floor and I unhinged her bra.

"I'm so upset with you right now." She tried to hide her smile.

"Hmm." I slid off the edge of my desk. "What if I did this?" I pushed her yoga pants over her ass and slowly pulled them down her thighs. Her skin pebbled beneath my touch. When her pants reached her knees, I released the fabric and they fell to the floor.

She gulped. "I can barely look at you I'm so angry."

"I figured. I'll respect your wishes then." I zipped my pants back up. "I'm going to go take a shower."

"Professor Hunter..."

"Don't worry, I'm taking you with me." I lifted her over my shoulder and carried her out of my office.

Chapter 19

Monday

Penny's lips traced my collarbone.

I groaned and slowly opened my eyes. Light was shining through the blinds. And I'd never seen Penny's hair look so bright. The morning sun made it look like there were a million different colors in the strands.

She kissed my collarbone again then underneath my chin.

"Mmm."

"I like waking up next to you," she whispered.

"I could get used to this." I ran my fingers through her hair, letting them disappear into the symphony of colors.

She laughed. "So what does the elusive Professor Hunter usually do when he wakes up in the morning?"

I just wanted to stare at her. "Are you a morning person?" I mumbled.

"I signed up for classes late and got stuck with all 8 a.m.s. I've gotten used to waking up early."

"Well." I reluctantly rolled over and looked at my alarm clock. "You're like clockwork then. It's 7:30."

"Is Comm the only 8 a.m. class that you teach?"

"Yes. It's funny, I didn't want to teach it at all. I kind of got stuck with it. But I'm so glad that I did."

"Me too." She kissed my collarbone again.

I really liked when she did that. And I liked last night. How easy it was to show her parts of my life I'd kept hidden. I wanted to keep doing that. And that meant answering all her questions. She wanted to know what my morning routine was. I yawned and sat up. "I usually go for a run before breakfast. But I just want to hang out with you today. What do you want for breakfast?"

"What do you usually have?"

"Ellen usually fixes me something. But I gave her the next few days off."

"Is that your chef?"

Ellen was a lot more than that. My friend. My surrogate mother. One of the only other people in this world that gave a shit about me. "She cooks and cleans and does everything that I don't know how to do." Which was a lot of things. "You'll like her. Come on, let's get up." I lightly slapped Penny's ass.

Penny laughed and climbed out of bed. Instead of any of the little satin nightgowns I'd bought her, she was just wearing one of my t-shirts. And I'd never seen her look sexier.

"Does Ellen know about me?"

"Yes. She was the one who went grocery shopping for you." And bought all those clothes. "She's excited to meet you."

Penny followed me into the kitchen. "And she's the one who buys you juice boxes?"

"Mhm. She's a keeper." I opened up the fridge. "How about a bagel?"

"That sounds perfect."

I grabbed two bagels, sliced them, and put them in the toaster. I was glad I at least knew how to do this. "Do you want some coffee?"

"Do you have any orange juice?"

"That I do." I poured us each a glass.

"So I was thinking a little about my speech. And I'm not really sure what to talk about this time. Usually I was flirting with you or losing my mind. I guess I should just do something normal for once?"

I wasn't sure Penny was capable of normal. Everything she did was extraordinary. But I was biased. And we both knew it. "I wouldn't worry about it too much." I winked at her.

"I haven't even thought about a topic yet, though."

"Certainly you'll get an A. You're sleeping with your professor, after all."

"What happened to no perks?"

"Well, Miss Taylor. That concept kind of flew out the window when I fell in love with you."

"Oh yeah?"

"Yeah." Besides, even though she was nervous when she did her speeches, she was my only student that put any thought into them. She deserved the good grades I gave her. The toaster popped and I grabbed our bagels and some cream cheese.

"Maybe I should give detailed instructions on how to seduce your professor."

Well, that was adorable that she thought she seduced me. I took a bite of my bagel. "You didn't seduce me. I seduced you."

"No way. Short skirts, my best push up bra, uncalled for texts, and my unbelievably illicit answers in class seduced the crap out of you."

Fair. But I'd gotten her to storm into my office hours. We were sitting here because I always got what I wanted. And I only wanted her. I was borderline stalking her for Christ's sake. It was a game of cat and mouse, although I was pretty sure I was actually a much more sinister animal than a cat. I was the hunter and she was my prey. The thought made me frown. I tried to shake it away. *Breathe.* "I had you right where I wanted you."

And I was pretty sure she knew it. Because she had no rebuttal.

"So what do you usually do after breakfast?" she asked.

"Go to class."

"What other classes do you teach?"

"I teach that grad class twice a week. And I have a few 300 and 400 level marketing courses."

"That's vague. Tell me what the 300 level ones are and I'll try to sign up for one next semester."

"You probably shouldn't take any more of my classes."

"But I like taking your classes. It means I get to stare at you the whole time."

"Which is very distracting."

"You seriously don't want me to take your marketing classes?"

"Well, I was thinking about it. And I think after this semester it really would be best if we disclosed our relationship to the dean. Maybe after winter session? That way your Comm grade won't be in jeopardy." And maybe if I was lucky, I'd somehow be able to keep my job.

"Which means I can't take any more of your classes?"

"It does."

"Pros and cons," she said.

"We can spend more time together at night that way. We won't have to worry about people seeing us together around campus. It'll be really nice." It was probably all wishful thinking. The dean had every right to fire my ass, even though I technically hadn't broken any rules. Which was why I was working on that new camera design for my next business venture. I was pretty sure the tech was already perfect though. I certainly used it a lot.

"I'll think about it," Penny said. "So what do you do after breakfast on the weekends?"

"Work."

"On your new company?"

IVY SMOAK

"There's always something to do." I shifted in my chair. I should have told her about this last night, but she'd been rather distracting with her wandering hands. "Actually, there's something I wanted to discuss with you."

"Okay." She was looking up at me with a worried expression. She was probably afraid I was going to tell her something awful. And I hoped this wouldn't be. I really wanted it to go well.

"My brother is coming back from Costa Rica this weekend," I said.

"That's fantastic. I can't wait to meet him. I want to get to know your family."

That was great, but it was a little more than just a visit. "I invited him here indefinitely. Earlier this month. We weren't together and..."

"James, that's fine. He's your brother. It'll be fun."

Hmm. "Yeah, he's definitely fun." And for just a second...I felt a little nervous. I took a sip of orange juice. Rob was younger than me. More fun. He certainly had less baggage. He was a better fit for someone like Penny. He'd make her laugh every day. He could love her in public.

Breathe. I could make Penny laugh too. And I could love her in public soon enough. And it wasn't like she was a teenager anymore.

"Where will he stay?" she asked.

"There are guestrooms in the hallway before my office."

"Did you not want me to stay over while he's here?"

"Were you thinking about staying over more?" I smiled. I liked the sound of that.

"Well, you were right about your bed. It's a lot more comfortable than mine."

"Is that the only reason?" I pulled her into my arms.

"I'm only in this relationship for the sleeping arrangements. Did I not make that clear when we started this?"

Naughty girl. "No, you failed to mention that."

"Well now you know." She smiled up at me. "I'm going to go brush my teeth." She unwound herself from my grip and disappeared back into my bedroom.

I smiled to myself as I pulled out my phone. I shot Rob a text, confirming that he'd be here this weekend. I'd already told Ellen and Penny that he would be. And the last thing I wanted was for him to flake on me.

My phone buzzed with an incoming text: "Be late and miss out on my surprise? Never. I hope it's two hookers."

I laughed. *Why two? Nope.* I didn't want to know.

Penny walked back into the kitchen and I slid my phone into my pocket.

"I'll be right back," I said. When I grabbed my toothbrush from the holder, it was already wet. Did Penny use my toothbrush? I wasn't sure why, but it made me smile. That she felt that at home. I probably should have put one out for her though. I quickly brushed my teeth and went back out into the kitchen. When I saw her sitting there, I couldn't stop smiling.

"What?" Penny asked. She could probably tell that I was amused by this. Or maybe she was embarrassed that she'd done it?

"Did you use my toothbrush?" I asked.

"Maybe?"

I laughed. "You are definitely making yourself at home. Even though you're only after me for my sweet sleeping arrangements, you can stay whenever you want. You'd move in for good if it was up to me. I only brought up Rob because I wanted to warn you that we were going to have company for a while."

"I know. So what do you want to do now?" she asked.

"I can help you with Stat."

"All my notes are in my dorm. Besides, lame. We have a day off."

"So you want to do something more fun?"

"Yes. But I can't really go anywhere with my secret professor boyfriend and a huge bandage on my forehead."

I closed the distance between us and grabbed her chin.

She tilted her face up to me and I slowly took off her bandage.

"There, that's better." My phone buzzed. I hoped it wasn't Rob asking for three hookers instead of two. And it wasn't. It was Ian. "Hunter," I said as I answered the phone.

Ian laughed. "So formal. Apparently Penny has a delivery at the front desk. And before you ask, no, I don't know what it is. I have eyes on the front desk of course, but there are a lot of packages down there."

Why would Penny have a delivery here? I swallowed hard, fearing the worst. There were only a few people who knew my address. One of them being Isabella.

"Want me to go grab it for you?" Ian asked.

"No, I'll come get it." I didn't want to drag anyone else into this in case it was a fucking bomb or something. "Thanks." I hung up and turned back to Penny. "You have a delivery."

"What? Here?"

"Apparently so." I was hoping she'd say she gave the address to her parents or something. But she seemed just as confused as me. *Fuck.* I walked into my room and quickly changed into jeans and a v-neck t-shirt.

I wasn't scared of Isabella. Not really. But for some reason my heart was racing. If Isabella was off her meds, it was really bad. The way she was in high school was a little…murdery. I tried to shake the thought away as I walked out of my room.

Penny looked nervous too for some reason. "I haven't given anyone your address, Professor Hunter."

Yeah. This was definitely Isabella's doing. "I know. It's rather curious." I kissed her forehead next to her stitches. Whatever this mystery package was, I knew it wouldn't be good. I just wanted to have this one day where we could relax and be happy. Just us. And it was already falling apart. "I'll be right back."

I got onto the elevator. What if it was pictures of me from that night Isabella drugged me? I was pretty sure my stomach sank as the elevator descended.

My phone buzzed again with another text from Ian: "Be careful. The package could be from Isabella."

Yeah. I stuffed my phone back into my pocket. We were on the same page. I nodded to the small camera that I knew was in the elevator.

If it was pictures…what were they pictures of? Could it actually be images of me fucking her? I felt like I was going to be sick. I didn't want it to be true. I reached for the rubber band around my wrist, only to remember it was no longer there.

Breathe.

No matter how hard I tried to remember that night, I couldn't. All I remembered was leaving Ian's car and then waking up feeling like my head was going to explode.

It wasn't the first time I'd blacked out. But it was the first time I'd done something I really regretted. All the fights back in college weren't great, but at least I hadn't fucked someone and not remembered it.

Breathe.

Dr. Clark said it was different than a normal blackout. Because I didn't choose to overindulge. But I had grabbed the drink Isabella handed me. A drink I shouldn't have been having because I'd been overindulging that whole week. In that sense, there was no difference. The blame was on me. And I didn't want to fucking see whatever Isabella had sent.

The elevator doors parted and I made my way to the front desk. Ian was right. There were packages everywhere waiting to be picked up. And a huge audacious bouquet of flowers in the center of the desk. I eyed the packages warily, almost like I was expecting to hear a ticking noise.

"I was told there was a package for Penny Taylor?"

The guy looked in his notebook. "Yup." He pointed to the ugly bouquet. "I guess someone has a secret admirer."

Wait, what? "I was told it was a package."

"Sorry," he said. "Should have said flowers."

I just stared at him. "You're shitting me."

"What?" the guy said.

Fuck my life. "Who are they from?"

"I didn't look at the card," he said.

I sighed. I didn't actually need him to look. Penny's admirer wasn't a secret. Because there was some dick in my building making passes at her. Brendan. It had to be him. No one else knew my address. Seriously, who the fuck was this Brendan guy?

All I knew was that he was rich, or he wouldn't be living here. And despite his stupid flower arrangement, he did have good taste. Because he was after my girl.

I grabbed the vase and headed back to my apartment. *Brendan.* I needed Ian to run a background check on this asshole. I shot Ian a text as I got back onto the elevator.

"Brendan who?" Ian asked.

"I don't know his last name. Some asshole who sent Penny flowers. He lives in this building."

"Lol. Another guy sent her those flowers?"

Shut up, Ian. I gave the middle finger to the camera in the elevator.

"Lol," he texted again.

I was pretty sure I would have preferred the bomb from Isabella.

Chapter 20

Monday

I could barely even see through the huge bouquet as I made my way back into my apartment. I set the vase down on the kitchen counter and turned to look at Penny.

"Are these from you?" she asked.

"No, Penny. I don't know who they're from." But I certainly had a guess.

"Probably my parents." She walked over and grabbed the envelope.

"Probably." I tried to keep my voice even. I stared at her as she opened the card.

What had she said that asshole said to her? Something about how if things are so hard between us maybe we're not meant to work things out. *Fuck him.*

Penny looked up at me, like she was trying to gauge my reaction to this.

But I wasn't giving her anything.

She slid the card back into the envelope and set it down on the counter. "They're from Brendan."

No shit. "A friendship rose kind of thing?" I raised my eyebrow. *Wishful thinking.*

Penny sighed. "No. He likes me. I'll talk to him..."

Fuck no you're not going to go talk to him. "Get dressed."

"What?"

"We're going out." I needed to get her out of this apartment before Brendan showed up. Because if he did, there was a high probability that I'd assault him.

"Okay."

I grabbed our dishes from breakfast. If I didn't do something useful with my hands I was worried I might throw the vase against the wall. *Breathe.*

"James?"

I ignored her as I washed the dishes. I just needed a minute to calm down. And to think about where I wanted to take her.

She retreated into my bedroom.

I wanted to take her somewhere far away from here. Away from freaking Tyler and Brendan and anyone else who had a death wish. Somewhere we could go unnoticed. Somewhere we could just be us instead of a professor and his student.

I placed the last dish in the dishwasher. I knew exactly where to take Penny. I pulled out my phone and shot Ian a text: "I'm going to New York for the day."

My phone immediately buzzed with his response. "Great, I'll drive."

"You can stay here."

"Oh, right. Incognito. I'll take a separate car and follow you there."

"Or you can just stay here," I typed back.

"Not if you're going to New York. We both know what happened last time you were there."

Actually I had no idea what the fuck had happened the last time I was there. But I was pretty sure that was his point. "Don't be an obvious tail, Ian."

"Me? Never."

I looked up from my phone when I heard footsteps. Penny reappeared in a pair of jeans, a sweater, and some brown leather boots. She looked beautiful, if a little apprehensive of me.

I slid my phone into my pocket and leaned against the kitchen counter.

"I'm sorry," she said as she approached me.

But I could feel the distance between us. I ran my hand through my hair. I just needed to fix this. "Let's go."

"James."

I forced a smile onto my face. "I feel like when you call me by my first name I'm in trouble. I don't want to fight."

"I don't want to fight either."

"Good." I grabbed her hand and pulled her toward the elevator. As soon as her hand was in mine, it felt a little easier to breathe. "I need to pick up some things."

"What kind of things?" she asked as we stepped onto the elevator.

"Well, my girlfriend needs her own toothbrush."

She laughed. "Sorry, I didn't know what to do."

I pulled her against me as the elevator doors slid closed.

"I don't want to go back to reality tomorrow."

I smiled down at her. "Me either."

"Let's just run away together."

"Just name the place." I wasn't sure if she meant it, but I did.

She sighed and pressed her the side of her face against my chest. I ran my hands down her back and stopped when they were on the small of her back. I wanted to freeze time. Just like this. Everything was better when we were in our own little bubble.

"Let's do something fun today," she said. "I don't want to go shopping."

I was happy to hear that she didn't want to go shopping. I'm not sure I'd ever dated anyone who liked me more than my Amex. "Good, because we're not just going shopping."

She looked back up at me. "But you just said we were going to go buy toothbrushes."

"Yeah." I tucked a loose strand of hair behind her ear. "I lied."

The elevator doors dinged and opened. I grabbed her hand and led her toward my cars.

Ian was wearing a baseball cap and was just climbing into his Tesla. His whole deal screamed security detail that was trying but failing to blend in. But Penny was just staring up at me.

"Wait, then what are we doing?" she asked.

"It's a surprise." I opened up the car door for her. She smiled and climbed in. I closed the door behind her. Today was going to be fun. I wouldn't go anywhere near Isabella's favorite spots. Which was easy, because I'd made a habit of that years ago. Penny and I would be able to blend into a sea of people. We could just be a normal couple for once.

I climbed into the car and started the engine.

"Am I at least dressed okay?" Penny asked.

"Not at all." Really, she was. But I loved messing with her. The flush spread across her cheeks.

"What? Let me go change then. What should I be wearing?"

"That would kind of take away from the surprise." We drove in silence for a few minutes. Once we turned onto the highway, she finally broke the silence.

"Can I at least have a hint?"

I pressed my lips together, trying to think of a good one. "I'm hoping to change your mind about something."

"About what?"

"I already gave you your hint."

She smiled at me and turned to look out the window.

I did want to change her mind about New York. When I left the city, I swore I'd never go back. But I'd meant what I said to Matt on the phone. I wanted to go back to how things used to be. The four of us. My friends were in New York. I wanted to be able to go back to the city and feel like I could breathe. I glanced at Penny. If she was with me, I knew I'd be able to.

She snored lightly and I smiled.

I looked in my rearview mirror to see Ian's car still a respectful two cars back. I pressed my foot down on the gas. Ian would like the challenge.

Penny didn't like when I sped. But if she was sleeping…I could get to the city in record time and have fun while doing it. I pressed my foot down harder on the gas.

***

I pulled into an empty spot and cut the engine. Penny was still fast asleep, which gave me a few minutes to plan out the rest of our day. I shot off a few texts to Ian on things I needed him to arrange.

My phone was on silent, but I saw his response come through. "You're lucky neither of us got a ticket."

"I would have paid for your ticket," I texted back. "Don't pretend you weren't happy to properly test out your new car."

"I'm more excited for pizza."

I frowned at the text. "You're coming in? I just gave you a bunch of stuff to do."

"I'll blend in and handle everything while I'm eating. Speeding makes me hungry."

I laughed and slid my phone back into my pocket. I knew he'd handle it. He always did.

I turned to Penny. She looked so peaceful while she was sleeping. I almost didn't want to disturb her. But she'd asked for a fun day. And I knew exactly how to give that to her.

"Hey," I whispered. I placed my hand on her cheek.

Penny slowly opened her eyes. She stared at me for a moment and then looked out the window. "Where are we? Philly?"

I laughed. "No, not Philly."

"Are we in New York?"

"I don't think you've experienced it the same way that I have."

"Because I'm not rich?"

I shrugged. "I want to show you my New York."

She glanced at the clock on my dashboard. "You like speeding."

"I tend to do everything efficiently."

"You mean fast."

I bit the inside of my lip. What did she mean by that? I thought about what Brendan had said to her again. He was dead wrong. He was just trying to get into her pants. What she and I had was more than that. "Penny." I grabbed her hand. "I know what I want. I want you. All of you. I know that I'm older than you. And I may be ready for something more serious than..."

"I didn't mean anything by it."

I wasn't so sure about that. "Still."

"I'm running just as fast beside you." She squeezed my hand.

Maybe I was just overthinking her words because of those stupid flowers. I wanted to believe that we were good. I leaned toward her until my lips were an inch from hers. "Okay," I whispered. But instead of kissing her, I opened her car door from the inside and then got out.

The city was loud. When I'd moved away last year, I'd told myself I wouldn't come back. I'd hated the city. I'd hated everyone here. I'd hated the way I was when I was here.

But with Penny beside me?

I couldn't really explain it. It just…it felt like maybe it could be home again. Maybe I could be okay here. As long as she was beside me.

She joined me on the sidewalk and clasped her hands behind my neck. She looked so happy. How could I not smile when we were together?

She stood on her tiptoes and kissed me.

Yeah, I could definitely get used to New York again with her by my side. Even if all we ever did was visit.

"I like New York better already," she said.

"Well you're about to like it even more." I pointed to the building we were standing next to. "Because Totonno's Pizzeria is *the* best pizza."

She laughed. "You brought me all the way to New York to prove a point?"

"One of the reasons." Mostly I just wanted to be away from campus with her. I opened the door to the pizzeria.

The checkerboard floor and walls covered in frames of newspaper clippings, awards, and black and white family photos…it all felt so homey. Honestly I felt more comfortable here than I had in the apartment I'd shared with Isabella. Isabella refused to step foot in this quaint shop. But Penny seemed perfectly content.

"This is your favorite pizza place?" she asked.

"Yes. Grab us a seat." I walked up to the counter in the back while Penny sat down. Ian was at a corner table. He lowered the newspaper that was covering his face and winked at me.

I remembered him being more subtle than this.

But…in his defense, I actually remembered very little of my adult life in New York. Ian was good at his job. Or else I wouldn't still be alive standing here.

I quickly ordered and then joined Penny at the table she'd chosen by the window.

"This place doesn't really seem like you," she said as I sat down across from her.

"What do you mean?"

"You tend to be kind of…extravagant."

I smiled. "Not always. I used to come here to eat all the time."

"What was your favorite part about living here?" She put her hand in the center of the table.

I immediately grabbed it. "There's always something to do."

"So you've been pretty bored in a college town?"

"Hardly. You're very entertaining." I smiled at her, but she was looking at someone over my shoulder. Fuck, she wasn't suspicious of the creep in a baseball hat in the corner, right? I forced myself not to follow her line of sight. It had been a while since I'd had Ian following me around. We were both off our game.

"You know that women stare at you everywhere we go, right?"

Oh. That's what she was looking at? "Is that so? I haven't noticed."

"You must have noticed. Everyone drools over you. I mean, look at you."

"I'm too busy looking at you."

Her cheeks flushed. "You're out of my league."

"You're out of your mind." If anyone was staring over here, they were probably looking at her, not me.

She bit her lip. "Why me?"

"What do you mean?"

"If you wanted to date a student..."

"I didn't want to date a student." Not at all. I'd tried so hard to stay away. I lifted her hand and kissed her knuckles. "Are you asking why I'm attracted to you? Or why I love your personality?"

"Both I guess."

"You don't have much self-confidence. It's rather curious."

"Why would I? No one's ever looked at me the way that you're looking at me right now."

"I know you don't see it. But you are always the most beautiful girl in the room. I enjoy that you don't see it. It's intriguing how naive you are. You're very alluring."

"Alluring?" She laughed.

"Yes. I find you unbelievably sexy." I stared into her eyes. "Every inch of you."

Her cheeks flushed even more.

"Did you want more intimate details? Because I could go on for days describing the blue of your eyes with the small flecks of green in the sunshine. Or the freckles on your shoulders. Or that birthmark on the inside of your ankle. Or how your ass jiggles just the right amount when you walk. Or how your breasts fit perfectly in my hands. Or how you get a cute little wrinkle in your forehead when you frown at me. Or how it makes me feel when you bite your lip when you look at me. Or the intoxicating smell of you. And the taste of you." I swallowed hard. *Maybe I should taste her right now.*

Chapter 21

Monday

I didn't want pizza anymore. I wanted her. And even though Ian was watching us, no one else in the pizzeria was.

I tried to push away the thought away. I was having fun getting to know her even better. And I already knew her body. I liked telling her all the reasons why I'd fallen for her. "And the way you're looking at me right now...it's sexy as hell."

Her throat made that adorable squeaking noise I loved.

"So if you refuse to see how beautiful you are, you'll just have to accept the fact that I'm attracted to you. And for things that aren't physical." I paused and kissed her knuckles again. "I love that you're down to earth. I love that you're shy. It's refreshing that you don't seem to want to be the center of attention everywhere we go. I like that you just want to be beside me instead, captivating me alone. I love that you're open to second chances and quick to forgive. Yet you're extremely stubborn as well, and I love how that challenges me. I love how intelligent you are. I love that you like experiencing new things. And I love that you're a hopeless romantic, or else we wouldn't be sitting here right now."

Each thing I told her made her cheeks even rosier. "I'm a hopeless romantic because I chose you? Why is that hopeless?"

"I told you that I wasn't good for you, yet here you are. Besides, you had plenty of other options."

"I didn't."

"Tyler and Brendan?" *Fucking assholes.*

"I was always going to come back to you. I can't stop thinking about you. I can't and I won't."

We both remembered when I'd told her to stop thinking about me. I was glad she liked defying me. "See...hopeless romantic."

"I don't like that phrase. It makes it sound like we're doomed."

For some reason I thought about Isabella. I swallowed down the lump in my throat. The divorce would be behind me soon enough. Max was a professional. He'd get me the leverage I needed. "I think we've already been through the hardest things."

"I hope so."

I lowered my eyebrows as I stared at her. Was there something else bothering her? "So really, the question is why did you choose me?"

"You're joking, right?"

"I'm curious." I wanted to know why she wanted someone with tons of baggage instead of someone her own age. Although, if Tyler was her only option who was closer to her age, I didn't have much competition.

"It seems as though you have plenty of self-confidence."

"Is that one of the things you like?"

"Yes. I like that you always seem so sure of what you want. Even if what you want scares you."

I put my other hand on top of hers, so that her hand was sandwiched between mine. I wanted her to keep going. The only person I ever heard analyze me was Dr. Clark. I'd much rather hear Penny's opinion.

"You know how good looking you are. You're classically tall, dark, and handsome. When I see you I get butterflies in my stomach. And when you touch me I get chills." She suddenly looked nervous. "I've never been so attracted to someone in my life."

"That's how I feel about you."

She laughed.

"Penny. I do."

Her eyes locked with mine. I hoped she could see how sincere I was being.

"You're also dark and brooding and mysterious. But when you let me in, when I get to see glimpses of the real you, I fall harder and harder. Like the juice box thing."

"You like that my parents didn't let me drink apple juice out of a box?"

"No, I like that you told me that. You're cute."

I lowered my eyebrows again. "I'm not cute." What the hell kind of description of me was that?

"Yes you are. You're being adorable right now."

I couldn't help but smile. *Adorable? Really?* That was even worse than cute.

"And I love that you're..." her voice trailed off and she looked down at our hands, "...domineering."

I laughed. Now that was a much better way to describe me. "You mean in bed?"

She shook her head. "Yes, in bed. But in everything else too. I'm indecisive. I'm so bad at choosing things."

"You chose me."

"I did. But you saw all the stupid stuff I did along the way," she said.

"Which was my fault."

"No. It was because I'm a mess."

I smiled at her. *Me too, baby.* "Do you know what I am currently enjoying most of all?"

"About me?"

"Yes about you."

She gulped. "What are you enjoying most?"

"How insatiable you are."

"Insatiable? How so? By wanting to spend time with you?"

"In bed, mostly."

Her eyes grew round. "I don't think that's true."

I laughed. "If I wanted to, I could have you coming in the bathroom before our pizza arrived." All I needed to do was pull her away from prying eyes. She'd spread her legs for me whenever I told her to. She loved almost getting caught. "Or maybe I could do it right here. I believe I owe you an orgasm with an audience after the office blowjob incident."

She gulped. "But you liked that."

"I did. And you'd like this." I brushed my foot against her leg. "Besides, I promised you I'd retaliate." I hitched my foot on a leg of her chair and pulled it closer to the table. The chair squeaked against the floor.

"I thought you were joking." She was saying one thing, but practically begging me with her bright blue eyes.

"I would never joke about pleasing you." One of my hands left hers and disappeared beneath the table. I placed it down on her knee and slid it up her thigh, higher and higher until her breath caught.

"Professor Hunter..."

My hand froze when the owner of the pizzeria, Marie, arrived with our pizza.

"James! It's so good to see you," she said. I'd missed her thick Italian accent. I had nothing against Grottos, but this right here was real pizza. She placed it down on the table.

I let my hand fall from Penny's thigh and shook Marie's hand. "It's been ages, Marie. I was in the city for the day and this was the first place I stopped."

"We all miss you here. And who is this?" She turned to Penny.

"This is my girlfriend, Penny."

"It's a pleasure to meet you," Penny said. She reached out her hand to shake Marie's.

"No, no, the pleasure is mine." Marie leaned down and hugged her. "Every Monday James would come here and have lunch. Always alone. Always glum. I'm so glad he has finally met someone. You better make him happy," she said in a voice a little more serious than I expected. When Marie released Penny from her hug, she smiled at me. "It's so good to see you, James."

"You too, Marie," I said. She gave me one last smile before walking way. I didn't realize that I always looked glum when I was here. I put my hand back on Penny's thigh for just a moment. "Another time then. I will get you."

Penny smiled. "Why did you eat lunch alone every Monday?"

"Just a habit." I grabbed a slice of pizza.

"Why did she think you were single? You still wore your ring when you lived here, didn't you?"

I exhaled slowly. "No, actually." I hated how all our conversations seemed to revert back to Isabella.

"Why?"

"I stopped wearing my wedding ring the first time I confronted Isabella about her infidelity. I thought she'd feel threatened and stop. I thought maybe the idea of me sleeping around would bother her. It didn't."

"Did you? Sleep around?"

Is that really what she thought of me? "No."

"I'm sorry, I didn't mean to pry."

"It's okay. I want you to be able to ask me questions. But I don't want to talk about her." For the love of God, I never wanted to talk about Isabella again. "I just want to focus on us."

"Okay." She stared at me for just a moment.

I wasn't sure why I kept ruining moments like this. *Breathe.* We were just talking. It wasn't like she was the paparazzi shoving a camera in my face. She wasn't trying to get some inside scoop to flash on the front page of the paper. I took another deep breath.

"So this is the best pizza, huh?" She held up her slice.

"Fold it before you eat it. Trust me."

She followed my instructions and took a big bite. Her eyes immediately lit up.

"What's the verdict?" I asked.

"It's freaking fantastic."

I smiled.

She took a few more bites and then slowly swallowed. "What?" she asked. She rubbed the side of her mouth. "Do I have something on my face?" She wiped the other side. "Where is it?"

I hadn't even realized that I'd been staring at her instead of eating. "Come here, I'll get it for you."

She stood up and walked around the table. She squealed as I grabbed her wrist and pulled her into my lap.

I silenced her with a kiss. "There's nothing on your face." I pressed my forehead against hers. "You're perfect."

"Hmm." Her hands settled on my shoulders. "I think you're the perfect one."

I swallowed hard. There was still a lot she needed to learn about me. Dr. Clark was right...I needed to tell Penny everything. Isabella wasn't the worst skeleton in my closet. And that was really saying something. But it was easy to dismiss Dr. Clark's words in the back of my head when Penny was in my lap.

I breathed in her exhales. For so long I hadn't known what it meant to live in the present. Yoga certainly didn't help. Telling myself every day that I was a worthless piece of shit didn't do it either. But this right here? I could live in this present. With her.

She pulled back slightly to look at me. "What are we doing next?" she asked.

"Next? You mean, you want more than a two-hour drive for pizza? Huh."

She laughed. "If this is all you have planned, that's fine with me. But I don't want to go home just yet. Can we stay a little longer?"

Did she seriously think I brought her all the way to New York just for a good slice? I wanted her to see my New York. I wanted to see if we could fit here. Because as easy as it was to be in the present with Penny, I knew that present was complicated.

One slip and we could easily be thrust into our future pretty quickly. And I didn't know where that future would lead us. Here? Or would we stay in Delaware?

"What's wrong?" she asked, her eyes searching mine.

"Nothing." And there I went again…losing the present. I didn't need to think about all that right now. Today was just for us to have fun. And to show her my hometown. "I was just trying to think of what I'm going to do with you."

"Do with me?" She laughed. "You make it sound like I'm some animal that needs to be wrassled into a cage."

Huh. I certainly wouldn't mind seeing her naked in a cage. Honestly, it was easy picturing her anywhere naked. My hands slid to her ass. "I think I have an idea." I'd actually already planned out our day. With the help of Ian of course. Hopefully he'd gotten it all done between spying on us and eating.

"If it involves the Central Park Zoo, I'm out. Because I didn't love the way your eyes lit up at the idea of me in a cage."

I laughed. No, my ideal date with Penny in New York was certainly not going to the zoo. What was I…five? "How about you finish your pizza and I'll show you."

"Deal. Are we going to the Empire State Building? Or the Statue of Liberty? Oh! Rockefeller Center?"

What? I also wasn't some basic ass tour guide. "No. Better."

Chapter 22

Monday

I slowly pulled my car to a stop. A valet rushed over.

"What's this?" Penny asked.

"One of the best hotels in the city."

Penny stared up in awe at the gold veranda and the modern glass building it was attached to. "Why are we going to a hotel?"

"I have a surprise for you." When I'd given her a closet full of clothes, her eyes had grown round just like they were now. I loved how cute she looked when I surprised her. I winked at her and climbed out of the car.

I handed the valet my keys and opened Penny's door. I grabbed her hand and escorted her to the entrance.

A doorman nodded at us as he opened the door. "Good afternoon and welcome."

"Thank you," I said.

Penny looked like she was worried that she shouldn't be walking on the marble floors. But then she was distracted by the mirrors and gold accents on the walls. And the huge chandeliers that hung from the ceiling. She'd once compared herself to a Disney princess when she was with me. I wanted to give her a day where she felt like that again. After putting her through so much hell.

I pushed the thought aside as we walked over to a plush lounge chair. She sat down as I walked up to the counter. I gave the woman my name and she pulled up my reservation. *Thank you, Ian.* I handed her my card and leaned against the counter.

A bellman came out from the back room. "Welcome back, Mr. Hunter. It's good to have you staying with us again."

The few times I'd been back to the city since I moved away, this was where I'd stayed. Well, except for those unaccounted-for hours when I'd apparently been in Isabella's bed. *Breathe.*

"It's good to be back," I said. And it was. It had been a long time since I'd felt comfortable in the city again. I would have been worried that this guy recognized me. But they were discreet here. Besides, Ian would let me know if anyone had tipped off the paparazzi. The last thing I needed was for Penny and me to show up in a tabloid.

The woman smiled and handed me back my card and gave me a keycard for my room.

"Right this way, sir," the bellman said and stepped toward the elevator.

I turned back around to get Penny. Ian was sitting on one of the other lounge chairs busy looking at something on his phone. Penny didn't seem to be aware of him at all. She saw me waiting and quickly hurried over. And she immediately slid her hand into mine. Right where it belonged.

I smiled down at her and we followed the bellman.

"James, is that you?" a familiar voice said.

Mason had just stepped off the elevator. I'd just been thinking how I wanted to reconnect with my friends. But...I kind of wanted to do that one on one with each of them. We couldn't exactly talk freely in front of Penny about everything that had happened.

But it was really fucking good to see him. It had been far too long. "Mason. Good to see you." I would have hugged him, but I swear it was like I could feel the distance between us. Even though we were standing in the same place, it felt like we were still in different states. So I just put out my hand.

He shook it. Apparently he felt it too.

I'd fix this. I was going to fix everything.

"I see that you finally took my advice." Mason glanced at Penny. His eyes trailed down her body.

I really didn't like the way he was looking at her. And what advice was he talking about? I tried to think about our last conversation. I couldn't remember. I'd probably been wasted. But I did remember what Rob had told me when I called him the other night. That Mason was starting a sex club.

Mason's eyes were still glued to Penny.

I lowered my eyebrows. *Stop looking at my girl like that.* The sex club thing combined with the way he was staring made his comment clear enough. He probably thought Penny was a hooker or something. "No," I said. "I thought you would have heard. I'm getting divorced."

"Oh, I'm sorry, man," Mason said. And then he shook his head and started laughing. "Geez, that's a lie. I'm not sorry at all. I'm surprised it lasted as long as it did."

"You two never did get along." The understatement of the year. We all hated Isabella. But again…I wasn't going to get into all this with him right now.

"No, not at all. So, who is this then?" Mason stared back at Penny.

"This is my girlfriend, Penny." It felt so normal saying that out loud. And good. Really fucking good.

Mason smiled. "Girlfriend? You didn't wait around long. Nice to meet you, Penny." He put his hand out for her.

She shook it. "It's nice to meet you. How do you two know each other?"

"James and I grew up together. Oh, the stories I could tell you..."

"Maybe another day," I interjected and laughed. I needed to tell Penny more about my past myself first.

Penny smiled. "I'll have to hold you to that."

Mason smiled back at her.

I really didn't like the way he stared at her.

"Well," Mason said and looked down at his watch. "I have a meeting I need to get to. If you ever change your mind, you have my number, James." Mason winked at me and walked away.

Okay yeah, he was definitely talking about going to his sex club or something. If his parents were cutting him off, it was probably something shady. And I wanted nothing to do with it for a number of reasons.

"What was he talking about?" Penny asked as soon as Mason was out of earshot.

"Yeah, you don't want to know. Let's go to our room."

We stepped onto the elevator with the bellman. Instrumental music flitted through the speakers.

Penny looked up at me.

I smiled down at her, wondering if she was thinking about me pressing her back against the wall of the elevator in my apartment. Either way, it was just good to see her smiling. I stared at the freckles along her nose. Now that I knew how young she was, I could see it. I wondered if Mason could see it too.

I shook the thought away. I didn't really care what anyone else thought. Mason and I had been through a lot together over the years, but I knew he'd be happy for me. No matter what age Penny was.

The doors dinged and opened. The bellman guided us down an equally ornate hallway to our room.

"If there is anything else you need, please don't hesitate to call the front desk. Turndown service is at nine. Have a good afternoon."

"You too," I said. I slid the access card into the reader and opened the door.

Penny gasped and walked past me. "Oh my God." She practically ran up to the window. We had the most amazing view of the city and of Central Park. That's why I'd chosen this hotel and this room.

I walked up behind her. "I told you that I could get you to like New York." I pushed her red hair to one side and kissed the back of her neck. My hands slid to her waist.

"It's beautiful."

"You should see it at night." I kissed her neck again as my fingers traced the waistline of her jeans.

She turned around to face me. "Are we spending the night?"

"I haven't decided yet."

"But I have to go back. I have classes."

I sighed. "Me too." I ran my nose down the length of hers and pressed my forehead against hers. "But I don't want to go back." I was worried about coming here. But I felt…free. Free to be with her in public. I hadn't realized how much I wanted that. How important it was. But I wanted her by my side at all times. I hated going to class and pretending she meant nothing to me.

Penny wrapped her arms around my back and pressed the side of her face against my chest. "Me either."

I breathed so much better when she was with me. I ran my fingers through her hair.

She looked back up at me. "I know I've made mistakes. Thank you for forgiving me. Thank you for letting me back in."

I didn't want to talk about Tyler and Brendan. Or Isabella. The past was better kept in the past. I knew that better than anyone. "Thank you for forgiving me."

She kept staring up at me. "You're different here."

"Different?"

"More relaxed, I guess."

"Well I'm not Professor Hunter here. I'm just...me."

She smiled. "James. I still need to get used to saying that."

"You do. Because Rob will give me hell if you go around calling me Professor Hunter." I laughed. Rob was going to give me hell no matter what. I'd been so adamant that I hadn't started teaching in order to hook up with hot students. Rob was going to have a field day with this development. I'd never hear the end of it.

"So, *James*. What would you do on a Monday after eating lunch alone?"

I smiled. "I'd go back to work."

"Was your office around here?"

"Well." I looked out the window. "There." I pointed to one of the buildings in the distance. It overlooked Central Park too.

"Is your headquarters still there?"

"It is."

"Your company must do really well."

"It's not my company anymore. But yes, it does." I smiled back down at her. I never thought I'd be standing here feeling this good. When I'd walked away from everything...I was hoping my life could be different. But I wasn't sure I actually believed it could be. Until Penny fell into my arms in that coffee shop.

"And what about after work?"

I unwound my arms from around her and walked over to the bed. There was a white box on the bed with a red ribbon around it waiting for Penny. Ian really was the best of the best. I had no idea how he'd gotten all this done in time. "Sometimes I'd grab drinks with some of the guys I worked with." Rarely, really. "Or I'd have dinner back at my place." I usually preferred to be alone. At least once I changed career paths.

"Do you still have an apartment here?"

"No. Not anymore." I'd handed a lot over to Isabella in hopes of her signing the damn papers. None of it worked. But Max would be getting back to me by the end of the week. It would all be over soon.

"What did you do after dinner?"

"It would depend on my mood." I grabbed the box. "Tonight it's your decision." I handed Penny the box.

"What are the options?"

"Open it."

She pulled the red ribbon free and lifted off the top. She picked up a red, silky dress and let the box fall to the ground. The dress was adorned with a sheer red material with small flowers embroidered in it. She'd look like a fucking goddess in it.

"It's beautiful," she said. She was staring at it like she had the hotel entrance. Like she'd never experienced such luxury. I wanted to change that for her.

"So, I have tickets to an art gallery opening on the Upper East Side. And you can wear that. We can go shopping for whatever else you want. I already have reservations at Eleven Madison Park."

"What is Eleven Madison Park?"

I smiled. It was honestly so refreshing that she had no idea what I was talking about. "It's one of the most prestigious restaurants in the city. I want to treat you to a night as one of New York's elite."

"New York's elite?" She laughed.

And my smile just grew. "Or you can wear exactly what you're wearing. And we can go to a comedy club that I love in East Village. We can walk through Central Park and we can eat at the Tavern on the Green before the show."

She folded the dress and put it back in the box. "I think I'd like to go to the comedy club."

I definitely wanted to see her in that dress at some point. But her skipping the fancy evening gave us a lot more time just the two of us. I should have known she'd do the unexpected. I grabbed her waist and pulled her against me. "God I love you."

She laughed as she looked up at me. "Was that a quiz, Professor Hunter?"

"No. I would have been happy doing either thing. I've just never met anyone who'd choose option two." Yes, she'd look amazing in the dress. But I preferred her in nothing at all.

"And you're happy that I did?"

"Yes." My hands slid to her ass. "Besides, now we have more time for other things."

"You do realize that we came to a hotel with no luggage? And we're probably not staying the night."

Exactly. I unbuttoned and unzipped her pants as I kissed the side of her neck. "Your point is?"

"The people at the front desk probably think we're having an affair."

I bet they do. I let go of her waist and sat down on the edge of the bed. I hooked my index fingers in the belt loops of her jeans and pulled her closer. I pushed her sweater up a few inches and kissed her stomach. "Well, if they already think so..." I kissed her a little lower. I looked up at her and raised my eyebrow, daring her to make the next move.

But she just stared at me, suddenly shy. Like she was waiting for me to give her the green light to become the little seductress I knew she was. I leaned back and pulled my shirt off by the nape of the neck.

She bit her lip as she stared at me. She knew exactly what I wanted.

I was daring her to strip for me. All this talk about cages and sex clubs had gotten to me. But I didn't need to go to Mason's sex club. Because I had my own private show with the sexiest girl in the city.

Do it, baby. I could already feel myself getting hard. *Strip for me.*

Chapter 23

Monday

Penny's eyes trailed down my abs. And I was pretty sure she understood what I wanted now, because she slowly pulled off her sweater.

Yeah, this look was better than any dress. I was glad that the lingerie I'd gotten her hugged her tits so perfectly. I forced myself to stay still. All I wanted to do was bury my face between her tits, but I wanted her to keep stripping for me. I liked watching her go from shy to bold.

Her cheeks flushed under my gaze. She pushed her jeans down over her hips and let them fall down her legs.

I swallowed hard. No dancing. No music. But it was the fucking sexiest strip tease I'd ever seen.

She reached behind her back and unhooked her bra.

Fuck yes. The material fell to the floor but my eyes were glued to her. Her nipples hardened. She was as turned on from this as I was.

She hooked her fingers under the lace of her thong.

I couldn't wait any longer. I leaned forward and pulled her thong down myself. My hands glided over her firm ass and down the back of her thighs. I breathed in the alluring scent of her. Fuck, I wanted to taste her. I was suddenly starving.

She laughed as I pulled her down on top of me.

I kissed the base of her neck and rolled over on top of her. "Besides, I promised you an orgasm." I got off the bed and knelt beside it. "I'm a man of my word." I wound my hands around her knees and pulled her ass to the end of the bed.

Fuck, she was already glistening. I spread her thighs wider and kissed the inside of her knee.

"Insatiable," I whispered against her thigh.

She propped herself up on her elbows to watch me ascend higher.

I liked teasing her. But I liked pleasing her more.

"You're insatiable too," she panted.

"Hmm." I exhaled when I reached the apex of her thighs. "Is that so?" I made one long, slow stroke against her wetness. I groaned. *So fucking sweet.* I should have known she didn't need to be warmed up.

Penny collapsed back down on the bed.

I unzipped my jeans as I kissed her thigh again. My dirty girl didn't need my tongue. She needed my cock. I pulled her off the bed and onto my waiting erection.

She gasped. "Oh God." She tilted her head back, savoring the feeling of me stretching her.

I grabbed her hair and tilted her head the rest of the way back, leaving a trail of kisses down her neck. Her skin was just as sweet as her cunt. My hands fell to her hips and I started guiding her up and down my length. *Just like that, baby. Ride me.*

She moaned.

I needed more. I needed her at my mercy. I leaned over her and bit her lip, pulling her back toward me. I grabbed her ass and stood up.

She clasped her hands behind my neck and wrapped her legs around my waist.

"I want all of New York to know you're mine," I growled, as I pressed her back against the window.

Her body shuddered against mine. "James..."

I thrust deep inside of her.

"James," she moaned, forgetting whatever protest was on her lips.

I grabbed her hands and unwound them from my neck. I pushed them against the glass and held them firmly as I thrust in and out of her faster and faster.

She tried to move one of her hands.

I spread her arms farther apart and pushed the back of her hands more firmly against the glass so she couldn't move at all. Then I tilted my hips, hitting that spot that drove her crazy.

She moaned and the glass squeaked as her ass slid against it. I hoped her ass left a print on the glass. I hoped everyone at this hotel knew she was mine. I hoped someone did see us from down below. I couldn't claim Penny back in Delaware. But I could claim her here.

I kissed her hard, silencing her next moan. Her legs tightened around my waist as I fucked her for the whole city to see.

Each thrust had her gripping my cock tighter. She tried to move her hands again to no avail. Her body was completely under my control. The way I loved it.

She clenched around my cock.

"Come for me, Penny." I kissed her again and groaned into her mouth as my cum filled her.

She shattered in my arms, her pussy gripping me even tighter.

Fuck.

My chest rose and fell as we both caught our breaths. I released my grip on her hands. She immediately ran her fingers down my biceps, like she couldn't wait even a second to touch me now that she was free.

"You're so sexy," she said.

I laughed and collapsed to my knees, pulling her down with me. I held her against my chest and sighed into her hair. I wasn't sure I knew how to go back to dating her in secret.

***

It was a beautiful fall day, and Penny opted to sit outside at the Tavern on the Green. The small lanterns in the tree above us blew in the breeze. I couldn't think of a more romantic setting.

"Is he a good friend of yours?" Penny asked as she looked at the menu.

"Who? Mason Caldwell?"

"Mhm."

"We used to be really good friends." I shrugged. "We fell out of touch after school." There was a really good reason for that. But this was the one thing I couldn't talk about with Penny. The only thing I had to keep from her. Because I'd made a promise to my friend Matt. And I wasn't going to break it. I cleared my throat. "Our parents are still close. And the ad agency Mason works for has helped me out before."

"He seems nice. I've never met any of your friends."

"You find out who your true friends are when things aren't easy anymore. Turns out I didn't have many."

"He didn't even know about your divorce. From my experience, you don't open up very easily. Maybe you're being too hard on your friends."

I smiled. "You're probably right." She was definitely right. I'd meant what I said to Matt. I missed the way we all used to be. But I wasn't sure there was any going back, no matter how badly I wanted to.

Penny looked out toward Central Park.

Even though she claimed to not like New York City, she seemed to really enjoy Central Park. We'd been walking around just talking for hours just the two of us. Well, and Ian. But she didn't know that. I eyed him a few tables over. He was texting again, and I couldn't help but wonder who he was so engrossed in talking to.

"Do you eventually want to move back here?" Penny asked.

I ran my thumb down her palm. I was starting to think that maybe I did. I could see us here. I could see it more clearly than back in Delaware. But that all depended on what she thought. "Not if you don't like it."

"I like it when I'm with you."

I pressed my lips together as I stared at her. "We can go wherever you want, you know. It doesn't matter to me. Wherever you'll be happy." I had a feeling that no matter where we ended up, as long as she was with me, we'd be good.

"After I graduate?"

"Yes." I tried not to sigh. It felt like a lifetime away.

"You talk so easily about our future," she said.

"That's because I already know that you're in my future."

"But there's still..."

"I will never run away from this feeling. I'm not letting you go." I really did not want to talk about Isabella right now.

Penny stared at me. And for some reason I knew whatever she was about to ask me next, I wasn't going to like. How many times was she going to bring up Isabella?

"How many children do you want?"

I frowned. I was not expecting that turn of events. "What?"

"You want to talk about our future. So let's talk about it."

Breathe. Years ago, I thought I might become a father. I didn't want it. And I still felt guilty every day, because the baby didn't make it. Like I'd willed it not to exist.

So this wasn't the first time I'd thought about what kind of father I'd be. And I already knew the answer. I'd be shit. Just like my father. I could barely take care of myself, let alone an infant. I didn't do well when people relied on me. The pressure that came with that… I knew how I'd fare. I'd slip. "I'm not sure I'd be a very good father."

"Why would you say that?"

"I'm…" my words trailed away when the waitress walked up. I was relieved for the pause in the conversation. Because I knew where it needed to head, and for just a little longer I wanted Penny to stare at me with stars in her eyes.

"Welcome to the Tavern on the Green. I'm Lexi and I'll be your waitress this evening. Can I get you both something to drink?"

I glanced at the wine list. And then I remembered Penny was only 20. *Nope, not happening.* "We're actually ready to order. We'll both have the cioppino. And could we just have two glasses of apple juice?"

She looked a little surprised. "Sure. I'll be right back."

Penny smiled at me. "Apple juice? You can have a drink if you want."

"I don't want one." I sighed and let go of her hand. This seemed like a good time to rip the Band-Aid off. The perfect time really. It wasn't like she could exactly run away from this discussion like she was so fond of doing. I'd driven her here. She was stuck with me. *Stuck.* I wasn't sure I liked that thought. I wanted her to love me despite my flaws. But I certainly wouldn't blame her if she did want to run.

I glanced over at Ian again. He was staring at us now over his newspaper. Like he knew I was finally about to tell Penny the truth about something. And he wanted to hear all of it. He saw me looking and ducked back down.

I almost laughed. Ian knew the truth, and he hadn't run away screaming. *But I paid him to stay.* The only people around me were ones that I paid. I swallowed hard. *Here goes nothing.*

"We don't have to talk about kids," she said.

Oh. Is that why she thought I was upset?

"I'm sorry, that was such like a weird thing for me to bring up. We only just started dating. I just..."

"No. It's fine." I took the out. We'd talk about my problems later. "I've just never thought much about it." Not for years anyway. I never thought I'd actually find someone that I wanted a family with.

"That's okay."

If she wanted to talk about this, I'd talk about this. "Do you want kids?"

"One day. I'd want at least two. I always wished I had a sibling growing up."

"Hmm." I took a deep breath. I could do it, right? Take care of someone if I truly loved them? I'd promised myself to keep Penny safe after all. And if Penny wanted it...I'd give it to her. I wanted to give her everything she'd ever dreamed of. I'd be better than my father. I would be. For Penny's sake.

And for just a second, I could picture it. Actually, I pictured me, Rob, Mason, and Matt all playing in the Caldwells' backyard. But my friends weren't married. And they were barely speaking to me. Our kids weren't going to grow up together the way we had. "Two sounds good then."

Penny smiled at me. "So is that why you think you'll be a bad father? Just because you don't want kids anytime soon?"

"No, that's not it." I grabbed her hand again. "I just haven't spent much time around children." Zero time really. None of my friends were even married. Not that I'd been hanging out with them anyway. And kids felt permanent. Nothing in my life had felt permanent before. Including me. I glanced at my old office building in the distance, remembering when I wanted to jump out the window.

"I don't want them anytime soon," Penny said, pulling me out of my thoughts.

"Good. I want you all to myself for as long as possible."

"So what exactly is cioppino?"

I laughed. "Trust me, you'll like it."

I glanced at Ian again. He'd gone back to texting. Seriously, who was he talking to? "If you'll excuse me for one moment," I said. "I need to use the restroom."

I made my way inside the restaurant and texted Ian: "Who are you texting so much? Does someone know I'm in town?"

"No, you're good. Jen asked me for a ride and we just got to texting."

What? Why? Seriously, did Ian have a thing for my sister? "If she needs a ride you can go get her. Penny and I are fine here."

"Are you sure? She'll wonder why you're not visiting while you're in town."

The last thing I needed was for Jen to tell my parents that I was dating one of my students. "And that's why you've signed an NDA."

"No need to remind me, boss. But I can go?"

"Yeah, go." I wanted to be alone with Penny. For at least a few hours. I wanted to savor every minute of it while we could just be a normal couple. *Normal?* I sighed. *No.* What I needed to do was savor every minute before she saw me for who I really was.

Chapter 24

Monday

As we walked out of the Upright Citizens Brigade Theater Penny was still laughing. I just wanted to keep hearing the sound over and over again. No more tears. No more fighting. Just this.

"That's so cool that Amy Poehler used to do improv here," she said.

I smiled down at her. "So you liked your choice?"

"Yes. Today was perfect." She looked up at the sky, like she was searching for an answer to something. "It's weird not being able to see the stars."

"Pros and cons."

We walked slowly back toward the hotel. It was nice walking through the street holding hands. We'd never be able to do this on Main Street. But we could do this every night if we moved here. If we started over.

I took a deep breath. I just hoped to God that I could handle starting over again. Because I was really tired of fresh starts. I wasn't sure if we had much of a choice though. She liked this just as much as I did. How much longer could we keep our relationship a secret? Maybe disclosing our relationship to Dean Vespelli would be for the best.

I heard music playing in the distance. I smiled, the song pulling me out of my thoughts. "Come with me." We jogged through Central Park until we came to a guitarist. He was strumming his guitar and singing.

Penny laughed as I twirled her around in the middle of the sidewalk and then pulled her in close.

My hand lingered on the small of her back. It reminded me of when I'd first walked her home in the rain. I'd told myself to stop. I should have known I'd never be able to. And I wouldn't change a damn thing. I smiled. Really, not one damn thing. Because this moment couldn't be more perfect.

The wind blew, sending her red hair in a million different directions. I pushed it away from her face.

She laughed as she stared into my eyes. "Do you know this song?"

"I believe it's called Hands Down." I twirled her again and placed both of my hands on her waist.

"Every day I spend with you I fall harder and harder."

Me too, baby. I leaned down and kissed her. When the song ended I didn't pull away. We kept swaying to the loud sounds of the city. I didn't want this moment to end. But I knew I needed to get her back home. I knew all our moments like these had to be limited for now. "I should get you home."

"Does that mean going home with you? Or are you sending me back to my dorm?"

I laughed. "I'd like to bring you home with me." *Always*. I didn't want to go to bed unless she was next to me.

"I don't want tonight to end." She slid her hands into my hair and pulled me back down to meet her lips.

I could kiss her all night. I could stand in the middle of Central Park for the rest of my days and die a happy man.

She deepened the kiss.

I groaned and slowly pulled back. "I love you, Penny."

"I love you, James."

***

I yawned and reached out, but my fingers came up empty in the sheets. I slowly opened my eyes. Penny wasn't in bed next to me.

But I heard her muffled voice in the other room. She must be on the phone with Melissa or something. I closed my eyes for another second. But then I heard another voice. Who was Penny talking to? Maybe she was on speaker phone?

I grabbed my phone to see what time it was. I had a dozen missed calls and messages from Ian and… *Shit.* Half of them were from Isabella. *What the fuck?*

I clicked on one of them. "Real mature, James. You're forgetting the fact that all the cards are in my hands. You should be begging me on your knees, not having me followed around. I never took you for a stalker."

How the hell did she know I hired Max?

Penny kept talking and then I realized that I knew the other voice. It was a little hard to forget it when it had been screaming at me for the past few years.

No. No, no, no. I pushed the sheets off of me just as I heard Isabella call my name from the other room.

God Damnit.

"James, get the hell up!" Isabella yelled.

It only took me a second to burst out of my room. I stared at Penny, scanning her from head to toe. I didn't actually think Isabella would hurt her. But I just needed to make sure. She was wearing one of my t-shirts, and she looked perfectly fine. Minus the fact that there were tears pooling in the corners of her eyes.

What the fuck had the two of them been talking about? I glared at Isabella. Her cold, calculating smile spread across her face as her eyes wandered down my body.

Screw me. I should have thrown a shirt on. I really needed to stop getting into these situations with her. Just thinking about it made a lump form in my throat.

"How did you get in here?" I gritted out. Seriously, where the fuck was Ian? He was here to prevent exactly this situation from happening. And no, I hadn't really believed that Isabella would hurt me or Penny. But there was something off about the way she was staring at me. I couldn't really pinpoint it. But she was definitely off her meds.

I walked over to Penny and stepped in front of her.

"Don't be so cold James. I'm your wife, after all."

I ran my fingers through my hair. "Get out of my apartment." *You fucking psycho.*

Isabella ignored me. "I see that you aren't being very discreet with your new *girlfriend.* She's a little young for you, don't you think?" She looked at Penny. "And really not your type at all."

Oh, fuck off. As if my type is you?

I pulled my phone out of my pocket. I'd told Penny the lies Isabella wanted me to. But I was done playing whatever sick game she wanted me to play. I wasn't taking any part in it. This ended now. Hopefully with her getting dragged out of here screaming. "Get out or I'll call the cops, Isabella."

"Hmm, so now we can add threatening to the list?" She grabbed a manila envelope off the table behind her. She slowly undid the tabs and pulled out some photographs. She tossed them on the table. "On top of blackmailing?"

You blackmailed me first, you fucking bitch. I took a deep breath. I really didn't want Penny to be a part of this. "Isabella..." I said and started toward her.

"I'm glad the girl that you're currently fucking is here."
She said it in a disgusted way.

Isabella wished that's all it was. But I was pretty sure
she was here because she knew differently.

"Now she can know what kind of man you really are."

I grabbed the photographs and turned them face
down on the table. I didn't need to see what they were. I
knew how much Isabella loved spreading her legs. And
Penny certainly didn't need to see that shit.

"You didn't give me a choice," I said as calmly as I
could. Now that I was closer to her, I knew I was right.
There was definitely something off about her eyes. But
hopefully she could still have a conversation about this.
Because I couldn't be married to her for one more fucking
day. She'd dragged this thing out long enough. And breaking into my apartment and saying God knows what to
Penny? This ended now. "Why do you have to make everything impossible? Do you enjoy torturing me?"

"Yes." Her voice was cold.

For Christ's sake. "I just need you to sign the papers."

"What, so that you can be with her?" she scoffed.
"You must be joking."

"What I do now is none of your business. Sign the papers," I said firmly.

"This is ridiculous. She doesn't even know you."

"Neither do you."

"And whose fault is that?"

"You can't blame this on me."

She laughed. "You know, the press is going to have a
field day when they hear about how my husband cheated
on me with a student. It's so cliché, don't you think?
They'll love it. The university probably won't love it as
much, though."

If she had such a problem with cheating, maybe she shouldn't have cheated on me. Not that I was upset about that. I was grateful that she'd done it. Because it had led me here. And I was not letting her ruin my new life. Or Penny's life. "I'll leak the photos."

"No you won't. How do photos of me screwing another man help you in any way? All it shows is that you can't satisfy your own wife."

"No. It shows that you have a history of infidelity that makes your claim to anything that's mine invalid."

"And she doesn't do the same for you?" she pointed at Penny.

I really hated that Penny was here witnessing this shit show. But I didn't know what else to do. I'd tried everything to get Isabella to sign the papers. This was my last option.

Breathe. "I don't want anything that's yours," I said. "Sign the papers now and you get half. Wait and get nothing."

She pulled out some more papers from the envelope. "I already did, you egotistical asshole." She threw them at me.

I stepped to the side and let them flutter to the ground. Had she really signed them? I leaned over and picked one of the pages up. Her signature was there. As clear as day. And it felt like this weight was lifted off my shoulders. Like I was free. Like it was finally okay for me to live my fucking life.

"You signed them?" Penny said from behind us.

I turned around to look at her. She looked so…small. And frightened. And hurt. *I'm so fucking sorry, Penny.* How many times was I going to make her feel this way?

Isabella stared at Penny. "He's all yours. Good luck. You're going to need it. He's fickle."

Each word out of her mouth made my blood boil even more.

"He gets bored easily. He's going to eat you alive."

"Isabella! Enough!" She'd signed the papers. I didn't need to even try to pretend to be civil with her anymore.

"What, are you afraid I'm going to let something slip that you haven't told her?"

Fuck, is that what they'd been talking about?

"Stop running, James. Stop throwing yourself into new things. Get some help. She's not the answer and you know it." Isabella walked over to the elevator and pressed the button.

The doors opened and closed and she was gone. The apartment was eerily quiet after her screeching voice stopped. I looked down at the paper in my hands again. She'd signed it. She'd really signed it. I set it down on the table and turned to Penny.

I wasn't sure what to do. I didn't know what they'd been talking about before I woke up. And I knew I didn't love anything Penny had just witnessed. I wanted to close the distance between us, but I didn't know how. Because a part of me knew that Isabella was right. Penny didn't know me. Not really. Hell, Dr. Clark had been trying to get me to tell Penny the truth for weeks.

But I was scared of what the truth would do to us. Because I needed her. Yes, fucking *needed*. And all the power was in Penny's hands. I felt…out of control. I felt lost. And I knew it was partially because seeing Isabella made me think about blacking out again. I didn't know how to acknowledge what may have happened when I blacked out the last time I saw her.

And Penny was the only one who ever made me feel better. The only fucking thing. But there might as well have been a canyon between us.

"What am I not the answer to?" she asked.

"What did she say to you while I was in bed?"

"James."

I swallowed hard.

"You're hiding something from me. Tell me."

"You need to get to class," I said.

"James." Her voice cracked. "Why won't you tell me?"

"We can discuss it tonight." Tonight. That gave me time to figure out what the hell I could say to her to make her stay. A few hours, at least. My heart felt like it was ricocheting around my chest. I'd been so focused on getting Isabella to sign the papers. I thought I'd be happy. But instead, I felt like I was seconds away from another panic attack.

It was like Penny could tell how much I needed her. She closed the distance between us and wrapped her arms around me.

I immediately relaxed. If she was still here…whatever Isabella had said to her in private wasn't so terrible. Right? I hugged her back. I felt calmer with Penny in my arms. With her cherry perfume invading my senses. And I realized I wasn't just rattled from what had happened with Isabella. I was rattled because of what could have happened.

"Are you okay?" I asked.

"I'm okay." Penny kissed the scruff beneath my chin.

This should have been a happy moment. I was divorced. We could be together without Penny feeling bad. But I only felt panic wrapping around my chest.

"I need you," I said. She could make me feel better. I just needed to know that we were okay.

"I need you too."

"No. I mean, I *need* you. Right now." I grabbed the back of her neck and kissed her hard. I needed her exhales.

I needed her body beneath mine. I needed all of her. Because I was guilty of exactly what Isabella said. Penny was my fucking vice.

I moved my hands to her ass and lifted her legs around me. I carried her back into my bedroom.

Penny always gave me what I needed. And maybe that was part of the problem. I could never stop because she kept offering me more and more of her. And I was greedy for all of it.

I was relying on her to make me whole. And that wasn't fair. She'd never agreed to fix me. Because she didn't realize how broken I was. *Yet*.

Chapter 25

Tuesday

I knew going back to reality after spending a day in New York would be hard. But I never expected for it to be this fucking hard.

I wanted to be happy that Isabella had signed the divorce papers.

Instead, I had a loop of "what ifs" going round and round in my head. Penny had helped calm me down. But she'd left for class and my first class of the day wasn't until later. So all I could do was think about Isabella standing in my living room. And there was only one person I wanted to take it out on. Ian.

But while I waited for him for over an hour, I just got angrier. I was paying for an extra apartment for him *here*. His salary was exorbitant on top of that. And he'd seriously dropped the ball. I clenched my hand into a fist and then opened it over and over again, trying to let go of the desire to punch someone.

The elevators finally dinged and Ian stepped out. He opened his mouth to say something, but I cut him off before he could give me whatever excuse he had.

"What the fuck, Ian? I pay you more than any security guard in the country and you let Isabella walk into my apartment like she owns the place? Where the hell were you?"

"I called you as soon as I got the alert on my phone, James. I tried to warn…"

"But where *were* you?!"

"You said it was okay to drive Jen yesterday. You said…"

"Yesterday! Not all fucking night!" I stared at him. His hair looked a little askew. And his t-shirt was wrinkled. I knew he'd probably been speeding back here this morning. That explained his appearance. Or…it could be something else. "Is there something going on between you and my sister?"

Ian frowned. "No. Nothing. She asked me for a few rides around town and I was just helping out."

"All night?"

"Well, she's going through some stuff and we got to talking. That's it."

I really didn't want to hear about this. I couldn't deal with whatever drama Jen was having with whatever new idiot boyfriend she had. I had real fucking problems. But I also really needed to know. Because if Ian's head was somewhere else, I obviously couldn't rely on him. "Ian, if you're sleeping with my sister I need you to be honest with me. Right now."

"I'm not fucking Jen." He looked a little horrified by what he'd just said. "I mean sleeping with. I'm not. This is coming out wrong. I meant I'm not making love to her. Fuck, I'm not doing any of that, James."

I laughed. Because this weirdly reminded me of talking to Penny's dad.

Ian smiled too. "I'm not," he said.

"Good."

He nodded. "Good then."

I sighed. "But what the fuck, man? Isabella broke into my apartment…"

"And I tried to call you several times."

"My phone was on silent. You calling from hours away wasn't helpful. Isabella did exactly what you're supposed to prevent. You were supposed to be here."

"I'm sorry."

I took a deep breath. I didn't need to keep beating this point over his head. He knew he'd fucked up. I sat down on the couch. "It's just a fucking mess. Before I woke up she told Penny God knows what."

"Well then look," Ian said. He pulled out his phone and sat down next to me. "If that's what you're actually upset about…"

"No, I'm pretty damn pissed at you too."

He shrugged. "Well, let's just see the footage okay?"

Oh. Right. I nodded. I'd been full of this panic and rage that I hadn't been thinking clearly. Of course I could see what the two of them spoke about. I stared down at the video on Ian's phone.

Isabella had been sitting alone in my dining room for a long time by herself. Sitting there so still it barely even looked like she was breathing. The smile on her face looked like it was glued on. Nothing about her looked real. Like if she turned her head, her neck might crack. And it was the first time in a long time that staring at her reminded me of the way she'd been in high school.

But the weirdest part about her sitting there so still was that she was staring directly at the camera. Like she knew it was there. And I didn't like that at all.

"It looks like she knows about the cameras," I said.

Ian shook his head. "That's not possible."

I knew that. And he knew that. But we both stared at her staring.

"I'll change the passwords just in case," he said.

I nodded. That would give me piece of mind.

The tape showed Penny finally emerging out of my bedroom. At first, she didn't notice Isabella. But then Isabella cleared her throat.

"How did you get in here?" Penny's voice was barely a whisper. She looked terrified. Did she know who it was sitting there? Probably. She'd looked up pictures of Isabella online.

"I'm his wife."

Well, if Penny wasn't aware, she was now. I couldn't think about a more awkward situation. What a fucking mess.

Penny tugged on the hem of the t-shirt she was wearing. It was one of mine. And I could tell how uncomfortable she was. This was exactly the feeling she told me she wanted to avoid. She finally opened her mouth. "I..."

"Don't embarrass yourself. I know all about you, Penny. I like to keep track of who my husband is currently screwing."

Penny glanced at the bedroom door, probably hoping I'd wake the fuck up too. I wish I had.

Isabella pulled a manila envelope out of her purse and set it on the table. "Don't flatter yourself. James definitely didn't mention you the last time I saw him. He was occupied by other, more pressing matters."

Oh fuck you, Isabella.

Penny didn't say a word.

"Oh, did he not tell you? You were together at the time, weren't you? It was only a week ago." She put her elbows on the table. "I know exactly how he works. I know exactly what he wants. And clearly you can't give him what he needs. If you could satisfy him, he wouldn't have come crawling back to me."

"He did tell me."

"So let me guess," Isabella said, ignoring Penny's comment. "You've given him quite the chase. Or is the fact that you're a student enough?"

"What do you mean?"

"He only wants what he can't have. You must see that. As soon as you say you'll stay, he'll leave you."

That wasn't true. Okay, fine. Maybe it used to be true. I loved the chase. But my life was different now. I was different now. And I wasn't fucking going anywhere.

But Penny had nothing to say to that. Isabella's lies were manipulating Penny. Just like Isabella's lies in the tabloids had. And I hated witnessing this shit.

"You do see it," Isabella said. "I can see it in your eyes. You just realized that this..." she waved her hand around the apartment, "...is all a lie."

"I don't think you know him as well as you think."

Isabella leaned forward and raised her eyebrow. "Is that what he told you?"

"He didn't need to."

"I've known him since we were kids. I know him better than you ever will. And if you'll excuse me, I need to talk to my husband in private." She stood up.

"I think you should go," Penny said.

That's my girl. One of the reasons why I loved her. She was shy and sweet until suddenly she was fiery as anything.

Isabella laughed. "Penny, I'm doing you a favor. Trust me, you don't want anything to do with him."

"If he's as bad as you say, then why haven't you signed the papers?"

Isabella put her hand on top of the manila envelope. "I'm actually here to discuss that."

Penny just stared at the envelope.

"You look relieved. You shouldn't be. I can tell that you're just as addicted to him as he is to you. That would be sweet in any other situation, but not in this one."

Oh, fucking hell.

"What are you talking about?" Penny asked.

"He really hasn't told you?"

Why was Isabella such a bitch?

"Told me what?" Penny asked.

This was about what I'd expected. I was ready to come clean tonight to Penny. But this guaranteed it. This was what Penny had been asking me once Isabella left.

"I think you already know," Isabella said. "You just don't want to believe it. Besides, James is bad at hiding his shortcomings."

"We love each other. That's all that matters."

Damn right.

"How old are you, Penny?"

I shook my head. Isabella already knew the answer to this. She was just being a bitch.

"Right. You're young. You don't know what love is. Have you ever even been in a serious relationship before? Can you even tell when someone is lying to you?"

"He's not lying to me."

"Withholding information is just as bad as lying. It's something that you should know. You did that to him, did you not?"

How the hell does Isabella know all this?

Penny glanced at the bedroom door again. Begging me to wake the fuck up. "If James didn't talk to you about me..."

"He has his sources and I have mine," Isabella said, cutting Penny off. "So how about you get to class. What I need to discuss with him is none of your business."

"It is my business."

Isabella sighed. "Remember that I tried to warn you. But fine, we'll do this your way. "James!" she called. "James, get the hell up!"

I hit the pause button on the video. "That's enough."

"I kinda want to see the rest," Ian said.

I glared at him.

He cleared his throat and shoved his phone back into his pocket. "Well…tell me happened after that then. I'll help you come up with a solution."

"You'll help me like you helped me keep Isabella out of my apartment?"

"Take it out on me all you want. But you were going to have to tell Penny the truth about your past eventually."

I sighed, leaned back on the couch, and stared up at the ceiling. "Isabella signed the divorce papers."

"Really?"

"Yeah."

"So shouldn't we be celebrating?"

"I don't know." I turned back to him. "I thought I'd feel relieved once it was over. But all I can feel is this dread in my stomach. Penny wants to know what I've been hiding from her. I told her I'd tell her everything tonight. Isabella signing the papers should have made today one of the best days of my life. But tonight could make it the worst."

"You really think Penny would walk away?"

"She should."

Ian shook his head. "She loves you."

"She doesn't know me. Not really."

Ian shook his head again. "I think you've shown her the good, the bad, and the ugly already and she's still here. You two have had arguments before. Really bad ones. And you always make up."

"This is different. It's not a discussion that we can both move forward from. I'm sick, Ian. I'll always be sick."

"What's that line that people say? That you'll love each other in sickness and in health?"

I laughed. "In wedding vows?"

"Yeah. Besides, you're good right now. You're better when you're with her."

"That's a lot of pressure to put on her."

Ian shrugged. "Like I said. You two have already been through a lot and you're still together. You're her professor, for fuck's sake."

I laughed.

"And makeup sex is hot."

I stopped laughing. "Stop watching us have sex."

"I didn't say *your* makeup sex was hot. I just meant in general."

"Voyeur."

Ian laughed. "I'm just doing my job. Trust me, that's not my kink. Although I do like the forbidden aspect. I just prefer sleeping with my boss's sister."

I glared at him.

"I'm kidding." He laughed even though none of this was funny. "Well, I need to go shower. It was a loooong night."

I didn't like these jokes at all. "Stop it."

"If you stop putting your phone on silent."

Okay, fine. That was a little funny. "Deal."

"And tell Penny the truth. It'll be fine." He slapped me on the back and stood up.

"Ian?" I said before he walked away.

He turned back to me.

"When you found out the truth about me…did you consider quitting?"

"You really think I was in any place to judge you?"

"That's not what I asked," I said.

He shoved his hands into his pockets. "No, I didn't consider quitting. I knew you needed me."

I appreciated his honesty. And I was glad that he stuck by my side through that past several years.

But I didn't want Penny to stay with me because she felt obligated to. I wanted her to stay with me because she couldn't picture her life without me in it. But obviously I was glad Ian hadn't said all that about his feelings toward me. That would have been weird.

"I almost forgot to ask, but have you checked your mail today?" Ian asked.

Speaking of weird...that was a very strange segue. "No, why?"

"Something came and I was curious what it was. I've had the guy at the front desk start sending me pictures of anything delivered. Luckily it wasn't the guy you had fired this morning. Because he's actually been very accommodating."

Yeah, while I was waiting for Ian, I'd had some new guy at the front desk fired. He shouldn't have let someone into my apartment without my permission.

"And getting the pictures will make sure we don't have another flower incident on our hands. I'll be right back." He walked over to the elevators.

I sighed. The last thing I needed today was for Brendan to send Penny more gifts. What the hell was that asshole's game? I stared at the camera in the corner of the room as I waited for Ian to get back. There was no way that Isabella had gotten access to the system. No fucking way. So...how did she know so much? Maybe someone had just told her about the cameras. She said that I had my sources and she had hers. Who the hell was her source?

Ian stepped off the elevators holding a black envelope. He handed it to me.

Scrawled on the front in embossed gold font was "James and Rob."

I looked up at Ian. "Who knows that Rob is visiting me soon?"

Ian shrugged. "I figured you'd told someone."

"No." I never really spoke to anyone. I opened the envelope and pulled out an invitation, if you could really call it that. All it had written on it was an address for a bar in New York with a date and time a couple weeks from now. The address seemed vaguely familiar, but I was pretty sure I'd never heard of the bar before. I turned over the envelope, searching for a return address.

"It was hand delivered," Ian said, knowing that what I was looking for wasn't there. "And I already watched the security feed. It was a courier who dropped it off, so that's a dead end."

"I haven't told a soul my address, Ian."

He frowned. "Well...Isabella has it. And it was delivered this morning after she left."

I pressed my lips together. Isabella had stormed out after signing the papers. It seemed pretty clear that she was done with me. "Why would she send this invitation to me shortly after she signed the divorce papers? And why wouldn't she have just left it at the front counter when she was here?"

"Because she's crazy. And I know it doesn't make any sense, but it did kind of seem like she knew about the cameras. She was staring directly into the lens on the feed before Penny woke up. Maybe she knows about the ones downstairs at the front desk too."

I didn't like this at all. Yes, it made zero sense for Isabella to have this delivered to me. But somehow that just made me think it was her.

"You're sure no one else knows your address?" Ian asked.

I nodded. *Wait.* "I may have mentioned to Matt that Rob was visiting. Maybe. I don't remember. Or Rob may have mentioned it to Matt or Mason. And Rob knows my address."

"Oh." Ian nodded. "Good. I was definitely worried, but that makes sense." He looked down at the invitation again. "The Caldwells are probably trying to bury the hatchet."

"Yeah. That must be it." We used to meet up for drinks every now and then, trying different bars. It made sense. It was still weird that they didn't sign it though. And they could have just texted me.

The invitation didn't look like something Matt or Mason would send. But...I didn't know them that well anymore. That was the whole point. And I really hoped that hanging out again would bring us closer together.

I stared at the invitation for another second. Maybe it was an invitation to Mason's new sex club. That would explain the secrecy of the whole thing. But I thought I'd made it pretty clear to Mason that I wasn't interested in that. I put the envelope down on the coffee table. I'd text Matt or Mason about it later. First I needed to get back control of my life that Isabella was trying to unravel.

Chapter 26

Tuesday

I'd told Penny I'd tell her the truth tonight. The day somehow ticked by extremely slowly and way too quickly at the same time. And now I was sitting in my car outside her apartment, debating whether to call her or just drive off the side of a cliff or something. But Delaware was frustratingly flat. I'd barely even seen any hills.

What the fuck am I doing? I pulled out my phone and shot her a text before I could chicken out: "I'm outside."

She didn't text me back. Penny and I didn't play dumb games. If she wasn't texting me, she was probably just coming right out. I took a deep breath and drummed my fingers on the steering wheel.

A few minutes later the door to the back of her dorm building opened and there she was.

I climbed out of the car and walked around to the passenger side door. But instead of opening it, I pulled her in close. I'd missed her all day. I'd been stressed all day, and she always made me feel better. I wished we could go back to New York and just be us.

"Someone will see..."

I silenced her with a kiss. I didn't care if someone saw. I needed her. And she needed me too, because she immediately kissed me back. She needed the same reassurances that I did. That we were going to be okay.

Penny's cheeks were flushed when I finally pulled back. "You look so beautiful," I said.

"You look so handsome." Her eyes wandered down my neck to where a few of the buttons of my dress shirt were undone.

I strongly doubted I looked good right now. I'd been a fucking mess all day worrying about this conversation. Even the distraction of tweaking my security system didn't distract me like work normally would.

I just had this fear in my head that this was going to be goodbye. And I knew I couldn't take it.

I opened up the door for her. She climbed in and I closed it behind her. I took another deep breath as I rounded the car and got in. I buckled my seatbelt and then I just sat there. I didn't know where to go. I didn't know how to start this conversation. I didn't want to.

"Are we going to your place?" Penny asked.

"It's too stifling." I didn't want to go back there. Picturing Isabella in my apartment made it hard to breathe.

"Maybe we can go for a walk?"

"We can't. Not here."

"You just kissed me outside of my dorm. It's dark. It's fine."

Fair point. And the fresh air would be nice. "Okay." I pulled the car into a parking spot and got out. Penny climbed out before I had a chance to open the door for her.

"I'm not used to dating a gentleman," she said, the flush back on her cheeks.

"I know." I smiled at her. I was good for her. I really was. Or…I could be.

I grabbed her hand and we walked toward the green. The area between the dorms was filled with a manicured lawn, walkways, and benches. And the chilly air had sent most of the students back to their dorms. There was barely anyone out on the brick paths. I kept my eyes trained on the ground though, hoping to avoid anyone's gaze. The last thing I needed was for my almost-stalker Kristen Dwyer to pop out of nowhere and recognize me. Shit, this was a bad idea. I was pretty sure she lived in one of these dorms.

But it was easier to breathe outside. Especially with Penny's hand in mine. Our feet crunched on the fallen leaves. I tried to focus on the sound as we veered down a side path, farther away from the dorms. It was a little easier to breath over here. We reached a bench that seemed particularly shadowed, and I gestured for her to sit.

I stared at Penny as she sat down. The dim light made her look younger for some reason. She just looked so...innocent. Sitting there staring up at me with her big blue eyes. Or maybe I just felt old because of the conversation we were about to have. I didn't want to tarnish her. But hadn't I already?

I sat down next to her and took another deep breath. "I need to know exactly what she said to you this morning." I already knew. But I wanted to see what Penny had to say about the encounter. What things she was hung up on. What she'd openly tell me about. Because she wasn't the only one with trust issues.

"She already knew about me," Penny said.

"I didn't..."

"I know. She made it clear that you didn't do much talking last time you saw her." She shrugged.

Fucking Wizzy. I sighed. "I'm so, so sorry." I hated how much this hurt Penny. And I hated how thinking about that night made me feel like I was going to be sick. Would that ever go away?

"No, it's fine. Really. I see the appeal."

I frowned.

"Yeah, I'm joking. She's horrible." Penny smiled, but I could tell it was forced.

I put my hand on her knee. "There was a new employee at the front desk. He's been fired."

"James, it wasn't his fault."

"Yes, it was." No, it really wasn't. Partially, sure. But my phone being on silent shouldn't have allowed an intruder to break into my home. I'd fixed the problem.

She opened her mouth and closed it again like she was going to protest. But then she changed direction. "She said you only want things you can't have. That's why you like me. Because I'm a student."

"But I do have you." I'd made mistakes, lashing out and saying we were just fucking. But it had just been in the heat of the moment. I'd also told Penny I loved her. She was my girlfriend. I did have her.

"She made it seem like you'll get bored with me and move on to something else."

Well, it didn't seem like Penny was holding anything back. Which was good. But I didn't love that she was believing all these lies. *Breathe.* "I'm not going to do that, Penny."

"I know. You wanted to know what she said."

Oh. So she didn't believe Isabella? That was good. But…Isabella hadn't lied about everything.

Penny grabbed my hand. "She said that you're addicted to me."

"I am." I didn't even hesitate in my response. Despite everything Dr. Clark said, I knew better. He was wrong about this one thing. And Isabella was a bitch, but she was right about this. I was addicted to Penny. Every inch of her.

Stop. I clenched my jaw. I didn't want to believe I was actually addicted to Penny. And wouldn't Dr. Clark know?

This was his job. He said this was love, not addiction. Maybe he was right.

"She made it seem like that wasn't a good thing."

Yeah, fuck. I squeezed her hand but didn't say anything. I'd tried all day to think of a good way to talk about this. But I was still coming up empty.

"And she said you were withholding information from me. That's it. We didn't talk for that long."

I nodded. That was everything. Penny hadn't held anything back. And it was time I did the same. "Saying I'm addicted to you is a bad choice of words. I love you. I love spending time with you. I love being with you. I missed you today."

"I missed you too." She stared at me for a moment. "What is your type?"

"What?"

"She said that I'm not even your type."

"I don't have a type." Unless shy, sweet girls from Delaware were a type. I immediately shook the thought away.

"Are you sure it's not tall brunettes?" She smiled at me.

"No." I laughed uneasily. "She's definitely not my type." I wasn't attracted to Isabella. Not physically. And I definitely wasn't attracted to her awful personality.

"So you like redheads?"

"You're the only redhead I've ever been with. I don't have a type. You're it. I don't want to be with anyone else. Just you." Sometimes the truth came easily to me. I wasn't sure why it was so hard other times. I pressed my lips together. I actually knew why. It would be easier to tell a stranger the truth. This was hard because I loved Penny. And I didn't want her to look at me differently.

"Don't you trust me?" she asked. "Whatever it is you need to tell me you can."

"I do trust you." There was no reason why I shouldn't. She'd told me everything Isabella had said. I was the one with the issues here. Filming Penny without her consent. Hiding huge chunks of my life from her. I felt a raindrop and looked up at the sky. For some reason I just kept staring up. Like the rain would give me the answers. The drops fell faster until it was full on raining.

And I realized we were just sitting in the rain. Penny had just been in the hospital. What the fuck was I doing? I'd promised myself I'd take care of her. I stood up. "Let's get back to the car."

"James, tell me."

"You're going to get a cold."

"James, tell me!"

"I've already told you. More or less." I raked my fingers through my hair. I had tried. A few times. "I thought you understood." Another lie. I knew the random slip ups and comments I'd dropped weren't enough. I wanted them to be, but they weren't. We needed to have a real conversation about this.

"Understood what? What am I not the answer to?" She stood up.

I just stared at her getting drenched by the rain. *I'm a monster, Penny. Please don't make me say it.* Standing in the rain staring at her like this reminded me of when we were apart. And it felt like I was losing her all over again.

"What did she mean when she said to stop running?" asked Penny. "What are you running from? Don't push me away again. Don't do what she said you would."

"I was trying to protect you. I told you that."

"But what are you trying to protect me from? Why do you think I shouldn't be with you?"

I didn't want to say it because I knew it was bad. Obviously it was bad. Why couldn't we just keep going the way we were? Why did she have to know about my demons?

"It can't possibly be that bad. Just tell me what it is."

"Damn it, Penny." I pulled her against my chest and kissed her. *Don't make me say it, baby.* I was angry. I was tormented. And the kiss was fucking hot. God, I loved when she was mad at me. My hands slid to the small of her back. I needed to touch her. I needed to know that we were going to be okay. I pushed her shirt up slightly so that my palm was against her skin.

"Stop." She pushed on my chest. "Stop using sex as a weapon."

"I don't..." I looked down at her face. She was already looking at me like I was a monster. I released her from my grip and took a step back from her. "I didn't realize I was doing that."

"Tell me what you're hiding. You told me no more secrets. Don't you want us to work? Tell me!"

"I have told you! I told you that I was drunk all of college. I told you that I've had sex with dozens of women. I told you I threw myself into my career in order to avoid my life. Everything I did was so that I didn't have to face reality. Whatever horrible thing you can think of, I've probably done it. I told you I wasn't a good man. I told you that."

Rain dripped from her eyelashes as she stared at me. And she didn't say a word. Not one fucking word.

"I'm an addict, Penny." And as soon as I said it, I wanted to take it back. Just saying it out loud made me feel weak.

For a second, she just looked confused. But then something shifted. I saw it. That recognition crossing her face. That she understood what this really was. That she was my drug.

But I didn't want that to be true. I loved her. I loved her so damn much. And I didn't want that to be twisted into something sinister. Couldn't this one thing in my life be good? Just this one thing? "Penny? Say something."

"All this talk about forever..."

"I mean it."

"But what happens when you get bored with me? Will you go off chasing your next high?"

"No." I lowered my eyebrows. "I'm not addicted to you." This time I believed the words. Yes, I felt desperate. Like I might lose her. But it was more than that. My chest ached at the thought. This was more than addiction. And maybe it was a little twisted. But this was love too. "It's different with you, it's not the same."

"How do you know?"

I took a deep breath. "I was trying to avoid my life. I was miserable. Every day I felt like I was suffocating. I needed an escape. But I'm happy now."

"Because of me? Or because of teaching? Or what?"

"It was my decision to come here."

"Because you walked in on Isabella..."

"Yes. But I came here for *me*. I'm living the way I want to live. I'm not answering to anyone else. I don't need an escape anymore." *I just need you.*

"Isabella said you needed to get help."

"I've gotten help."

"So you're not addicted to drugs, or alcohol, or work, or...sex anymore?"

"No. I haven't been addicted to anything since I left the city. I was living a life that wasn't mine there. I was numb. Those things made me feel alive. They sustained me. They were a choice I could make for myself."

"So you chose to do them? That doesn't make you an addict, James. If you had control over your choices..."

"I couldn't stop, Penny. Whenever I was able to pull myself out of one thing, I just moved on to the next." My words hung in the air.

She stared at me exactly how I'd been afraid she would. Like she thought I'd easily move on to someone else after her. And that wasn't fucking true. The more I talked about this, the more I realized how different it was with her.

"Don't look at me like that," I said. "I'm not addicted to you. I'm not going to move on. I need you in my life. I need you, Penny." *Need.* Fuck, I knew how that sounded. Every word out of my mouth had a double meaning. "Penny, I've made so many mistakes. But I was young and stupid."

"You're still young."

"Okay. But I'm not stupid anymore." Well, sometimes. I forced smile. But none of this was funny.

"Addicts are like...it's not something that goes away, is it?"

"No, it's not."

"So, how do you control it?"

My eyes searched hers. It was like I could already feel her pulling back. The age gap between us really did feel larger than before. I was piling all this crap on her when all she should be worried about was her next Stat test. But I did had control over this. At least when we were together. I'd slipped when we were on a break. But I could control it. I was taking steps, anyway. "My therapist helps me with that."

"You have a therapist?"

"I do." I stared at her for a moment. "He doesn't think I'm addicted to you either." Maybe she'd believe Dr. Clark more easily than she'd believe me. But I had a hard time believing Dr. Clark sometimes too.

"You talk about me?"

"Yes."

"He knows that you're dating a student?"

"Doctor patient confidentiality. He did advise me against it. I think he's glad that I ignored his advice though."

"Why?"

"I'm happier when we're together. Everyone can see that." *Can't you, Penny?* It was weird, standing in the rain so far apart. It made me feel so distant from her. I didn't like that feeling. It made my chest feel tight. *Breathe.* The last thing I needed to add to this conversation was a panic attack.

"Why didn't you just tell me?" she asked.

"Because I liked the way you looked at me. Like I was strong and in control. It made me feel like I could be those things for you. I thought everyone could see my demons when they looked in my eyes. You never did. You just saw me. I didn't want that to change." That was the whole truth.

"I don't think any differently of you."

Her words should have been comforting, but it looked like she was going to burst into tears. Not because she was upset for herself. Because she was upset for me.

I swallowed hard. "You do. You're looking at me right now like I'm weak."

"I don't think that you're weak. You're incredibly strong for overcoming something like that."

But I hadn't overcome it. That was the whole point. I'd have to carry around this shit forever.

I shoved my hands in my pockets. We were both completely drenched. And the distance between us was unbearable. "I don't want you to leave me," I said slowly. "But if this is too much..."

"No. James." She closed the distance between us and I'd never been more relieved. "I'll never let you go."

Her words made the tightness in my chest ease. "I'm not addicted to you."

"You keep saying that. And all I can think about is how rude it sounds." She smiled at me.

"I don't understand how you can keep choosing me. I'm..."

"Perfect."

That was definitely not what I was going to say.

"Everything that you've been through has made you who you are. And I love the man I see in front of me. I love you so much."

It started raining harder. And I remembered what Penny had told me about the rain. That it reminded her of me. And it felt like some kind of sign. I'd shown her the darkest side of me and she wasn't running away screaming. She was standing by me. And we really should have been celebrating today. I'd been waiting over a year for Isabella to sign the papers. And I'd been waiting a lifetime to feel free from all of that.

"I'm divorced." I almost had to yell it over the rain.

"I know." Whatever I'd seen cross her face after learning about my addiction was gone. She was staring up at me with stars in her eyes again.

And if she was still here, we were all in. "No more of this waiting nonsense?"

"No. My heart is yours."

I smiled. I wasn't sure I'd ever heard anything sweeter. "I'm divorced!" I picked her up and twirled her around.

Penny's laughter was infectious.

I set her back down on her feet. I couldn't wipe the smile from my face.

She rubbed her palm against the scruff on my cheek. "You're all mine."

"All yours, Miss Taylor." I turned my head and kissed her palm. And I'd stay clean for her. I would.

Chapter 27

Tuesday

Something had shifted in the air. Maybe it was the weight off my shoulders from telling Penny the truth. Or maybe it was the thunder booming in the sky. Penny was right, the rain always reminded me of her and our first kiss. Regardless, it was like I could feel the electricity cackling between us.

When the elevator doors closed on the way up to my apartment, I wasn't sure who moved first. But my fingers tangled in her wet hair as I slammed her back against the wall. Her lips tasted like the rain. And I realized that for the longest time, they'd taste like sin. But not tonight.

For so long I'd been concerned about being her professor. Being older than her. Being a bad influence.

But now everything was more simple. I was a man. She was a woman. And she was fucking mine.

The elevators dinged and I grabbed her thighs and lifted her up. She immediately wrapped her legs around me. I was pretty sure I knocked something off the kitchen counter as I carried her into my bedroom. But I didn't care. All I wanted was more of her.

She didn't care that I was a monster. But maybe that was the whole point. She made me feel like I wasn't.

Penny loved me.

The real me.

I slammed her back against the doorjamb as I tried to pull off her shirt. But it was sticky from the rain.

"The. Bed," she said between kisses.

But she didn't realize how desperate I was for her. This was what I'd wanted to do to her when I'd pressed her against the side of my car. When I'd told her to stop thinking about me. All I wanted to do was fuck her senseless.

"James." She laughed as she put her hand on my chest. Her lips were swollen from my kisses. "Put me down so I can somehow take off my clothes."

Put her down? Hmm. There were some visions in my head of things I'd been wanting to do with her. I couldn't even count the times I'd masturbated to the image of her on her knees right in my bedroom. How many times I'd dreamed of devouring her sweet pussy. Before I'd even kissed her.

And I was done beating myself up over this. Penny wanted me just as much as I wanted her. I knew we were more than just a professor and his student. I wasn't even sure how much longer I'd be her professor. But there was something I wanted to do while I still was.

I slowly lowered her feet back down to the ground. She took a step toward the bed, but I grabbed her wrist. She turned back to me and looked up at me with her big innocent eyes.

But we both knew she wasn't all that innocent. I peeled her wet shirt off over her head. Followed by her jeans and thong. She blushed as I unhooked her bra.

She reached for the hem of my shirt, but I caught her hand. "Get on your knees, Miss Taylor."

Her throat made that adorable squeaking noise I loved. But she didn't make me repeat myself. She knelt down and stared up at me.

I sat down on the edge of the bed. "Do you have any idea how many times I fucked my hand while thinking about you?"

She shook her head.

"I pictured you in my office. In my bed. In my shower." I put my elbows on my knees and leaned forward.

The heat in her gaze made me feel hot all over.

"The first time you texted me, I had my hand wrapped around my cock. Don't tell me I'm the only one, Miss Taylor. Did you touch yourself and wish it was me?"

"I…"

"Show me," I said. I could so easily picture her in her uncomfortable bed in her dorm, running her fingers along her wetness. Snuggled up next to my sweater. Trying to be quiet so no one would know the dirty thoughts running through her head.

She slid her hand up her thigh. For just a second, she paused at the top of her thigh. But then she locked eyes with me and slid her index finger into her wetness. Her lips parted slightly as she moved her finger in and out.

I resisted the urge to fall to my knees and replace her finger with my tongue. "What did you picture when you touched yourself?" I asked. Because I'd fucking pictured this. I wasn't sure why, but I really loved her being completely exposed to me while I was still fully clothed.

"You," she said.

"I'm going to need more than that, Miss Taylor." My erection was straining against my jeans and we'd barely even started.

Her cheeks flushed even more. "I pictured you pulling me into a dark room. Where no one could see us."

I watched her nipples harden. "And then what?"

"You'd tell me you couldn't stop thinking about me as your hand wandered up my thigh." She closed her eyes like she was still dreaming. "I'd grab your tie. You'd press my back against the door and cage me in." Her hand started to move faster.

I'd pictured this same scene. Having her in a dark room, completely unseen. "Stop," I said.

Her hand froze. She watched me stand up and walk over to the lights. I switched them off as thunder boomed in the distance.

When my eyes adjusted to the darkness, I stared down at her. "Come here."

She shifted forward onto all fours. And crawled. To. Me. *Fucking Christ.* If I wasn't in love already, that would have done it.

I put my fingers underneath her chin. I'd felt like I was slowly dying before I met her. But she made me feel alive. "Do you know what I pictured while I stroked my cock?"

She didn't respond.

"Your lips wrapped around me." I undid my button and zipper with my free hand. "Letting me tell you exactly how I like it. Teaching you. Be a good girl and suck your professor's cock. And then I'll give you your fantasy."

She didn't even hesitate. Her lips wrapped around my cock like she was as greedy for this as I was. I buried my fingers into her wet hair. I loved being her professor. But she didn't really need much instruction here. Her mouth was already fucking perfection. I still fantasized about it though.

"Show me how far you can go down, baby," I said.

She complied.

My tip pressing against the back of her throat felt amazing. But there was one thing that would make it better. "Use your hand at my base."

She lifted her hand, wrapping her fingers around where her mouth couldn't reach.

"Just like that," I groaned. "In sync with your mouth."

Her head bobbed up and down on my cock.

"Just a little tighter," I said.

Her lips wrapped tighter around me.

Fucking hell. "If you relax your throat, you can take more of my cock. Can you relax your throat for me, Miss Taylor?"

I wasn't sure if it was what I called her, or the rain turning her on even more, but she shifted forward. My tip went into the back of her throat and she gagged.

I groaned. "Just like that, Miss Taylor. Gag on my cock."

She moved down even further.

Jesus. I gripped her hair tighter and pulled back before I exploded down her throat.

She looked up at me with her big blue eyes. They were a little watery from choking on my cock. But I could tell she loved every second of that.

"Your turn." I helped her up as I kicked my bedroom door closed. It wasn't a dark closet or anything. But this would do.

Her throat made that squeaking noise again as I caged her in against the closed door.

"I can't stop thinking about you, Miss Taylor."

She smiled up at me. "This is so much better than my fantasy." She grabbed the front of my shirt and tugged me toward her.

"And what happens next?" I whispered against her lips.

"You fuck me against the door, Professor Hunter."

God, this girl was everything I'd ever needed. I lifted her up and slammed my cock inside of her as her back hit the door.

I should have been making love to her. We'd been through so much to get here. But I knew what my girl liked.

"Do you like being a little slut for me?" I whispered into her ear.

She moaned.

"Do you like riding your professor's cock?"

Her nails dug into my back.

I thrust into her harder, savoring the feeling of her gripping me. "You like sneaking around with me, Miss Taylor?"

"Professor Hunter," she moaned.

Fuck. "I love you." I knew I'd broken away from her fantasy. But I really needed her to know.

She grabbed both sides of my face. "I love you." She kissed the tip of my nose.

And for some reason it made me laugh.

Which made her laugh too. She gripped my cock even tighter.

God. I pulled her off the door and we both laughed as we tumbled into my bed. I caught myself so I wouldn't crush her. I stared down at her splayed beneath me.

She reached up and ran her fingers along my jaw line. "My fantasy has changed."

"Yeah? How so?"

"I want this. Right here, right now." She pressed her hand against the center of my chest.

And I felt it again. Her warmth spreading into my cold soul. My fantasy had changed too. I grabbed the outside of her thigh, hiking her leg up.

She moaned at the change of angle.

Penny and I weren't some quick fuck. And I was going to spend the rest of my life worshipping her body.

***

Our wet clothes were in a heap on the floor and our naked bodies were intertwined on my bed.

"I think you might still be addicted to sex," Penny said.

I laughed and kissed the top of her head. "Maybe it's just because I like using it as a weapon with you?"

"I'm sorry."

"No, you're right. You're...frustrating. Sex is the only way I can seem to control you." And I really liked controlling her. Especially when her response was to fucking crawl to me.

"Control me?" She rolled onto her side and perched her head up on her hand. "Hmm. I could control you in bed."

"No, you couldn't. I'm stronger than you."

"I could tie you down."

"Good luck trying. It'll end up being you tied to my bed. Which doesn't sound bad at all." I actually really liked the sound of that. I needed to tell Ellen to buy me some rope. I pressed my lips together. Or maybe I should buy it myself. She'd ask too many questions.

"Maybe later. James, did you really blackmail her?"

I sighed and rolled over to face her. I figured this question would come at some point. "That wasn't much of a segue." I stared at her for a minute. Maybe I should have felt bad about blackmailing Isabella, but I didn't. Because I had everything I wanted now. Penny. "It's the last thing I could think of to do. I know it was stupid. I wanted to be with you. I didn't want her to control my life anymore. You said you wanted to wait and I had no intention of waiting."

She looked amused by my answer. "I like that you're bad."

I laughed. "You do?"

"I've spent my whole life being good. It's fun being bad for a change."

"What, do you think dating a bad boy automatically makes you a bad ass?"

She laughed. "Absolutely...*Professor Hunter*."

"Touché." Penny was a good girl. For me. At least most of the time. But she was also kinky as hell. I loved every side of her.

Her eyes locked with mine. "I don't care if people think this is wrong."

I reached out and tucked a loose strand of hair behind her ear. "We should probably talk about that."

"Isabella's threat? You think she'll really reveal our relationship?"

There was nothing stopping Isabella now. She'd already signed the papers. She'd gotten half of what was mine. She could tell anyone whatever she wanted without any repercussions. And I knew she came off looking better in this scenario than I did. Especially with her spin on the "facts." I didn't want to get into a media war with her. I didn't want anything to do with her. So I needed to get out in front of this thing. "I think it would be best if we go to the dean in the morning."

"But..."

"It's better if he hears it from us." We'd agreed that we were all in. And I meant it. I also knew what that meant. We needed to tell the dean. We needed to tell her parents. We just needed to come clean to everyone.

"I don't want you to get fired."

I swallowed hard. "Yeah, me either." Just thinking about not teaching anymore made my chest feel weird. Coming here had saved me. Teaching had saved me. And I didn't know what would happen if I had to walk away. But getting ahead of this would hopefully mean I didn't have to. "I know you're worried about what will happen. I told you it's not explicitly against the rules. And I don't think that anyone's complained."

"So you think nothing will happen?"

"I hope nothing happens. But I don't want you to worry about it." This was all on me, not her. I kissed her forehead and climbed out of bed. I pulled on a pair of pajama bottoms.

"Where are you going?"

"Get some sleep. I need to make a phone call."

"To who?"

"My lawyer." My eyes trailed down her naked body. "I won't let anything happen to you. We'll figure this out." If I'd had any lingering doubts, tonight would have confirmed everything for me. Penny and I were meant to be. And I'd promised myself I'd protect her. That meant getting in front of this situation.

Chapter 28

Tuesday

"I'm sorry, you did what?" my lawyer Litt said.

I sighed and sat down behind my desk. "Are you really going to make me repeat myself?"

"You slept with a student?"

What was he not getting here? "Yes. And I want to disclose it to the dean tomorrow."

"I need a lot more information than that."

"Look, the details don't matter…"

"The details absolutely do matter here, James."

Breathe. "I had Ian check out the university's policies. And there's nothing explicitly listed against it."

"Well, Ian's not a lawyer. You should have called me weeks ago."

"That's why I'm calling you now. I just want to know what the next steps should be."

"The next steps? James, stop sleeping with your students."

"*Student.* Singular." Why did everyone just assume I was fucking all my students? Shit, the dean would probably just assume the same thing. "I'm forwarding you a copy of the university's code of ethics." I sent off the email. "I just need you to comb through it and help me out here."

"Does Isabella know?"

Why the hell did people keep asking me that? I was starting to regret not telling every media outlet about my ex-wife's love of infidelity. *Breathe.* In this one instance, I actually wasn't the monster. She was. "What I do is none of her business. You saw the signed papers."

"But you started sleeping with your student before the divorce was finalized. You know how that looks."

"I really don't care how it looks. I just want to keep my job. Look at the papers and call me back."

"James, I'll be honest with you. Regardless of whatever it does or doesn't say in the code of ethics…this isn't going to end well. I think you need to be prepared to walk away from whoever this girl is."

"I'm not doing that."

"Then you're probably going to need to walk away from your job."

"I called you so that I wouldn't have to walk away from anything. Find a loophole. Figure something out."

"Give me a few hours," he said. "But my best recommendation is to not tell the dean anything. At least until the end of the semester."

I thought about Isabella. And how angry she'd been. There was no way she wouldn't leak this to the press before the end of the semester. She'd want to beat me to it and save face.

But it wasn't just about her threats. I knew the consequences of loving someone in secret. Back in high school, Matt had done that. And that was a series of events that no one would have seen coming. But an innocent girl had died.

I wouldn't love Penny in secret. I'd love her out loud. Besides, if there was one thing I'd actually learned in therapy, it was that the truth was always better. I'd finally told Penny that I was an addict. And I'd never felt closer to her. I wasn't going to take one step forward and then two more back.

"No," I said. "I'm telling the dean tomorrow. Just find something to give me my best chance of keeping my job."

"Give me a few hours," he said. "But I'm not a genie." He hung up the phone.

I stood up and walked over toward my windows overlooking Main Street. I loved my work here. And I loved Penny.

But I think I always knew in the back of my head that I'd have to make a choice here. Teaching was my fresh start. I'd poured everything I had into it. I had a good routine here. Structure. I was worried what would happen if I lost that.

My phone buzzed. I looked down to see a text from Ellen. It was like she knew I was struggling.

"I'm coming in tomorrow. I did not leave you enough meals for this long and I'm concerned that you're starving."

I laughed. Well, I wasn't starving. But I appreciated her concern. "See you tomorrow, Ellen," I texted back.

I knew who I actually needed to talk to. I pressed on Dr. Clark's name and pulled my phone to my ear.

He answered after a few rings. "James? Is everything alright?"

"I...I don't really know." It felt like someone was closing their fist around my heart.

"I've been looking forward to our next session. To see if you went through with everything. You said you were done torturing yourself for your past mistakes. You acknowledged that you're allowed to be happy. So what happened?"

"I told Penny the truth."

"Ah. You showed her the real you. And?"

"She didn't run away screaming." The pain in my chest eased slightly and I smiled. She hadn't run away. Instead she was lying naked in my bed.

"That's good. So why the late-night call then?"

Main Street was quiet down below. A sound I never heard on the streets of New York. I couldn't hear honking cars or sirens. Just…silence.

"I don't want to keep my relationship with Penny a secret anymore. I'm going to tell the dean tomorrow morning. I think."

"You think?"

I turned away from the window and sat back down at my desk. "I called my lawyer asking for advice, and he thinks it would be better if I waited to disclose my relationship with Penny until the end of the semester."

"And you don't want to wait?"

"I'm not even sure I have a choice," I said. "Isabella will leak it in a matter of days anyway. It's better to get ahead of it."

"So why the hesitancy on your end?"

"I don't want Penny to doubt my intentions here. By keeping our relationship a secret, isn't that what I'd be doing? The last thing I want her to think is that I'm embarrassed or something. Because I'm not." I knew that didn't answer his question. I was rambling. Trying to make sense of the thoughts swirling around in my head and the fear gripping my chest.

"I believe you. I still don't see the problem."

"My lawyer thinks I'll probably be fired."

"And how does that make you feel?"

I ran my hand across my desk. "I'm worried. This job has been good for me. The structure and routine that I've needed. You said yourself how necessary that is for me."

"This relationship has pulled you away from your routine though. In a good way."

"But I slipped."

There was a long pause on his end. "Do you think that maybe Penny is the key to you being content? Not the job?"

"I only slipped when I started dating her. I was in a really good place before I ran into her."

"Were you really?"

I frowned. "Wasn't I?"

"James, I never once saw you smile during a session before you met Penny. Not a single time."

I swallowed hard.

"Let's look at this from a different angle. Say you do get fired tomorrow. You do need something to focus on. Something to preoccupy your mind when Penny is in classes during the day."

"I'm working on some stuff."

He waited for me to elaborate, but I didn't want to go into the logistics of my security system that really hadn't worked. I needed to put more time into it.

"Alright," he said. "Good. And you'll still be surrounded by people who care about you. Penny. Ellen. Ian."

"And Rob," I said.

"Your brother?"

What other Rob would I be talking about? "Yeah. He's going to be visiting this weekend." That was misleading. He wasn't visiting for just the weekend. I was pretty sure he had nowhere else to go. He'd be staying indefinitely.

"Hmm," Dr. Clark said.

"Hm?"

"You've taken a step away from all your family and friends with your move. It's a lot to quit your job, start hanging out with Rob again, and being in a new relationship."

Fuck my life. I knew he'd think it was a bad idea. "I want to work on repairing my relationships."

"You do?"

"Of course I do." Why the hell wouldn't I?

"Well, that's good. But it might not be the best time. In the midst of so much change, James."

I shook my head. "This isn't all about me. Yes, I'm worried about quitting. But this is about Penny too."

"Well let's talk about that for a moment. What would you getting fired do to her? Or maybe you don't get fired, but you still come clean to the dean? How does that affect her?"

I pictured Penny in class. How shy and nervous she was during presentations. "Well, first of all, I wouldn't be her professor anymore." Which really fucking sucked. "Under either circumstance, really. She'd have to take the class over."

"I'm sure she's not looking forward to that."

"No. She definitely won't be."

"What else?" Dr. Clark asked.

"There will be rumors. Things can so easily be twisted."

"What kind of rumors do you think will spread?"

I shook my head. "Better grades for sexual favors. That kind of thing."

"That certainly wouldn't make her feel good," he said.

"I'm sorry, what is the point of this exercise?" I asked. "I know none of this is good."

"Well, say the worst happens. You get fired and Penny gets expelled."

"I won't let her get expelled for this."

"James, her fate isn't in your hands. Let me say it again. Say the worst happens. What then?"

"I'd help her get accepted into another university. We'd move. Maybe we'd go to New York." Penny claimed she didn't love the city. But she definitely had a good time there with me. And I meant what I said...I did want to repair my friendships. I knew things were especially tense between me and Matt. But he needed me. And I was finally in a place where I could help him.

"So she'd have to leave all her friends behind? Retake all her classes? And is her family in Delaware? You expect her to move away from everything she knows and loves?"

Well, fuck. "She loves me."

"James, I want you to close your eyes for second."

"Why? I don't need to mediate right now, I just need to calm down enough to figure out what the best course of action is."

"Close your eyes."

I laughed. "Fine, Doc." I closed my eyes.

"Take a deep breath for me."

"Are you going to try to hypnotize me or something? Because I really don't think..."

"James, breathe."

I took a deep breath.

"I want you to put yourself in Penny's shoes. Do you remember when you were a sophomore in college? A million years ago?"

"Not funny."

"A little funny," Dr. Clark said.

I shook my head.

"Picture yourself back in college. Surrounded by all your friends. Picture one of your best memories."

I took a deep breath and pictured myself at the Gryphon Club, a final club at Harvard. Mason and I had been accepted freshman year, but we got to live in the mansion sophomore year. The two of us always had fun.

But it was always better when it was all four of us. Me, Mason, Rob, and Matt. I remembered a weekend where Matt and Rob were visiting. They were two years younger than Mason and me and they were seniors at Empire High at the time. We'd wanted to give them a taste of how fun college was.

"Did you choose a memory?" Dr. Clark asked.

"Yeah, one of the best nights."

"Tell me all about it."

I closed my eyes tighter as the memory came back...

Chapter 29

Friday

A million years ago, according to Dr. Clark

"Why would you choose to live in an all-boys dorm?" Rob asked as he tossed his duffel bag on my bed.

"It's not a dorm," Mason said. "It's a final club. And it's fucking awesome. We throw the best parties on campus."

"Is it even technically on campus?" asked Rob. "It was like a five-minute drive. At least, that's how long the driveway made it seem." He collapsed onto the leather Chesterfield sofa and frowned. "And why is your room decorated like we just walked into the Caldwell's mansion?"

Matt laughed. "This place does remind me a bit of home." He tapped the wood paneling with his knuckles and stared at the built-in bookshelves. "Minus the fact that you have gryphons outside your creepy mansion instead of gargoyles."

"And the fact that it's filled with only men," Rob added.

"Would you stop being annoying for five seconds?" Mason said. "You're lucky you're even here. It's very exclusive."

"Not that exclusive if they took your ass."

Mason smacked Rob in the back of the head.

I ignored them and walked over to Matt. He turned away from me and looked out the window. He looked worse than the last time I'd seen him. There were dark circles under his eyes. And I'd heard that the Empire High Eagles had lost their last three games. Rumor had it that their leading wide receiver had been benched because he'd shown up drunk to practice too many times. Matt was their drunk wide receiver.

"How are you doing?" I asked.

He cleared his throat. "Ready to fuck some shit up," he said.

Was he though? Because he looked a mess.

"Speaking of fucking shit up, we brought some delicious homemade brownies," Rob said and pulled out a plate of brownies. There were already several missing.

How did brownies have anything to do with fucking shit up? But I was hungry. I grabbed one and took a bite. I wasn't sure who they were homemade by, but they were actually pretty tasty.

Mason grabbed one too. Rob pulled out two and tossed one at Matt.

I had no right to judge Matt. I'd showed up drunk to high school plenty of times. Or high. I was actually high right now. But I also didn't have a whole team depending on me. I was just fucking up my own life. So yeah, I wasn't judging. But I was worried about him. I just wanted one weekend where we could just be...us again. The four of us against the world. The way it used to be. Before everything broke.

Matt turned away from me. "So what's the plan for tonight?" he asked Mason. "Because I need a drink."

Matt did not need a drink. Neither did I. But it was Friday. And I was a little worried that half the time I looked as sad as Matt did. My girlfriend had suddenly stopped talking to me several weeks ago. I'd tried to call her and her number was disconnected. I would have been worried about her, but I knew she was fine. She just didn't want to talk to me. Because even though she'd changed her Facebook account to private, she seemed eager enough to accept a friend request from a new fake account I made that didn't show my face. It wasn't even a good fake account. I had like one friend and one picture.

So that was done. And honestly, maybe I wasn't that sad. Because the more time that passed, the more I realized I didn't miss her. Back in high school we made sense. When I first met her, I liked that she wasn't part of my world. But she made it pretty clear that all she wanted was to be a part of it. The more time we spent together, the less I liked her. But I found that was the case with most people. Except for my three friends in this room.

"Well, like I was just telling this idiot," Mason said and pointed to Rob. "The Gryphon Club throws the best parties on campus."

"But if it's a secret club, how do you throw parties?" Rob asked. "Because whoever you invite will know about said secret club. Meaning it's not a secret anymore."

"I swear to God, Rob, I will kick your ass."

"I knew you missed me," Rob said.

Mason laughed. "I did not. But just so all of you know, I'm not getting shitfaced tonight. I have a game tomorrow, and unlike some people in this room, that matters to me."

Matt groaned. "I was only drunk for a few games. Besides, we suck this year. Our quarterback is trash. He makes you look like Eli Manning."

"I'll take the compliment," Mason said. "But three games, man? Come on. If you keep that up there won't be a spot for you here."

"In this all-boys dorm," Rob said. "Oh, the horror."

Matt laughed.

"No," Mason said. "On the Harvard football team."

Rob shrugged. "So do you guys all shower together too? Because I stopped by the bathroom and I only saw one big community shower. And there was a tub. What the hell is up with that?"

"Yeah, what kind of pervert would want to take a bath every night?" Matt asked.

"You don't have to take a bath," Mason said. "But it's there if you want it."

Matt frowned. "But who would want that?"

"It's actually great for sports recovery to sit in cold water for a few minutes," Mason said.

Rob shook his head. "I don't think that sounds right. But forget the weird bath for a second, you didn't answer my question. Is there really only one bathroom for all of you?"

Mason shrugged. "There's one on each floor. But yeah. Why are you guys making this so weird? They're just like locker rooms."

"With a bath though," Matt said with a laugh.

Rob laughed too. "Don't tell me…there's a daily dick measuring contest in the showers."

"If there was, you'd lose," Mason said.

Rob laughed. "No, you would. Big boy, small dick. Facts."

"I'm going to kill him," Mason said and turned to me. "I'm finally going to do it."

"Bring it on," said Rob.

"Give Mason a break," I said. "He's having a really hard time because the coach believes in celibacy during the season or something. He's on edge."

Rob opened his mouth and then closed it again. He glanced at Matt and then back at Mason. "Wait. So let me get this straight. You're not having sex. You're not drinking or doing drugs. And you have a small penis? It sounds like college sucks."

Matt laughed. "We need to remind our brothers how to have a good time." He rubbed his hands together. "Don't worry, we've got tonight covered."

"Um…" I looked at Mason and then back at our younger brothers. "No, *we* have it covered. We're showing you two the ropes tonight. And I'm not on the team. So unlike Mason, I still know how to have a good time."

"All. Boys. Dorm," Rob said. "No, you do not know how to have a good time. Luckily for the two of you, Matt and I are here." He pulled a bottle of tequila out of his duffel bag. "Now can you please direct us back to campus from this isolated creeper den?"

***

"Why are we doing this again?" Mason asked me as we followed Rob and Matt wherever they'd deemed appropriate after spending literally five minutes on campus.

"Because our party doesn't start for another hour," I said. "And it's going to be hilarious to see their faces once we show them up."

"True." Mason sighed. "But this fucking sucks."

I laughed. "It'll be worth it, I promise." But maybe I was going to eat my words, because Rob was heading up the steps toward the library. Mason and I both looked at each other. And then we quickly caught up to them.

"What are you doing?" I asked. "This is the library."

"I know," Rob said. "The kinkiest girls hang out in the library. They'll know where the best party is."

Mason groaned.

Seriously, why did Rob and Matt not trust us here? Apparently running Empire High had gotten to their heads. But they didn't know anything yet. Watching this plan crash and burn could be mildly entertaining, though. "Fine," I said. "After you." I gestured toward the front doors.

We walked into the library. I hadn't spent much time in here, but I knew this was probably a bad idea. Rob was...well, loud. And libraries were notoriously quiet.

Rob and Matt wandered around until we got to the Loker Reading Room. We stopped at the large columns and stared at all the tables of people studying. I looked up at the ornate curved ceiling of windows. It was my favorite part of the library. I kept meaning to sneak in here at night when all the lights were off. I bet it would be easy to see the stars through those windows when it was dark.

"I'm confused," Rob said. "I thought it was supposed to look like Hogwarts in here? It just looks...old." He stared at the wooden tables and wooden chairs.

"Why would this look like Hogwarts?" I asked.

"Didn't JK Rowling base the Hogwarts grand hall off this or something?"

"Pretty sure she based it on Oxford, man." Actually I knew for a fact that it was Oxford. But if I talked about this too much he'd call me a nerd and never want to go back to the Gryphon Club tonight.

"Why are there so many people in here on a Friday night?" Matt asked.

"Because we're at Harvard." This was one of the best schools in the country. What wasn't he getting?

"Shh!" someone said.

Matt laughed.

I was also almost 100% positive that Matt and Rob did not deserve to be accepted here. But luckily for them, I wasn't in charge of admissions. And even more luckily for them, our parents were *very* generous donors. Hell, I probably didn't deserve to be going here either. I'd never know for sure.

Watch this," said Rob with a wink. He walked over to the nearest table and sat across from a girl studying.

She did not look up.

He proceeded to talk to her.

She still didn't look up. But she did say something back to him.

"He's going about this all wrong," I said. "Why hasn't he lightly touched her arm to get her attention? It's all about that one touch. And eye contact." I leaned against one of the columns and folded my arms across my chest.

Mason shook his head. "Amateur."

Rob said one last thing to the girl, then tapped the table, and then walked back over to us. "I don't think this was the best place to come to ask about parties."

"And why is that?" Mason asked. "Because the hottest girl here wouldn't give you the time of day?"

"Is she the hottest girl here? I doubt it. But she did talk to me. And like I said, this isn't the right place to ask about parties."

"She didn't know of any?" Matt asked.

Rob sighed. "No, she did. But she said the Gryphon Club throws the best parties."

"That's what I've been trying to tell you all night," Mason said.

"Shhh!" someone hissed.

Mason shook his head. "Come on," he whispered. "Let's head back."

"Look, I admit that I was wrong," Rob said.

"Apology accepted," Mason said. "So let's go back to the Gryphon Club."

"I'm not talking about your off-campus frat orgy place. I'm saying I was wrong about coming into this library in the first place. Clearly these girls aren't that kinky. We need to find…" He snapped his fingers. "Wait. We gotta go to a floor that's more deserted."

I shook my head. "Rob…"

"We need to find the kinky library sluts who daydream of being pushed up against the deserted library stacks. I bet there's at least one girl upstairs waiting for exactly that to happen."

"That's a great idea," Matt said. He took a swig of tequila from a brown paper bag.

Had he had that the whole time? *What the fuck?* We were going to get arrested. I grabbed the bottle from him, but when I turned my back, Rob sprinted off. Matt ran after him. Luckily he didn't fall down the stairs or anything, because the bottle was already half empty.

Mason sighed. "I forgot what it was like hanging out with children."

I laughed.

"But when in Rome…" He grabbed the bottle from me and took a sip. He handed it back to me.

I was surprised he'd had a drink. But yeah…when in Rome, I guess. "Cheers, man," I said and took a sip too.

"Shh!" another person hissed.

"Want to just wait outside?" I asked.

Mason nodded. The two of us walked back outside. Mason sat down on the steps. "Is it weird that I'm a little proud?"

"Of who? Those two idiots?"

He laughed. "Yeah. You have to admit that the library was a good choice to ask about parties. As long as you ask the right girl. Which Rob did."

"True. And even though he didn't like her response, the pivot to finding a kinkier girl in the stacks? Pretty brilliant."

"We taught them well."

I smiled. "Too bad they forgot that we were the ones that taught them everything they know." I looked down at my watch. Our party started in half an hour. It was fine if we were late, but if we missed the whole thing, Rob and Matt would always regret it. Usually we'd save tonight's theme for much later in the semester. But we'd convinced our Gryphon Club brothers to move up the theme for tonight. Just for Rob and Matt. And they were too busy flirting in the library.

"They'll remember we know what we're talking about soon."

I took another sip of tequila as Rob and Matt burst out of the library doors.

"We've got it," Rob said.

"Don't rope me into this shit," Matt said. "The girl I asked said the Gryphon Club too. I think we should just head back."

Mason smiled and nodded at me.

"No, no, no," Rob said. "I met the most beautiful artist. There's a soiree starting in like 20 minutes. She's going to be painting for a bit or something and then we can hang out."

"Um…what?" I said.

"It's going to be a blast. I mean a soiree sounds fancy as fuck."

"Hmm." Matt stared at him. "Now that you're describing it better, a soiree does sound kind of fancy. And that artist did have amazing tits. Maybe we could just stop by." He pulled a blunt out of his pocket and lit it. He took one puff and handed it to Rob.

"Oh, they're high," Mason said. "That explains it."

And a little drunk probably. That all definitely explained it. "Honestly, I feel a little high too," I said with a laugh.

"Because of the brownies," Rob said.

"What?"

"There was pot in the brownies."

"Are you serious?" Mason said. "I told you that I'm not doing that shit right now. What the fuck?"

"In my defense, you told us *after* you'd already had a brownie. And then I didn't know what to say."

"You let me eat another one!"

"And for that I am sorry." Rob laughed. "Sorry," he said more firmly. And then he laughed again. "Fuck, I can't stop laughing, sorry."

I started laughing too.

"Fuck this." Mason stood up and grabbed the blunt from Rob. He took a long inhale, letting the smoke out through his nose. "Here's the plan," Mason said. "We're going to go to the Gryphon Club first and then do your thing."

And by that he meant we'd *never* do the weird watching someone paint thing, because they'd have a blast at our party.

"We should get going," Rob said. "I want to get my art on."

"Get your what on? What the fuck are you even talking about?" Mason laughed. "And what the hell is in this thing?" He coughed. "That shit is strong." But instead of handing it back, he took another hit.

"Exactly," Rob said.

I started laughing. "Exactly what? What is even happening right now?"

"Weekend!" Matt yelled.

I laughed even harder. I couldn't remember how many brownies I'd eaten. But I knew half the plate had been empty before Rob and Matt had even offered us any. They were high as fuck right now.

"Weekend!" Rob yelled too and then he howled.

"Fuck," Mason said. "Whenever he howls we're totally screwed."

Matt howled next to Rob.

"Shh!" someone said as they walked by us, even though we were only on the steps of the library instead of inside.

I couldn't stop laughing. I leaned back on the steps, trying to catch my breath.

Rob plopped down next to me and grabbed the tequila bottle. Matt sat down next to him. And Mason sat down on the other side of me and handed me the blunt.

"So why are we trusting this hot artist sending us to a strange soiree?" Mason asked.

"Because…tits," Rob said.

"To tits." Matt lifted the tequila bottle in the air.

I laughed. "To tits!" I yelled.

Mason started laughing as hard as me.

It felt like the four of us on the steps outside of Empire High all over again. Only tonight was going to be a million times better. It was only just getting started. And I could only remember good things happening whenever all four of us were high…

Chapter 30

Tuesday

"It sounds like you all had a fun time in college," Dr. Clark said, pulling me out of my story.

"Yeah." I smiled. "It was a good time. But that wasn't even the best part about that night. I was about to get there."

"Alright, but before you tell me about the rest of the night...do you ever think about changing anything?"

I stared at him. "About that night? Or more existentially?"

"Both."

I pressed my lips together. "I would have changed a lot of things about my life. But I'm happy about where I am now."

"So everything worked out the way it was meant to?"

I slowly nodded. "And who knows what would be different about my life now if I changed anything in my past?"

"That's a good point. But I need you to visualize something for me before we proceed. I need you to insert someone new into your memory. Just plop them right down into the middle of it."

I gripped my cell phone a little tighter. I already knew what he was going to tell me.

"Say you met someone just like Penny before your friends visited from out of town. Someone who you loved. Someone perfect for you. A fellow student at Harvard. Would you have given up the partying? Given up those memories with friends? Dropped out of Harvard and moved away?"

I swallowed hard. "I…" My voice trailed off. "Yes."

"You hesitated."

"Well, that situation doesn't make sense. Why would we need to drop out and move if she's a student with me at Harvard?"

Dr. Clark laughed. "Fine. Then she's your professor and she's about to be fired."

"I've never really had a thing for older women. Mason on the other hand…"

"James, I'm just asking you to visualize it. I want you to put yourself in Penny's shoes here. To see how she's feeling about the situation you're currently in together."

"Penny doesn't go out partying with friends every night. I think she prefers just hanging out with me."

"You're not answering my question," he said.

I shook my head. "Sorry, what was the question?"

"If you'd *had* to drop out of college and move away because you fell in love. Forget the why. It just is. Would you have done it? Even if it meant you would have missed out on all those memories with your friends?"

"A lot of college is blurry for me anyway. So yes."

Dr. Clark sighed. "But it's not blurry for Penny if she doesn't party as much as you did."

I mean…she parties a little. Or else she wouldn't be recovering from a concussion. "If I'd fallen in love with Penny back then, she would have been a good influence on me. Just like I'm being a good influence on her." I knew that was strange to say, given my history. But Penny hadn't been herself when we were on a break. Neither had I.

"But college students aren't really seeking good influences. They're supposed to be out there living their best lives. Having new experiences."

I looked back out the window at Main Street. I knew what Dr. Clark was saying. I did. "You think telling the dean is a mistake?"

"I didn't say that. I think honesty is always the best policy. I'm just trying to get you to see this from Penny's point-of-view. James, you're in a very different stage of your life than she is."

I swallowed hard. "We're on the same page now."

"And what·page is that?"

"She's my forever."

There was a long pause on the other end of the line. "So you intend to marry her?"

"I only just got out of one marriage." I forced a laugh. But apparently Dr. Clark didn't find it funny, because he sighed.

"Forever in most circumstances comes with a ring."

"But Penny's young. She…"

"James, that's exactly my point."

I took a deep breath and exhaled slowly. "Yeah."

"So despite the fact that Penny isn't out partying all the time…let's say she is having an amazing college experience. She's having just as good of a time as you were back in college."

"If she is, then I'm a part of that."

"Yes. But we need to go back for just a second. Before she met you. Was she having as much fun as you had back in college? Would she have wanted to mess any of that up?"

"Well, she did mess it up. She chose to pursue me, just as much as I pursued her."

Dr. Clark sighed again like I was exhausting him. "It's hard to put yourself in someone else's shoes. And we're honestly approaching this all wrong. Is Penny there? Could you put her on the call too and we can work through this together?"

I honestly didn't love the idea of Penny talking to Dr. Clark. It was one thing telling her about my messy past. It was another for her to be able to ask Dr. Clark questions. "She is here. But she's sleeping."

"Okay. Well, this is a conversation you need to have with her. I want you to ask her if she was happy before you met. Only she can really answer that. You need to hash it all out with open communication."

I didn't want her to think about being happier before she met me. And how could that possibly be true anyway? I truly did believe we were a perfect fit. Which meant I completed her just as much as she completed me. We were better together.

"And I don't want you to just talk about where she was in life before she met you. I want you to talk about where you'd like to be going forward. Together."

"Yeah."

"You don't sound thrilled."

"I haven't been thrilled for a million years." I laughed at my own joke. Since he said my being at college was a million years ago. But again, Dr. Clark didn't respond. Penny probably would have laughed. Hence why we were better together.

"Okay," he finally said. "You don't find your relationship with Penny thrilling?"

"It was a joke. Of course I find my relationship with her thrilling. She makes me feel young again."

"Because she's young."

"Yes. I get it. You don't need to beat me over the head with this anymore." But he was wrong if he thought Penny and I were really in different places in our lives. She was 20. She was allowed to fall in love and make rational changes in her life because of that.

"Okay. I want you to revisit your memory before you go speak to her. To give you more perspective."

"Alright?" I didn't know where he was going with this. Did he want me to insert Penny into the memory and see how the night would have gone differently? Because I wound up naked, and that probably would have still happened if Penny was there...albeit differently. We probably just would have wound up naked in my bed together.

"You're remembering this great night. One of your best nights. But were there some bad parts? Maybe it wasn't all sunshine and roses."

"Well, Rob accidentally drugged Mason when he was trying to be clean for the season. It almost got Mason kicked off the team. That was pretty shitty."

"I want it to be more of a reflection of *your* night, not Mason's."

"Okay."

"Keep telling me the story. But leave wiggle room as you go. Remember all of it. Not just the best moments now."

"All the gory details?" I said with a laugh.

"Every last one of them. Really think about every situation you were in as you tell me about your night. And when you're done, we can talk about what went wrong or what could have gone wrong. Or what could have been better."

"The night was insane. We were lucky we didn't get arrested."

"Good start. So what happened next?"

"We wound up naked in front of a bunch of strangers. Or wait. No, I remember more than that…"

Chapter 31

Friday

A million years ago again

"No, we need to climb it," Mason said as he stared up at the John Harvard statue. "And sit on his little head."

I couldn't stop laughing. "So you want to sit on his head like you're his hat?"

"Exactly. Because he's not wearing one. Why the fuck isn't he wearing a hat?"

Matt and Rob started laughing with me. Mason had been sober for over a month. And from how fucked up we usually were before his season started...getting back to that level after being clean had its consequences. The main one being that Mason wanted to sit on the head of the John Harvard statue like a little hat.

"But it's better than a hat," Mason said.

"How exactly?" The cool autumn breeze blew and I shivered. Actually, maybe a hat didn't seem like such a bad idea right now.

"It'll be like a double decker John Harvard statue. Because I'm going to make the same pose as him. I'll put my feet on his arms."

"Why the fuck?" Matt asked.

"Because! You'll see. Help me up."

I wasn't going to *not* help him up. My feet crunched in leaves as I walked over to the base of the statue. I put my hands out for him. Mason slid his foot into my hands and I hoisted him up.

He somehow gracefully got onto the cement block at the statue's feet. But the gracefulness stopped there. He tried to climb onto John Harvard's lap but kept sliding back down.

"Why is it so slippy?!" he yelled.

Rob was bent over laughing. "Did he just say slippy instead of slippery?"

Matt tried to say something, but I couldn't make it out through his laughter.

"Do they wax this thing or something?" Mason asked, as if any of us would randomly know the answer to his question. "So. Slippy."

"Stop saying slippy!" Rob said.

"NEVER!" Mason tried once more and somehow ended up sliding onto the statue's lap.

"You look like a little baby," Rob said through his fit of laughter.

"You look very little from my vantage point, son," Mason said in a weirdly deep voice in an undiscernible accent.

"Was John Harvard Scottish?" Matt asked.

"That was definitely not a Scottish accent," I said in a much better Scottish accent. Which just made us all laugh harder.

"I did it!" Mason yelled.

We all looked up. Mason was sitting on the top of John Harvard's head. I swear he'd just been in the statue's lap. How did he get up there so fast? Especially when the statue was so fucking *slippy*.

"How in the hell?" Rob asked.

"Bow to me, peasants!" Mason yelled and spread out his arms.

"I need a picture of this." Matt pulled out his cell phone and snapped a photo.

"I'm king of Harvard now!"

"I don't think John Harvard was the king of the university," Rob said.

"Bow. To. Me!" Mason lifted his arms again as he tried to stand up on the statue.

"Dude, don't…" Matt started.

But it was way too late. Mason immediately fell forward on the slippery ass statue and crashed down onto us. All four of us somehow wound up on the sidewalk groaning.

"Fuck," Mason said. He put his hand on my upper thigh as he tried to stand up.

I shoved him off of me. "Watch the package, man."

Mason laughed. "Oh my God. I know what we need to do. I need a package so bad."

Rob, Matt, and I all stared at each other.

"Good, sir," Rob said in a Scottish accent that wasn't nearly as good as mine. "Pray tell. What the fuck do you want to do with another man's junk?"

"What?" Mason said.

"You just said you need a package so bad."

"Yeah I did." He put out his hand to help Matt up.

Matt did not take his hand. "You can't have mine."

"What are you idiots talking about?" Mason asked.

I stood up and brushed off the back of my jeans. "Mason, you touched my upper thigh and then said you need a package so bad."

Mason laughed. "Wow. No. I don't want your package. Hunter dicks," he said with a laugh. "Tiny baby penises."

Matt started laughing.

"Projecting," Rob coughed into his arm.

"I need it!" Mason yelled.

"Is he asking one of us to molly whop him or something? Because nose goes." Rob touched his nose.

Matt and I both touched our noses too.

"You lost!" Matt yelled and pointed at me. "Molly whop Mason so he shuts up."

"I'm not molly whopping anyone with facial hair."

"So if he was smooth shaven you'd do it?"

"You know what I meant, Matt!"

Mason started laughing harder. "No. I don't want that."

"Then why do you keep asking for it?" Rob said.

"I meant I need the whole package. Of the woman variety. I need to put my dick in all the holes. Female holes. There's three of them." He got a big goofy grin on his face.

"Aren't you not supposed to be doing that?" Matt asked.

"Aren't you not supposed to be doing that?" Mason mimicked back in a very incoherent way.

Matt laughed. "That's not at all how I sound."

"Ah!" Rob yelled at the top of his lungs. "Speaking of holes, we're late."

"For what?" I asked.

"The soiree. There will be holes for Mason there. Come on." He tapped Mason's chest and started walking away.

"Did we agree to that?" Matt called after him. "I don't remember agreeing to that. Or…maybe I do."

"Did we agree to that?" Mason mimicked again with weird shoulder attitude this time.

"Dude, stop doing that."

"Dude, stop doing that. Bloink!" He lightly slapped both of Matt's cheeks at the same time and made a farting noise.

***

I wasn't even sure how it happened. My memory just jumped to the four of us in an empty white room.

"I'm confused," Mason said. "I see no holes. Dicks need holes, Rob." He groaned and looked up at the ceiling. "I need a hole!"

"Yeah," Rob said. "I'm confused too. Why did they send us in here?"

"How did we even get here?" Matt put his hands on the walls. "What *is* here? What even is life?" He banged his head against the wall.

Well, Matt was having a moment.

He banged his head again.

I pulled him away from the wall to stop him from getting a concussion.

"The door is locked!" Mason yelled. "We're going to die in here without getting laid one last time!"

The door immediately opened. I was pretty sure it hadn't been locked at all. I laughed. *Doorknobs.* Who the hell thought of putting a knob on a door? I laughed again. A knob was such a stupid thing to put on a wooden board.

An older man walked into the room wearing a beret that he had no business wearing.

"Aha! You've arrived. Just in time too." He snapped his fingers and a woman came running in with a clipboard and a plastic bag. She handed him the bag and then ran off just as quickly as she'd come.

"Here are your outfits," he said. "You have two minutes to change and then please make your way into the party. Any questions?" He pushed the bag into Mason's hands.

"I have questions," Mason said as he stared into the bag. "But also...I was a hat earlier."

"Um. Okay," the man said. "Just change and shimmy on out to the party." He turned on his heel and left the room.

"I didn't know there was a dress code," Rob said. "You think she would have mentioned that." He peered into the bag that Mason was holding. "Oh. Shit."

"What?" I asked and looked into the bag. I plucked out a big fig leaf. "What the hell is this?"

"What the hell is anything?" Matt said with a big sigh.

Rob laughed. "Now that I think about it, she did mention something about posing. And needing four guys to do it."

"Posing for...what?" I asked.

"For art, man. What else would we be posing for?"

"You didn't think this was important to mention?"

"I forgot. I'm high."

I laughed. "This isn't an outfit though."

"It must be a tasteful nude painting," Rob said. "I'm guessing we put the fig leaves over our junk."

"I'm not doing this," I said.

"Ready," Mason said. He'd already stripped out of his clothes and was holding a fig leaf in front of his dick. "What?" he said when he noticed I was staring. "Being naked is one step closer to getting that pussy. I bet there are some hot girls in there."

I turned back to Rob. "Are they going to be selling this painting or something? Where is it going to wind up? And how many people are out there?"

"Eh." Rob shrugged. "Who cares. Matt, stop stroking the wall and take your clothes off."

"Okay," Matt said and pulled off his shirt.

"This is a really weird thing to do on a Friday night," I said.

"It's a soiree," Rob said, as if that made in not weird. "You're just not getting it." He started to strip.

"Yeah, get on our level, James," Mason said, dead serious.

I laughed. "Fine. Whatever. But one of us is buying this painting when the night is over." I pulled my shirt off over my head.

"I'll buy it," Matt said. "I like art."

It didn't seem like he liked art based on the frown on his face. And I was wondering if this had anything to do with all the portraits he'd painted that were locked in his bedroom closet. I cleared my throat. We weren't talking about that tonight. Or ever. I'd given Matt my word. "Just as long as this painting doesn't end up in a museum somewhere."

"I'd look good in a museum," Mason said. "Maybe we can sell the photo of me owning the John Harvard statue."

That is not how I would have described what happened. I pushed off my jeans and boxers, grabbed a leaf, and put it over my junk.

"Let's do this," Mason said. He grabbed the doorknob. "Ah, it's locked!"

Rob walked to his side and easily opened the door. "You're so high, man."

"No, I'm sober. For the game."

The rest of us looked at each other. Did Mason actually think he was sober right now?

Rob cleared his throat. "Sure. Whatever you say. Arts and crafts time!"

The four of us left the room, and for some reason we walked in a single file line down the hallway.

"Wait, where did Mr. Beret say to go?" Rob asked.

"He said to shimmy on out to the party," Matt said from far away.

I turned around and he was just standing there staring at the wall outside the room we'd been in. I backtracked and linked my arm through his.

Matt laughed. "For an art party, there is very little color here."

He was right. The walls were a plain white out here too. And when we made it to the end of the hall, we walked into another blindingly white room.

There were women in fancy dresses and men in tuxedos standing at cocktail tables chatting. But the room hushed when we walked in.

"I think we're in the wrong place," Rob whispered.

I heard a spoon fall to the ground. *Yeah.* We were definitely in the wrong place. Because everyone else was wearing freaking clothes!

Mason looked down at his leaf. "When did I get naked?" he whispered.

I laughed.

Matt laughed too. "Why are we the only naked ones? Robert Hunter, you're in trouble, young man."

"Don't use my full name," he hissed. "This isn't my fault."

"How is this not your fault?" I asked. And then I laughed. "Fault is a strange word."

"I don't even think it's a word," Matt said. "I've never heard that before."

"Fault, fault, fault," Mason started saying on repeat.

"We're so high," Rob said. "Maybe this isn't even happening right now."

"But you're all seeing this, right?" I whispered. "A whole party of people staring at us? And they're all wearing way more clothes than us."

"I see it," Mason said. "I wish I was still a hat. Oh, fuck I'm getting hard."

"What? Stop it!" Rob hissed.

"It's too late. There's a hot girl at table two. Direct eye contact is my weakness."

I looked over and there was indeed a hot girl at table two smiling over at us.

"This leaf isn't big enough!" Mason hissed.

"Calm down, that leaf is twelve times the size of your small dick," Rob said.

"It's tenting! The leaf is going to rip."

"Get it together," Matt said. "Think of…bunnies or something."

"You know I love fucking on top of furs!"

Matt started laughing.

"My tip is showing!"

I looked down. And sure enough, the tip of Mason's penis was poking out at the bottom of the leaf. But I felt like he was holding the leaf all wrong. It was way too high up. What the hell was he doing? "You gotta put it lower," I said and reached for his leaf.

"Don't touch my boner, man."

"Yeah, I was definitely not trying to do that."

"Bloody wanker," Mason said.

I started laughing. "Are we British now?"

"I think I should just drop the leaf," Mason said. "It's the only way."

"Don't flash all these people," Rob hissed. "They're all staring at us. Are we screaming right now? I feel like we're screaming…"

"You're finally here!" a bubbly brunette said as she ran up to us. She gave Rob a quick kiss on the cheek. "I just need you and your friends over there and I'll start painting you."

I turned to where she was pointing. There were some cloth tarps laid on the ground and paint and brushes. But there was no canvas.

"Where exactly are you painting us?" Rob asked.

"Over there," she said again, but this time she pointed to the wall.

Rob laughed. "It's a mural? That's staying here? Forever?"

"That's the idea, yes," she said.

"I can't buy that wall," Matt said.

I laughed. "It's fine." Who cared if our asses were forever immortalized on this wall? Certainly not me. Had I ever said I cared? "Is there food?" I asked.

"Yes it's…" her voice trailed off as she looked over my shoulder.

I turned around to see Mason talking to the hot girl at table two. The girl at the table behind him was staring right at his exposed ass.

"If you'll excuse me," Matt said. "My brother's ass is out." He walked over to Mason, seemingly unaware that his ass was out too.

"Mason is going to need a better wingman than Matt," I said. I started to walk over toward them, but Rob caught my arm before I could.

"So, over there?" Rob asked. "Great. Let's get our art on." He pulled me away from Mason and Matt. Which was a mistake. Because I was a really good fucking wingman. Yup, I was the best. Matt and Mason were already retreating from table two. I would have got Mason fucking laid. The boy was in dire need of some holes.

The artist girl somehow wrangled us all into the poses she wanted. And we stood there perfectly still.

"Please stop moving," she said.

Okay…so maybe we weren't perfectly still. But this leaf was a plant. And plants weren't supposed to be this close to balls.

"Just be still," she said more firmly.

Did floating count as still? I was pretty sure I was floating.

Matt started giggling.

I looked over and Rob was poking at Matt's leaf with a sword.

"Where did you get a sword?" I asked.

"I'm the king of the jungle. Or something like that." He poked Matt's leaf again.

"Stop it," Matt said through his giggles.

The girl walked back over to us. "I need you all to not move."

"We're not marooving," Mason said as he tripped to the side.

"Did you just say marooving?" she asked.

"That's not a word."

"I know it's not a word." She looked up at the ceiling and took a deep breath. "You guys, please just be still. This is the first night of the exhibit. We're going to end up painting this whole room over the course of the semester, but this is the pivotal piece."

"Wait," Matt said. "What's going to be right next to us?"

"I don't know, someone else is painting that."

"I think we need to know what we're being painted next to. Like…is it lions? Because if it is, what if I do this?" He turned and lifted one of his legs like he was about to sprint. But he stayed perfectly still. "This way it looks like we're about to get on those lions and rule this fucking wall."

"No," she said. "We're not doing that. And Rob, stop poking him with the sword."

I looked over and Rob had the point of his sword close to Matt's butt. It made it look like Matt was running away from being anally impaled instead of being cool and running toward lions.

I burst out laughing.

"Oh no," Mason said. He sounded so devastated. "I broke it." His penis was poking through a hole in the leaf. "This wasn't the hole I was promised."

"What the hell is wrong with you guys?" She pulled the leaf off of Mason's erection, folded part of it down over the hole he'd made, and pushed it back in front of him.

"Nothing is wrong with us." Rob reached out and poked his sword against Mason's butt next.

"Stop it," she hissed. "You've lost your sword privileges." She grabbed it and handed it to me.

I smiled. "I'm the king of the jungle."

"You're not in the jungle!" she yelled. And then she looked surprised that she'd yelled. "Just...stop it. Be quiet. All of you." She stormed back over to the wall where she was painting us.

"I bet she gives great head when she's angry. Don't you think?" Rob asked.

"Unless she's a biter," Mason said. "Like the lions."

I couldn't stop laughing.

"I feel like we should do the running thing," Matt said. "It would be cooler next to the lions."

"There are no lions," I said through my laughter.

"Shhh," Rob said. Now that he didn't have his sword, he was perfectly poised. "I want her to just be a little angry. Not a lot angry. That's the secret to good head."

"I'm going to get blue balls," Mason moaned.

"Shh," Rob said again.

So I poked him with my new sword.

But then the artist cleared her throat. And there was something about the tone that made me stop. "I think we're in trouble?"

"You think?" Matt said. "We're being painted without lions."

The artist stared daggers at us as she continued painting the wall.

The party continued in front of us. Every now and then the people would casually look over at the wall and start talking and pointing. Presumably they were discussing the live art concept or some bullshit like that. While all four of us were ass naked, posed in weird positions, holding fig leaves over our junk.

"This is not fun," Matt said. "Boooo, Rob."

"It's not my fault," Rob said. "She tricked me with..."

"Tits," I said. "Yeah. It happens." Just thinking about tits made my dick start getting hard. *What the fuck?* It had been a while since I'd been laid too. I closed my eyes and pictured bunnies like Matt recommended. And unlike Mason who loved fucking on furs, the little guys calmed me down. I breathed a sigh of relief. I didn't want to be painted with my dick poking through a hole in the leaf.

Mason started laughing again. The brownies, and blunt, and alcohol had seriously fucked him up. I wasn't sure I'd ever seen anyone's pupils so big before. The bright white room probably didn't help. I was pretty sure we could be doing anything and he'd be having the time of his life. Which was fantastic for him. But the longer we stood up here, the more sober I got. And I'd just remembered the party we were throwing at the Gryphon Club. And now I was the only one who wanted us to get back there before the night ended.

"It's cold in here," Rob said and shimmied his shoulders a bit.

"That explains it," Mason said.

"Explains what?"

"Tiny penis syndrome." He giggled.

Rob glared at him. "You can't even see my dick. It's behind a leaf."

"Exactly. It's hidden behind a very small leaf."

"This leaf is like a foot long."

The artist cleared her throat again. We all froze.

"Wait, can you buy walls?" Matt asked. "Because now that I'm thinking about it...that's kind of what buying a house is. I'll try to buy a piece of this house."

"Or we could just sneak back in here later and paint over it," Rob said.

"Why would you paint over us?" Mason leaned forward to see the wall to our side. "We look good. Very realistic."

I craned my neck to see too. I had to hand it to the artist...we looked like fucking Greek Gods. "You can tell it's us though," I said.

"Can you?" Rob asked. "I don't know."

I laughed. "What other four idiots would wind up doing this on a Friday night during tops-optional night at the Gryphon Club?"

"What did you just say to me?" Rob asked.

"Oh. Oops. That was supposed to be a surprise."

"Why the fuck are we ass naked at this soiree when your weird frat has a bunch of topless girls roaming around waiting to be motorboated by yours truly?"

"Because you made us come here," I said with a laugh.

"But you left off very important details."

"Because it was a surprise."

"Okay, new plan," Rob said. He craned his neck to see the painting. "We've been here for like 12 hours."

"Maybe 20 minutes," I said.

"Same difference. She got what she needed from our bodies. New plan."

"I'm listening," Mason said. "As long as it involves that buffet." He pointed to where everyone else was getting to eat.

"Absolutely. We're going to run to the buffet, grab a bunch of food, and then run back to the Gryphon Club. On three. Three!" Rob sprinted off.

"What happened to counting!" Mason yelled.

"We needed a hut, hut or something," Matt said.

"Where are you going?!" the artist yelled. "You agreed to pose for four hours!"

Sorry…what? No. That wasn't happening. "Let's go!" I yelled and sprinted after Rob.

Matt and Mason followed. I grabbed a handful of chicken before Mason lifted the whole silver chafer.

"Stop!" she yelled.

But we'd all already grabbed our own chafers and were sprinting back to the hallway.

"Rob, grab our clothes!" I pointed to the room where we'd changed.

"On it." He ran into the room and we kept running. We pushed out the side of the building, laughing hysterically.

"Chicken," Mason said and plopped down on the stairs. He started double fisting the meat.

"I got mashed potatoes." I sat down next to him and he scooped up a handful of that too as I stabbed my sword through some chicken. Why didn't people still use swords as utensils? It seemed perfectly good to me. But the cold concrete under my ass did not seem as good. "Brrr my ass is cold."

"Brrrrr," Mason agreed.

"Ew," Matt said as he pulled the lid off his. "I should have opened it first. Who serves a whole tray of wilted asparagus?" He set it down on the steps next to him as we started feasting.

"Where is Rob?" Mason eventually asked.

I ate more chicken off my sword and frowned. "I don't know. He was right behind us."

We looked over our shoulders at the door.

"He probably got arrested," Matt said. "He was naked."

I stared at him. "We're all naked, Matt."

"I'm not na…" his voice trailed off when he looked down. "I don't remember that happening."

Mason and I both laughed.

"I love college," Rob said as he pushed through the doors behind us holding a bag of our clothes. "I knew she'd give good head."

He had lipstick prints all down his torso.

Mason laughed. "High-five!"

Rob high-fived him. "What did we get? Oh, score." He grabbed some chicken.

"I need my clothes," Matt said. "I'm naked."

"You'll never catch me!" Rob yelled and started running again.

"What the fuck," Mason said with a laugh. "I'm going to tackle his naked ass."

"You're going to tickle Rob's naked ass?" I asked.

Mason laughed. "I'm pretty sure I said tackle." He set his chicken tray aside. "Give me that sword."

I tossed it at him and he caught it with one hand. He lifted the sword over his head and sprinted after Rob.

Chapter 32

Tuesday

I smiled at the sound of Dr. Clark laughing. "I know, right? It was a great night. And I haven't even gotten to the party yet."

"James, what happened to trying to remember the bad moments as well?"

"Those were bad moments. Mason poked through his leaf and was giggling like a schoolgirl. And Rob was about to be slain with a sword. And Matt got asparagus in his chafer."

"And you?"

"I was having the time of my life with my best friends."

Dr. Clark laughed again, but my smile faltered.

My best friends. They *used* to be. I sat down at my desk and stared at the cryptic invitation that they'd sent me. When I got back to New York, I knew what I wanted to do. Mend my friendships. They wanted to meet up at a bar like we always used to. It was time to move forward from everything that happened. It was time to bury the hatchet, like Ian had said.

"Keep going, James. Remembering *all* the details for me this time, please."

"You said to pick a great memory. I'm just giving you what you wanted."

"But even the best memories have something that maybe wasn't perfect."

"I mean…we probably should have been arrested."

Dr. Clark sighed. "I'm more concerned about your feelings. Really think for me. Really immerse yourself into your sophomore year. What you were feeling. Wanting. Needing."

"Okay. I'll try."

"That's all I'm asking. Try to stay focused on what we're trying to discuss."

I took a deep breath. Dr. Clark was right. This night had started off amazing. But I was pretty sure it didn't end that way...

Chapter 33

Friday

A million years ago again

Rob jumped into a small fountain to escape Mason's flailing sword.

"What are you two jackasses doing?!" I jumped into the fountain and stepped between them so they couldn't reach each other.

"He said I had a baby penis," Mason said. "Does this look like a baby penis to you?" He gestured to his definitely-way-above-average-sized dick.

"Yes," Rob said. "Compared to mine."

Mason lunged for him.

I put my hands on their chests and shoved them back. "Stop it. Come on. Can't we all just be happy that we all have huge dicks?"

"I just want everyone to acknowledge that I'm packing a freaking elephant trunk," Rob said.

Matt belly flopped into the fountain, splashing all of us, and just missing hitting his head on the stone side.

And then somehow the great penis size debate had ended and we all started running around and splashing in the water even though it was fucking freezing.

Mason grabbed both sides of Rob's face. "Bloink!" he yelled at the top of his lungs.

I laughed. "Wait, Mason! We have to show them Tanner fountain."

"What the hell is a Tanner fountain?" Rob asked.

"It's pretty cool. It's all misty, especially on cold nights like this." I started climbing out of the lame little fountain, but Rob caught my arm to stop me.

"I'm not going to Tanner fountain," he said.

"Why not?"

He shrugged. "I don't know. I just got this weird déjà vu or something. I don't...I don't like that name."

"What name?"

"Tanner. It's a bad name. Bad juju. It's not for me. Right, Matt? Tanner sucks?"

"We don't know anyone named Tanner," Matt said.

Rob shuddered. "I know. But it's a very bad name. I have a feeling that if I ever meet a Tanner, I'm going to fucking hate him."

I shook my head. "But the mist is actually really cool..."

"That sounds flashy and stupid, just like the name Tanner."

Mason laughed. "You hate most people that aren't us. Bloink!" He slapped Rob's cheeks. The face ones, not the ass ones.

"What do you think the four of you are doing?" someone said from behind us.

We all turned around and stared at the campus security guard. And we were much more still than we had been while posing for that mural.

"We're invisible," Matt whispered.

The security guard frowned at all of us. "No, you are not invisible, son. And entering the fountain is against campus rules."

"We're invisible," Matt said again.

The security guard shook his head. "I've gotten calls about disturbances at the library tonight. And at an alumni charity live art event. Apparently four young men who were supposed to be tastefully posing in fig leaves stole a prop sword and lots of food."

Mason tucked the sword behind his back while I tried to cover my fig leaf with my hands.

"That wasn't us," Matt said. "Because we're invisible."

"I'm going to need the four of you to step out of the fountain."

"Isn't this guy our age?" Rob whispered to me.

"Yeah, it's like a campus job for students," I whispered back.

"Which means he has no actual authority. I think we should punch him."

"Better idea," I said. "Well, maybe try that too if my idea doesn't work. But first…let's rush him." I looked over at Mason and Matt to make sure they'd heard us.

Mason saluted me.

That seemed like a yes.

"Hut, hut!" Matt yelled and we all scrambled out of the fountain and charged toward the security guard.

He screamed at the top of his lungs. I wasn't sure if it was because of how intimidating we all were. Or if it was because we were all ass naked. But boy ran home.

"I'm the king of Harvard!" Mason yelled and lifted his sword in the air. He banged his fist against his chest.

Rob laughed. "Not on my watch." He shoved Mason backward into the fountain and stole the sword.

***

We showed up almost three hours late to our own party, completely drenched, and still high enough that we didn't really need the red solo cups someone shoved into our hands. But we downed them anyway.

"Holy fuck," Rob said as he saw a girl walk by in nothing but heels and a pair of cut-off jean shorts.

We were only standing in the foyer and you could already tell that this was the best party ever.

"You weren't kidding," Rob said. "Tops-optional is the best idea. But what's the actual theme for the party?"

"That's it," I said. "Just that. Tops-optional."

"It's a little lazy, honestly."

I laughed.

"But I love it."

"We figured you would," Mason said. "That's why we convinced everyone to move the party up to tonight. It's usually later in the semester."

"I knew you loved me."

Mason rolled his eyes.

"Now if you'll excuse me, I see my hot artist from earlier, and she looks like she desperately needs to be motorboated." He tossed the sword at me and walked into our house library.

"He's definitely going to fuck this up," Mason said. "Let's watch."

I laughed. "She already gave him head though." But we followed Rob into the library anyway. It was dark in here tonight and my final club brothers had removed most of the furniture. All that remained was one very heavy wooden desk, floor-to-ceiling mahogany bookshelves, a ton of books, and a number of old marble busts.

Rob was talking to a brunette who most definitely wasn't the artist from earlier. But he still immediately motorboated her. And she surprisingly didn't slap him.

"That's not the same girl, right?" Matt asked and cocked his head to the side. "Her tits look way bigger."

"Yeah, that's definitely not the same girl," Mason said.

"Um, why are you guys completed naked?" one of my final club brothers asked. "It's just tops, guys."

"Watch and learn," Mason said and patted his back. He walked up ass naked to one of the topless girls. She stared down at his dick, smiled, and then looked back up at him. He was making out with her in less than 30 seconds. And in less than a minute he had her back slammed against one of the bookshelves, her legs around his waist.

My final club brother shrugged and walked off.

"I still prefer pants," Matt said. He grabbed the bag off the ground that we had somehow managed to get back here safely. He pulled on his boxers, jeans, and shoes. I did the same.

The silence stretched awkwardly between us.

I cleared my throat. "Hey, if you want to talk about what happened with…"

"Nope," Matt said and downed the rest of his drink. "Let's just have fun, okay?" He gave me a forced smile and then walked away from me. Like he'd have more fun as far away from me as possible.

I sighed and leaned against the wall. Mason was still making out with the same girl. But Rob had already moved on to someone new again. Another brunette. Maybe he was making a run of it or something? Motorboating as many girls as possible? It didn't sound like a bad plan. But for some reason I didn't join in.

Instead, I pulled out my phone. I wasn't even sure why. Everyone who'd text me was here at this party.

I used to look forward to talking to Rachel or maybe even seeing her on the weekends. But that wasn't going to be happening anymore. I slid my phone back into my pocket and took a deep breath.

And I wasn't sure why, but instead of hitting on other girls and hanging out with my friends, I just stood there drinking alone. I walked over to one of the old marble busts on display. The library was filled with them, highlighting famous and successful Gryphon Club members. When I first joined, I didn't really care much about them. But now? Maybe that's what I wanted. To be famous. Or at least successful. To be immortalized here as a bust. *Bust.* I laughed.

Originally I saw Rachel as my ticket out of living like this. Or...she was supposed to be. I didn't need all...this. But she'd wanted it. My parents wanted it for me. All my friends wanted it.

I'd just wanted to be able to breathe a little easier.

Somewhere quieter. Where the people were nicer. I lit another blunt and took a deep inhale.

I closed my eyes, picturing a smiling face from my past. And all I could think about was the fact that I'd rather be in Delaware. I opened my eyes and shook the thought away. What the fuck was in Delaware?

I downed my drink and stared at the bust. Maybe focusing on being one of these would help me in some way. Give me purpose again. Or not. I was fucking high after all. I shook my head and walked over to Rob who was currently making out with yet another brunette.

"What are you doing?" I said when he finally came up for air and headed to get another drink. He'd found his pants again, but was still carrying around his sword. Or...more like using it as a walking cane. It worked somehow.

"What do you mean?" Rob asked. "But first, I have a question. What's in the basement? Because I've heard a lot of people whispering about something going down in there tonight."

"The basement is off limits to non-members. And non-pledges."

"But what is happening down there?"

I smiled. "I'm not allowed to tell you."

Rob gaped at me. "It's something kinky, right? Because I swear I saw someone with a cloak heading down there…"

"Enough about the basement."

"I also heard that one of these bookshelves is actually a secret door that leads to…"

"I'm not allowed to talk to you about that either."

"But…"

"Back to you. What's your end game here? You've made out with like five different brunettes tonight."

He looked at me like I'd lost my mind. "No I haven't. That was the artist from earlier. I've only made out with her all night."

"Dude, that's not the same girl," Matt said.

I wasn't sure where he'd come from, but I was glad he was back.

Rob shook his head. "Yes it is."

"It's definitely not," I said. "You've been hooking up with like every brunette here."

"Oh. Well, that explains why one of them slapped me when I talked about her giving me an amazing blowjob earlier. I was giving her a compliment. But wrong girl, I guess." He shrugged. "Damn, I think I might need glasses."

Mason laughed and grabbed both his shoulders and shook them. He'd found new clothes somewhere too. "You're just wasted."

"Not as wasted as you, big boy."

"So you finally admit it! I'm the biggest boy!" Mason hopped onto a nearby table. "I have the biggest dick!"

We all started laughing. The music turned to a more upbeat song and we all started jumping up and down. Including Mason. Who immediately broke the table in two.

***

"I'm going to be so fucked up during the game tomorrow," Mason groaned. He lay down on his bed, but I was pretty sure he'd be spending most of the night in the bathroom.

Rob plopped down on my bed with a similar groan. "But tonight was freaking amazing. I was wrong about this weird orgy frat thing. Topless night won me over. Best night ever!" But then his cheeks puffed out. He leaned off my bed and threw up in the trashcan.

Mason made a face like he was going to vomit too. He somehow held it together though.

Matt walked back into the room a little wobbly. He'd already been to the bathroom several times. But this time his eyes were a little red. I wasn't sure if he'd just snorted some cocaine or if he'd been crying.

My chest ached. Because I knew it wasn't really cocaine. I knew he'd been crying. And I knew who he'd been thinking of.

I did that too sometimes. Got so shitfaced that I cried in the showers. Remembering a girl that told me I'd be happier in Delaware.

Mason stumbled out of bed and stole the trashcan from Rob just in time.

"Fuck me," Mason said. "I'm going to be benched tomorrow."

"At least you finally got your holes," Rob said with a groan.

"Holes?" Mason looked so confused even though he'd gone on and on about holes earlier. "What the fuck are you saying?"

Matt laughed. But it was forced. I looked over at him and he immediately looked away.

"Holes are female parts," Rob said.

Mason just stared at him.

"For our dicks."

Still no recollection on Mason's face.

"Holes for our dicks."

"That's a gross way to describe a pussy."

"You started it! Fuck, give me that." He grabbed the trashcan from Mason.

"Lightweights," I said. I put my hands behind my head and stared up at the ceiling. But I knew by saying that…that maybe I was the one with the problem, not them. I swallowed hard. Yeah, I definitely had a problem. And we all knew it.

Matt cleared his throat. "I gotta go to the bathroom again." He walked out of the room.

The three of us looked at each other. And it was like we all sobered up at once.

Mason ran his hand down his face.

"I should go after him," Rob said. But I was pretty sure if he tried to get up, he'd throw up somewhere other than the trashcan.

"I got it," I said and climbed out of my bed. I hurried out of the room, but I didn't need to go far. Matt was just sitting in the hallway outside my room. His eyes were closed and his head was leaning back against the wood paneling on the walls. His cheeks were stained with tears.

Fuck. I let my back slide down the wall too. "Matt?"

He opened his eyes and looked at me. And then he shook his head. "I miss her," he choked out.

Matt only ever talked about this when he was really high or drunk. And I mean really, really fucked up. Because this was only the fourth time since her death that he'd mentioned her. Whenever we were sober, he always refused to talk about what happened. "I know."

"No you don't."

"I do…"

"You don't, man. I can't breathe without her. I can't…" his voice broke and he put his face in his hands.

I felt the tears roll down my own cheeks as I pulled his head against my shoulder.

I hated seeing him like this. And he was right. I didn't understand. Not really. Because I'd never really loved anyone. And I knew for sure that no one loved me.

Matt kept sobbing.

I ran my hand up and down his back.

Mason walked out of the room. He looked down at us and gave me a sad smile. He sat down next to Matt too.

But he didn't say anything at all. And maybe that's what Matt needed. I knew he didn't want to talk about it. At least, not yet.

Rob came out of the room too. He sighed. "Maybe not the best night ever."

Matt laughed, but it was forced.

"Make room for me," Rob said. He ducked under Mason's arm and somehow managed to lay down on all three of our laps.

"What are you doing?" Mason said. "Why are you mounting me?"

"I'm making Matt feel better. I'm the only one who knows how." He reached out and tickled Matt's side.

Matt started laughing. "Stop," he said.

Rob started tickling him harder.

"Why do you always fucking tickle me!?"

"Because it makes you laugh."

"Stop!" Matt yelled through his tears of laughter now.

Mason started tickling Rob's side in retaliation.

Rob yelped. "I don't need to be tickled! I'm already laughing!"

For some reason, I started tickling Matt too. And I was pretty sure he started tickling Mason. And Rob somehow managed to tickle me while still tickling Matt.

"Stop!" I said through my tears. I couldn't stop laughing.

And then one of our final club brothers walked by with what I could only presume was his younger brother who was also visiting for the weekend.

"What kind of weird off-campus orgy frat den are you a part of?" the younger boy asked.

And we all burst out laughing.

Chapter 34

Tuesday

"And how did relieving that night make you feel?" Dr. Clark asked.

I gripped my cell phone a little tighter. "It made me want to fix my relationships with my friends. And Rob. Starting with Rob. Which is good since he's visiting this weekend."

"That's fantastic. Tell me more."

"I miss them."

"I can tell. You've isolated yourself in Delaware. And you think it's time to stop doing that. I agree with you. That it's time to move forward."

"You do?"

"Well, earlier in the story, I wouldn't have been as sure. The four of you together are trouble."

I laughed. "Yeah."

"But later in the story? You finally showed me the other moments. The ones I was digging for. The hard ones."

"The end of the night is always shittier than the beginning."

"But what if none of it has to be shitty?" Dr. Clark asked.

I nodded. "You mean with Penny?"

"James, were you happy in college? Truly happy?"

I took a deep breath. "No. I was miserable. Yes, I had fun with my friends. But I was drowning. I didn't know what I wanted. I was...aimless."

"And when you're aimless, you..."

"Reach for vices." I swallowed hard. *Yeah.*

"And now? How do you feel right now?"

"Sober."

Dr. Clark laughed. "Besides sober. How does Penny make you feel?"

I smiled. "She makes me so happy. I don't remember ever really feeling like this before. Ever."

"So to answer my question from earlier. Now that you have the perspective of your own college years in the forefront...would you have given it all up? To be with Penny?"

"I would have traded it all to be with her. One hundred percent."

"So you weren't truly happy until you met Penny. And it might be the same case for her. If that's true...the two of you can go anywhere and face anything and be okay."

"You really think so?"

"I do. As long as you continue to be open and honest with her. Which includes having a hard conversation. Talking about her sophomore year and how she's feeling before and after meeting you."

"I don't think she felt like she was drowning before she met me."

"That doesn't mean you don't make her happier, James. That's the key here. You said something near the end of that night you were reliving. About how no one's ever loved you. We've talked about this before. About how you feel like you don't deserve love. That because of your past mistakes you're unlovable. But James, your friends love you. Even if you've drifted apart over the years, the four of you are bonded. That doesn't just fade away. And Penny loves you."

I swallowed hard. I knew that. I felt guilty for even thinking that back then. But now? I wouldn't think it about Penny. I knew Penny loved me. Even the dark parts. I'd shown her every side of me. And she wasn't running away. She was sleeping soundly in the other room. I yawned.

"Am I boring you?" Dr. Clark asked.

I laughed. "No, not at all. I just realized that I actually want to go to bed for once. Because she's waiting for me in my bed."

"Well I won't hold you up. But when you wake up tomorrow, I want you to talk about all this. I want the two of you to move forward as a team. Do you think you can do that?"

I nodded. And then I realized he couldn't see me. "Yeah. I can do that." I wanted us to be a team. "But…" my voice trailed off.

"Spit it out, James."

"You just said that when I'm aimless I reach for vices. If I'm forced to resign tomorrow after telling the dean the truth…I'll be aimless again. I'll slip." It hadn't been that long since I'd slipped the last time, and we both knew it.

"No you won't. Because you're going to focus on Penny. She's helping you, James. And we both know it. You've been different since you met her. You've been better for her."

I wasn't sure why, but I felt myself tearing up. "That's what I wanted. To be better for her." I'd been so worried for so long that I'd break her because I was broken. But maybe I had it all wrong. Not about being broken. I was a fucking mess. But I wasn't breaking her. Instead, she was healing me.

"And you told me you were focusing on a new business venture too, right? I think you'll be plenty preoccupied. No matter what the two of you decide together."

"Thanks, Dr. Clark. For that. And for taking my call so late."

"Any time, James. And call me if you need to talk after the meeting with the dean. I have to admit, that I'm rather invested in how this is all going to unfold."

I laughed. "Will do."

"Have a good rest of your night, James." He hung up.

And in the weirdest way, it felt like everything reset as soon as Dr. Clark hung up the phone. I'd promised myself that I'd be a better man for Penny. And…I was. Even Dr. Clark saw it. And now that I'd come clean about everything, I could be even better.

I pressed my lips together as I stared at the camera in the corner of my study. Okay, maybe I hadn't come clean about everything. There was still the issue of the cameras. But I'd tell her about those too. I'd get everything out in the open. We'd be on equal footing. And we'd make a decision together, weighing all the options before we did anything.

I stood up and walked out of my office. I knew it was past midnight. But Penny would want to have this conversation. I walked into the bedroom and smiled at the smell of cherries.

My eyes slowly adjusted to the light. I sat down on the edge of the bed and pushed a strand of red hair out of her face. I don't think I'd ever seen her look so beautiful. She looked ethereal in the moonlight peeking through the windows. And I felt it again. That she was healing me. Even touching her warm skin made it feel like the darkness was being chased out of me.

"I love you," I whispered as I traced her freckles with my thumb.

My lawyer didn't believe in us. But Dr. Clark did. Ian did. Ellen did.

And most importantly…I did.

Penny and I were a team. And we were going to get through this together. If I had to quit my job, she wouldn't let me slip. Maybe we'd move to New York. Maybe we'd stay here. All that mattered was that we were together. And that we decided our future together.

I put my hand on her shoulder.

She moaned in her sleep and I smiled.

"Penny," I whispered.

She moaned again and moved her head about, but she didn't open her eyes.

I wondered what she was dreaming about.

She moaned again and I smiled. I had a feeling she might be dreaming about me. I couldn't even count the times that she'd made appearances in my dreams. Ever since the first time she fell into my arms.

"Penny," I whispered again. I was just about to nudge her awake when my phone buzzed. My hand fell from her shoulder. I grabbed my phone and stared down at a text from Ian.

"James, can you head back to your office for a minute so I can call you? Something's come up."

I frowned. I stared back at Penny still sleeping peacefully. Whatever Ian needed, it could wait. Penny and I wanted to come clean to the dean in the morning. We needed to discuss this. I texted Ian back, telling him I'd call him in the morning.

But he immediately texted back: "It can't wait until morning."

I frowned and stood up. Ian wouldn't keep texting me if it wasn't important. I glanced once more at Penny peacefully sleeping in my bed and walked back out into the hall.

I hit Ian's name on my phone as I walked into my office.

"James," he said. "I'm really sorry."

"What's going on?"

"I already tried everything I could." There was a long pause. "It's bad."

My heart started racing. "Just tell me."

"It's Isabella."

For fuck's sake. Would this woman ever just let me be?

"She's…she's done something. And you're not going to like it."

I shook my head. "What could she have possibly done? The papers are signed. It's done. It's over," I added, as if that would make it true. But my stomach was already twisting into knots. All I could think about was Penny sleeping back in my bed. I just wanted to ignore whatever Isabella had done, climb into bed, and pull Penny into my arms.

"Ah, fuck," Ian said, delaying whatever horrible thing he was about to tell me. But then I heard him typing. And I realized that maybe something else had just come up. Like a string of bad events. Each one worse than the last.

For some reason my eyes landed on the invitation on my desk. It was the key to my fresh start with my friends. Hopefully a clean slate. But neither Matt nor Mason had signed it. And honestly, it didn't look like something they'd send. They wouldn't have sent anything at all. They would have just texted me or something.

I couldn't stop staring at the strange invitation. And then it hit me. I knew why the address sounded familiar. Mason had asked me and Matt and Rob to go there once to check out some real estate he was interested in. But Isabella showed up too and we'd all gotten into a huge fight.

So either Mason had finally bought that real estate and the invitation was to the grand opening of his sex club or something… Or Isabella sent that invitation as part of some crazy scheme to destroy my life. And I was scared that my friends might be collateral damage.

She was off her meds. And I knew what that meant. Rob, Matt, Mason, and I all knew what that meant. But I hadn't warned them. If something happened, it would be my fault.

I'd finally felt like a weight was lifted off my shoulders earlier today. Like I was free. But now it was back. Isabella preferred for me to stay in hell.

Penny was safe, fast asleep in my bed. That itself was a relief. But I had no idea where the fuck my friends were. And I had no idea what new game Isabella was trying to play with my life. All I knew was that when I saw her earlier, I recognized that hollow look in her eyes. And the last time I'd seen it, someone had wound up dead.

I took a deep breath. "Tell me what Isabella has done."

What's Next?

Professor Hunter and Penny know how to melt a kindle.
And I can't stop writing about them!

To get your free copy of a steamy bonus scene about
James and Penny, go to:

www.ivysmoak.com/devoured-pb

A Note From Ivy

My heart with this man! Getting inside James' head has been one of my favorite things. Trying to untangle and come to terms with all that hurt from his past. Who else just wanted to reach into the pages and give him a hug?

There was so much I didn't get to share from Penny's point-of-view in The Hunted series. All these new moments that I had been dying to write for so long. Like getting to see James and his friends in college! And that new steamy scene in Chapter 27! I'm still fanning myself.

I actually took a break from writing the Empire High series to focus on this installment because James really needed to find peace over what happened back in high school. And if you have no idea what I'm talking about or who "Lyn" is, go check out Empire High. Teenage James is to die for. And his whole backstory will make you love him even more (if that's even possible, haha).

I know I left you with a new question – what the heck has Isabella done this time? Well, don't worry. We're about to get to the bottom of that invitation. Get ready for all the feels!

I hope you loved Devoured. And thank you for continuing to make James Hunter my most popular hero.

Ivy Smoak

Ivy Smoak
Wilmington, DE
www.ivysmoak.com

About the Author

Ivy Smoak is the USA Today and Wall Street Journal best-selling author of *The Hunted Series*. Her books have sold over 4 million copies worldwide.

When she's not writing, you can find Ivy binge watching too many TV shows, taking long walks, playing outside, and generally refusing to act like an adult. She lives with her husband in Delaware.

TikTok: @IvySmoak
Facebook: IvySmoakAuthor
Instagram: @IvySmoakAuthor
Goodreads: IvySmoak

Recommend *Devoured* for your next book club!

Book club questions available at:
www.ivysmoak.com/bookclub